Wild Hearts

Book One of the Wild Hearts Trilogy

Sabrina Wagner

Stay Connected!

**Want to be the first to learn book news, updates and more?
Sign up for my Newsletter.**

https://www.subscribepage.com/sabrinawagnernewsletter

**Want to know about my new releases and upcoming sales?
Stay connected on:**

Facebook~Instagram~Twitter~TikTok
Goodreads~BookBub~Amazon

**I'd love to hear from you.
Visit my website to connect with me.**

www.sabrinawagnerauthor.com

Table of Contents

Prologue

Wild Hearts

Once in a lifetime.
Some of us are lucky enough to find it.
That special person who completes you.
The one you'd do anything for.
The other half of your heart.
Your kindred spirit.
Your mirror.

And in one weak moment,
You shatter your mirror.
Break it into a million pieces.
You destroy it.

After the pieces have fallen,
You look at yourself in the shattered remains.
And you barely recognize the person looking back at you.
Because without her,
You are nothing.

Chapter 1
Chris
Age 8

I sat there in Mrs. Donovan's third grade classroom, next to Kyla, trying to get through another day. I forgot to comb my hair this morning and put on yesterday's jeans. Who cared anyway? It was just another boring day at school. My brother Jim woke me up this morning. Now that he was in middle school, he got up super early and we shared a bathroom. Jim insisted on slamming doors and making as much noise as possible. I swear he thrived on pissing me off. I tried to put my pillow over my head, but I just couldn't fall back asleep.

I was an average kid who got average grades, and of course, I had to sit next to the smartest girl in the class. She was shy, so it didn't bother me too much, except days like today when Mrs. Donovan handed back test papers. I saw a bright red C on mine. I glanced over at Kyla's paper and yep, it had a bright red A on it. I quickly shoved my test into my desk and tried to forget about it. It was just a stupid science test, I tried to tell myself, but my dad wouldn't think so. He expected more. I could already hear him saying, "You're better than that, son." I blew out a breath and dropped my head to my desk.

As I sat there trying to come up with an excuse for my dad, there was a knock on the door. I lifted my head just enough to see the principal standing there. This day was going from bad to worse, and quick. Surely, he knew what I wrote in the bathroom stall with Sharpie, "Harry Ballz Rocks!". It was a compliment really and it was funny, or at least Trevor thought so when I was writing it. I mean, who names their kid Harold Ballz? Our principal's parents, that's who.

3

I looked back at Trevor with a questioning glare. He shook his head and shrugged his shoulders. If he didn't sell me out, then who did? I didn't think anybody else knew.

Principal Ballz stood there, talking to Mrs. Donovan and I saw her nod her head. He led a dark-haired girl with pigtails into the room, and I breathed a sigh of relief. He wasn't here for me.

"Good morning boys and girls," he said.

"Good morning, Mr. Ballz," the class responded, and I swear he cringed. It had to suck going through life with a name like that.

"We have a new student to our school and she's going to be in your classroom. This is Tori Russo. She just moved here from Ohio. Please make her feel welcome."

Tori gave us a nervous little wave and looked down at the ground. She had on a purple dress and fancy looking shoes. Great! Another girl in our class. We already had more girls than boys. Why couldn't the new kid have been a boy?

Kyla raised her hand. "She can sit next to me, Mrs. Donovan."

Mrs. Donovan looked at Kyla. "That's very kind of you. We'll put her desk between you and Chris."

Fucking great! Yeah, since my brother started middle school, I'd learned a lot of words I wasn't supposed to say, but that didn't stop me from thinking them. Why did I have to get stuck sitting next to the new kid? And a girl at that?

Mrs. Donovan scooted a desk between Kyla and me, then led Tori to her new seat. I tried to ignore her as she slipped into the chair next to me. I heard Kyla say, "I like your dress."

Tori answered in a harsh tone, "I hate it! My mom made me wear it for the first day. I'd rather be wearing jeans. Mom said I couldn't." Okay, so clearly, she wasn't a typical girl.

"Well, you look pretty," Kyla answered.

"Thanks, I guess. But how am I going to be able to run on the playground in this? It'll fly up when I go on the monkey bars."

4

Now I was really listening. Maybe I could get a peek at her underwear.

"Just don't go on the monkey bars," suggested Kyla. She was the queen of practicality.

Tori gave her a weird look. "That's the best part of the playground. I'm going on the monkey bars," she huffed.

Yeah, I was going to stick close to the new girl at recess. I was definitely going to get to see her underwear.

Chapter 2
Tori
Age 10

Kyla and I sat at the table in the lunchroom. Since my first day of school here, she and I just clicked. We were totally different, but I liked her. Today's hot lunch was hamburger on a bun and fries. Seriously, why did they call it hamburger on a bun? If it didn't have a bun, was it even a hamburger? It was a sin the school even called this food. Of course, Kyla brought her lunch. She had a turkey sandwich, an apple, and Oreos. I was so jealous. My mom always made me buy hot lunch. I wished she made me a lunch like Kyla's mom.

I sat there trying to choke down the disgusting hamburger and then I looked across the table. Chris was joking with Trevor and Jason, and had two French fries stuck up his nose. It was totally gross, but it was also funny. I let out a giggle.

Kyla looked over to what I laughed about. "That's so disgusting," she said.

"It's kind of funny. Don't you think?" I questioned.

"Not really," she said dismissively, as she took another bite of her apple.

I didn't care. I thought it was funny. I looked back at Chris and saw that he was looking at me. He quickly pulled the fries out of his nose and set them back on his tray. I just hoped he wasn't going to eat those fries.

Then he surprised me and popped them into his mouth. Now that was gross!

That kid was always doing something to get attention.

We were in fifth grade now and I was starting to notice boys. Not that they were noticing me, but I was sure they would soon. I already started getting boobs and I knew boys liked that.

We were in those awkward years, when our bodies were starting to change, and nobody wanted to talk about it.

Just last week we had that stupid assembly where they separate the boys and the girls and talked about *maturation*. That stuff was so embarrassing! I knew what happened. My mom already had "the talk" with me. It was weird thinking that the boys knew all that stuff about girls. But I guess we learned some stuff about boys too. I really didn't need to see that video!

After lunch, Kyla and I went out to the playground. She was wearing a dress and couldn't really run around, so she just stood there and watched while I hung upside down on the monkey bars. I swung by my knees and my shirt started to fall down to my face. I tried to grab it, but it was too late. I was pretty sure my training bra was showing.

"Get down off there!" Kyla yelled to me.

I released my knees and landed on my feet on the woodchips below. Just then, I was shoved from behind.

As I stumbled forward, I saw Chris run by. "I see London. I see France. I saw more than Tori's underpants!"

"Jerk!" I yelled as he ran by. But it was too late. He was already whispering to the other boys on the playground.

Why did boys have to be such jerks and so immature? Really! I looked over to where he was and shot him a death glare. He was pointing back at me and laughing.

I really hated him!

Chapter 3
Chris
Age 12

Everyone sat around in the basement and looked at each other nervously. This was the first boy-girl party any of us had been to. Usually, the boys had parties with boys and girls had parties with girls, but now that we were in middle school that changed.

Michael's mom and dad let him have a birthday party with both boys and girls. They served us pizza and pop and then went upstairs. Everyone sat around looking at each other with boredom, and honestly this party was kind of lame. It definitely needed some excitement, and I knew just how to do it.

"Anyone ever play Spin the Bottle?" I asked, glancing around the room.

"We're not playing that game," Kyla said. "We'll get in so much trouble."

"What are you? Chicken?" I asked, quirking up an eyebrow.

She got an embarrassed look on her face, and I couldn't help but push it more. "Who's too chicken to play Spin the Bottle?"

"Not me," Tori answered. She was fearless and never backed down from a challenge. I didn't want to admit it, but something about her intrigued me.

No one wanted to confess to being chicken. I had thrown the gauntlet down, and now everyone was considering it, especially since Tori seemed as invested in this as much as I was.

Soon Tori and I convinced everyone to play. Since Michael was the birthday boy, he spun the bottle first. The bottle landed on Crystal, and they snuck off into the closet. Her cheeks got red, but she went. Everyone started to giggle when the door shut. But they weren't in there long, so nothing probably happened. They sat back in the circle and Crystal picked the next person to spin. She picked me.

I clapped my hands together in anticipation and spun that fucker around. I was hoping it would land on Tori, but it ended up pointing at Kyla.

"No way! I'm not doing this!" she exclaimed while backing out of the circle.

"Fine, I'll do it for you!" Tori stood up. "I'm not afraid."

Tori had a look of determination on her face. She and I walked to the closet, went inside, and shut the door. It was pretty dark, and I wanted to do more than kiss her. Fuck, I didn't even care if I kissed her, I wanted to touch her boobs. They were bigger than most girls our age. Just one feel. That's all I wanted. My first touch of a girl's tits.

It was like she could read my mind. "Kissing only," she proclaimed. "Don't get any funny ideas."

"What are you talking about?" I questioned innocently.

"I know you, Chris Capizzio. Kissing only," she said with defiance. "You're not touching my boobs!"

I rolled my eyes, even though I knew she couldn't see me. "Fine, but you know you want me to."

"You wish! You gonna kiss me or what?" she asked.

I put my hands on her hips and leaned in to kiss her. My lips brushed against hers and I felt a jolt of electricity flow through me. Surprisingly, she lifted her hands to my shoulders and wrapped them around my neck. I pulled her in further and stuck my tongue out like I'd seen on T.V. She shocked me and opened her mouth. Our tongues touched and tangled together. I pressed in closer to her and she didn't pull away. It was sloppy and wet, but God, I loved it.

9

It seemed to go on forever. My dick hardened in my pants and that was the first time I had reacted to a girl like that. I'd had boners before, but this was definitely different.

"That's enough," she said pulling back. She may have ended the kiss, but it wasn't something I would be forgetting anytime soon.

Tori opened the closet and walked out. I had to adjust myself and pull my shirt down to cover my hard-on before leaving the closet. I was sure I had a shit-eating grin on my face, but at that moment, I didn't really care. That kiss was fucking amazing!

I knew I would never be the same after that kiss. I think I was in love!

Chapter 4
Tori
Age 14

High school. Ugh! I should have been totally excited, but I just couldn't seem to drum up the feelings to get there. Since we'd started, my best friend had gone AWOL. Cheerleading consumed most of Kyla's time and she'd made new friends.

I wanted her to, but I missed the connection we used to have. Don't get me wrong, we still hung out all the time, but I was jealous of her new friends. I think it was because they shared something I wasn't a part of. I could have done cheerleading. I had the skills. I just didn't have the desire. I didn't want to wear those little skirts and shake pom-poms. I was much more comfortable in jeans and a T-shirt.

I loved going and watching the football games, but from the stands. I didn't want to be in the spotlight, shaking my ass.

Kyla and I had been friends since my first day of school here. She was kind and sweet... almost sickeningly so... but I loved her. She encouraged me to get involved in something and so I joined Yearbook. I came to every game and took pictures. It wasn't all bad. I had a valid excuse for zeroing in on the guys' asses to take their pictures. Some of the pictures went to print. Others were just for me.

After the games, Kyla and I hung out with the other cheerleaders and the guys from the football team. Usually, we ended up at the empty field not far from the school and hung out by a bonfire. It seemed like everyone went to the bonfires... from freshman to seniors. Tonight, was no different, but being freshman, we were still the newbies.

Kyla was busy talking to the girls from the cheer squad and I sank into the background. It's not that she didn't include me, but it wasn't my scene. I wandered off to the side and watched from afar.

Suddenly, I wasn't alone. I could feel him creeping up behind me. My skin broke out in goose bumps, and I was on high alert. I hadn't forgotten the kiss we shared in the closet two years ago. I didn't want to like him. He was crass and kind of a jerk, but I couldn't help the way my body reacted.

"Hey," he said in casual voice.

"Hey," I responded. I didn't even turn around because I knew who it was.

"Wanna get away from here for a while? I've got some of my brother's weed. We should go smoke it together."

I didn't turn around. "I don't do drugs."

"Come on… it's just weed. It won't kill ya. It'll just make all of this so much more bearable."

I turned around and faced Chris. "What makes you think I need it?"

"Seriously? Your best friend is over there," he pointed to the bonfire, "and you're over here."

"I'm not mad," I said.

"I didn't say you were." He started to walk away. "Whatever. Suit yourself. I'll be over by that tree if you're interested."

I wasn't interested, but then again, I was. "Wait up!" I called to him. I sped up my walk to a jog, until we were side by side. "I've never smoked weed before."

"That's cool. You don't have to do it. I was just offering," Chris stated.

"Yeah, I know." I stopped walking. Chris turned to look at me questioningly. "What if it fucks me up? My parents will blow a gasket," I asked.

Chris laughed. "Did you just drop an f-bomb?"

I put my hands on my hips. "Yeah. What about it?" I glared at him. Was he making fun of me?

12

"Nothing." He shook his head. "I just didn't expect it. It sounded kind of hot coming out of your mouth."

Well, that wasn't what I thought he was going to say. "You didn't answer my question. Is this going to fuck me up or not?"

"Nah. It'll just mellow you out. You probably won't even have a buzz by the time we leave here," he assured me.

I started walking again. "Okay. I'll try it."

He smiled at me. "That's my girl!"

I smacked him in the shoulder. "I'm not your girl!"

He rubbed his arm, like I had really hurt him. "Relax! It was a figure of speech. You know kind of like... attaboy."

"Oh." I wrapped my arms around myself in a protective gesture. Chris and I hadn't really ever been friends, more like acquaintances. Two kids who had been thrown together since third grade. Sometimes I hated him and sometimes I thought he was actually kind of cool. Tonight, I was just glad I had someone to hang out with.

We walked past the trees and found a couple of rocks to sit on. He pulled the joint out of his pocket, along with a lighter. He put the joint in his mouth, lit the end, and sucked in. I watched him as his eyes closed and he held the smoke in his lungs. Finally, he released the breath he was holding and blew the smoke out.

He held the joint out for me to take. "I don't know how to do this," I said nervously. "How did you learn?"

"My brother. He and his friends always smoke weed." He shrugged his shoulders. "Finally, one day, I decided to try it."

I took the joint from his hand and held it to my lips. "How do I do this?"

"Just suck it in, swallow it down to your lungs, and hold it a few seconds. Then blow out the smoke. It's not rocket science."

I nodded my head, then followed his instructions. The smoke burned my throat and lungs. I tried to hold it in but ended up coughing out the smoke."

Chris patted me on the back. "You alright?"

"Yeah. Let me try it again." This time I embraced the burn and held the smoke in. I kept it in a few seconds, then blew out the smoke." My head started to feel a little foggy, but in a good way. I felt my muscles relax and a sense of calm washed over me. It wasn't what I expected, but it wasn't a bad feeling.

"How do you feel?" Chris questioned as he took the joint out of my hand.

"Really good, actually," I admitted.

He took another hit and I reached for the joint. He pulled it away. "You've had enough for one night. I don't want your first time to mess you up. Next time," he stated, like he was sure there would be a next time. "So, how come you didn't join cheerleading?" he asked.

"I don't like the skirts. Besides, I don't like to be on display. I'm kind of a fade-into-the-background kind of girl."

Chris laughed.

"What's so funny?" I asked.

"Tori, you couldn't fade into the background if you wanted to. You're way too pretty for that. Plus, you've got some killer curves."

I looked away. "Thanks... I guess."

"It's the truth. Just because you don't embrace it, doesn't make it untrue. All the guys on the football team talk about you."

I thought about what he said and let out a sigh. "What do you mean?"

"Come on, you're not that naïve. You're hot."

We sat there in silence. I let my mind race and I thought about that kiss in the closet two years ago. Suddenly I felt brave and uninhibited. "So... remember when we were in middle school?" I started.

"You mean that kiss in the closet?" he finished. I nodded. "Yeah. What about it?" It was like we were on the same wavelength.

"That was my first kiss," I said. I felt the blush rise up into my cheeks, but it was dark so I was sure he couldn't see it.

14

"Yeah, mine too. But it was an awesome first kiss." He bumped me with his shoulder.

"Yeah, it was," I admitted.

"You wanna try it again?"

"I'm still not letting you touch my boobs," I said. "But I wouldn't mind the kiss again."

"Awww… come on. You've got great boobs. They're even bigger now. Just one feel?"

I laughed. "Nope. There's got to be some mystery," I proclaimed.

"Fine! I'll take that kiss though. You know you want me." Chris laughed.

"Yeah, right." I scooted a little closer to him, until our legs were touching. I turned to face him, and he wrapped his arms around my waist. I put mine around his neck and leaned in. Our lips touched, and fireworks exploded through my body. Memories of that night in the closet came crashing back to me.

I didn't know what this feeling was, except that I really liked it. His tongue pushed at my lips, and I opened up for him. Our tongues tangled together, and it wasn't half as wet and messy as the first time. I felt consumed with the feeling and let the kiss go on for what felt like forever. His hands moved from my waist and started to move up my sides. I pushed him back and released the kiss. "Still good," I said. "You're going to make some girl really happy one day."

"I could make you really happy," he said with a smirk.

"In your dreams, Chris Capizzio," I taunted him. I stood up, walked out from behind the trees and back toward the bonfire. My panties were wet and the space between my thighs tingled. Getting involved with Chris was the last thing I needed to do. But if I ever did… I was sure he wouldn't disappoint.

Chapter 5
Chris
Age 15

Sophomore year and I made the varsity football team. I was the cornerback, and I was fucking fast. I was built lean, but over the summer I started working out like crazy, and what do you know? I had muscles underneath all this skinny.

My brother set up a gym in our garage and since he went away to college, the weights just sat there collecting dust. My dad was ready to get rid of it all, but I decided to give it a try. Once I started seeing my body change from scrawny to defined, it became an obsession. Every morning, I put on my headphones and lifted for an hour. Then I'd go for a run. I felt good and girls started noticing me. Now I just had to grow a few more inches.

The one girl I wanted to notice me, was still playing a cat and mouse game with me. She couldn't deny that there was chemistry between us. Those couple of kisses we'd shared, got my blood pumping and my dick hard. I knew she was affected too. Even if she tried to deny it.

I loved playing varsity, because you got to play under the lights instead of during the day. The stands were full, and the crowd cheered us on. It was way different than JV, when the stands were filled with our parents and maybe a few students.

The game was about to start when I saw my favorite photographer. Her lens was pointed in my direction, and I gave her a little wave. She lowered the camera from her face and looked at me over the top of it. She could try to hide it all she wanted, but I saw the little smile that played across her face. Tori lifted the camera back up and started taking pictures. I wondered if they all went to the yearbook, or if she secretly saved some of them for herself.

After the game, the guys and I headed over to the empty field by the school. Pickup trucks were backed in and formed a circle around the bonfire. Now that I was on varsity, I was part of the "In" crowd. I sat on the back of a tailgate with a beer in my hand, listening to Kid Rock blare through the speakers and watching the flames dance. I scanned the crowd for Tori. She always came after the games, but I hadn't seen her yet. I downed another drink of my beer and pretended like I wasn't waiting for her.

I felt her, before I saw her. Tingles always ran down my back when she was near. I nonchalantly turned my head to the left. Tori and Kyla were giggling and holding onto each other as they sauntered over to the fire. They walked up to some of the other cheerleaders and started talking.

I watched Tori from the back. God, she had a great ass! She turned her head and looked around. Her eyes locked with mine and I motioned with my head for her to come over. She quirked her eyebrow up at me but started walking my way. She was beautiful, yet she didn't know it. Her long dark hair flowed over her shoulders and rested on top of her big tits. The black T-shirt she was wearing, had me wanting to finally get my hands on her. I let out a low groan as she approached.

"Hey," she said.

"Hey," I answered back. I tapped the space on the tailgate next to me and she hopped up. She wiggled her ass back until she was seated comfortably. I handed her my cup, and she took a long drink.

"So… varsity, huh?" Tori asked.

"Yeah. I guess all those years of running from my brother finally paid off."

She let out a little laugh. "I guess. But I'm pretty sure you've put some work into it too," she said as she looked me up and down. "You're not so scrawny anymore."

"Pffft! I wasn't scrawny," I defended.

"A little bit." She held her thumb and forefinger up to show me.

I bumped her shoulder with mine. "Fine! I was scrawny."

"Seriously though...you look good," she said with a smile.

"Thanks. You want me to get you a drink?" I offered.

"Sure. I'll take a beer."

I jumped off the tailgate and walked over to one of the coolers. I popped the top off the beer and poured it into a cup for her. I hopped back up on the tailgate, so our legs were touching, and handed her the cup. "Get any good pictures at the game?" I asked.

Tori blushed and lowered her head into her cup as she took a drink. "A few." The words came out all muffled, like she was trying to hide them.

"Any of me?"

Again, she answered, "A few."

"You get my face in any of them or are they all of my ass?" I taunted her.

"Oh, please! Like I'd take pictures of your ass." She laughed.

"Oh, you would! It's not so scrawny anymore, remember?"

Tori threw her free hand up in the air. "Whatever!"

I draped my arm over her shoulder and pulled her into a side hug. She didn't pull away. Instead, she rested her head on my shoulder. "Seriously," I whispered, "why won't you give me a chance? I know you felt it in the kisses we shared. There's something there." I'd been trying to get her to go out with me for a while now and she always said no. Not in a mean way, but a no was still a no.

18

She lifted her head and our brown eyes met. Mine were dark like chocolate. Hers were soft and warm like honey. "I can't talk about this here. Go for a walk with me?" she asked.

I hopped off the tailgate and held my hand out for her to take. She scooted forward on the tailgate and looked down at her feet. I grabbed her by the waist and lifted her down. She held out her hand to me and I laced my fingers with hers.

We walked toward the trees where we kissed last year. "So, why not?" I asked.

"I don't want to ruin it," she said.

"What do you mean?" That didn't make any sense to me. Ruin what?

"We've really gotten to know each other over the last year. You're a good guy. And you're right. I feel it. But what if it doesn't work out and we've ruined this friendship for nothing. I don't want to risk that."

"Being together won't ruin it. It'll only make it better," I said.

"That's what you say now. But what if it does? If we were to break up, it would turn ugly. I don't ever want that."

We stopped walking when we got to the trees. I turned her and wrapped my arms around her waist. "Just so you know... I'm not giving up on you, Tori. I'm going to keep asking you. And one day, you'll say yes." I leaned down and touched my lips to hers. Her arms went around my neck and pulled me in close. The kiss started soft and gentle, then turned feverish. Our tongues twisted and tangled. My hands moved to her ass, and I pulled her into my hard-on. She let out a gasp.

I rested my forehead against hers. "Do you feel what you do to me?" I asked.

"Which is why we shouldn't do this," she said. "But God, it's so good. Kiss me again." Her words came out breathless and needy.

And I did. I kissed her again. Got lost in her. When we finally broke apart, we both had lust in our eyes. She made me want to take her back into the trees. I wanted to make her my first. I wanted to fuck her… bad. "You're going to be the death of me, Tori Russo. We better get back before Kyla wonders where you've disappeared to."

She didn't say anything. She just took my hand and led me back toward the fire. I didn't know what this was between us, but I was dying to find out. One day…

Chapter 6
Tori
Age 16

It was the summer before our junior year. There was going to be big party at the field. Kyla's parents wouldn't let her go, so I was going with my current boyfriend.

Matt was a senior. He was cute in a bad boy sort of way. His grades sucked, but he knew how to have a good time. We drank too much and smoked pot on a regular basis. The problem was I couldn't get Chris out of my head. When Matt and I kissed, it was hot and heavy, but the fireworks were definitely missing. It was nothing like kissing Chris. I rationalized it all, by telling myself that Chris and I should never be a couple. His friendship meant too much to me. What was the harm in trying out some other options?

Chris had climbed the ladder of popularity. He'd gotten taller and more filled out. The girls were all over him. He'd had a girlfriend here and there, but nothing ever lasted. It was exactly the reason I couldn't go out with Chris. We were good friends, and if I was being honest... next to Kyla, he was my best friend. He was a great guy. Just not the guy for me. His friendship was worth so much more.

I refused to risk my heart for Chris. I knew he could break it if I let him. I wasn't that invested with Matt. We had a good time together, and right now that's all I was interested in.

Matt picked me up in his old Camaro. It was cool. The engine rumbled when he pulled into the driveway. I opened the front door to go out when my mom stopped me. "Isn't he going to come to the door for you?"

"Really mom? This isn't the 1900's. It's the 2000's. He doesn't need to pick me up at the door."

My mom scowled. "Some things never go out of style, Tori. Like good manners."

"You don't even know him. Quit being so judgmental," I shot back at her.

"Maybe if he came to the door, I'd get to know him," she said in a huff. "Just go. Have a good time and be home by one."

I leaned over and kissed my mom on the cheek. "I will. Love you."

"Love you too!" I heard her say as I closed the door behind me.

I ran out to the car and opened the door. I slid into the seat next to Matt. He turned down the radio and leaned over to kiss me. "Want some?" he questioned, as he passed his joint over to me.

"Yeah. My mom's being a pain." I took the joint from him and sucked the smoke into my lungs. I let out the breath I was holding and took another hit.

Matt pulled the joint from me. "You're going to hotbox it. He took another hit and stubbed the joint into the ashtray."

"What's up your ass?" I questioned.

"Nothing. You know I hate these jock parties. Let's just go and get this over with."

Okay. I could do without the attitude I was getting. What was his fucking problem? This was not a great way to start the night. I sat back in the seat and started to think about our relationship. Matt never really wanted to do anything with my friends. He always wanted it to be just the two of us. When we did hang with other people, it was always his friends. I knew Kyla hated Matt, and now I was starting to see why.

We got to the party and Matt pulled a twelve pack out of his trunk. "I'm going to fucking need these tonight."

"Why are you being an ass? I hang with your friends all the time."

"My friends are cool," he responded with sarcasm.

22

I rolled my eyes, snagged a beer, and walked over toward the bonfire by some of the cheerleaders. I'd gotten to be good friends with them through Kyla. God, I wished she was here tonight. I tried to forget about Matt and his shitty attitude. I drank down a couple of beers and started to get a little buzz.

One of the guys from the football team came and stood beside me. He bumped his hip into mine. "Hey, Tori. What's up? Where's Matt?"

"Hey, Trev. I don't know where Matt is. He's kind of being an ass tonight." I shook my head in disgust.

"Well, he's moody for sure. I'm surprised you're even dating him. Want me to kick his ass for you?"

I laughed. "Thanks for the offer, but no thanks."

Trevor gave me a hug. "If you change your mind, let me know. It would be my pleasure."

"I'll keep that in mind." I laughed again.

When Trevor walked away, I felt a hand wrap around my arm and pull me backward. "We need to talk," Matt said in a pissed off voice. I could smell the alcohol on his breath, as he led me away from the crowd.

"What the fuck, Tori?" he yelled.

"What?" I questioned. I didn't know what he was so pissed about, but considering his attitude when we arrived, I wasn't surprised.

"Are we together or what? That guy had his hands all over you and you just stood there and laughed."

"What are you talking about?" I questioned. "Trevor gave me a hug. Big fucking deal."

"It is a big fucking deal!" he yelled. "Guys shouldn't be hugging you!"

"Oh, get the fuck over yourself," I yelled back and pushed him in the chest. "It was a hug. It didn't mean anything."

I saw the fire in Matt's eyes and that's when I knew I'd made a mistake. "It is a big fucking deal!" He pushed me back with a solid shove and I fell onto the ground, my ass hitting hard. "Quit being such a bitch!" he yelled.

Tears sprang into my eyes, and I quickly wiped them away. I refused to let them fall. I didn't know who was watching, but I felt the humiliation. This was going to get around school. I was so embarrassed. I didn't know if I should stay down or stand up and fight. My instinct was to fight, but I didn't want to make a bigger scene than we had already made.

Luckily, I didn't have to make that decision, because a pair of long legs stood between Matt and me. "Don't fucking touch her like that! What? Are you such a pussy, you gotta push a girl?"

"Stay out of it, Capizzio! This has nothing to do with you! She pushed me first and she's being a bitch!" Matt shouted.

"I'm sure she really hurt you, asshole! Get the fuck out of here before I punch your teeth down your throat."

"Fine with me. Bitch isn't worth it anyway!" Matt spouted off.

I watched him walk away. I felt humiliated, but also relieved. Chris bent down next to me and lifted me off the ground. "Come on, Tor. I got you," he said softly.

"Thank you," I said over the lump in my throat. I tried to be strong, I wouldn't let the tears come. Chris pulled me into his chest and wrapped his arms around me. I took in the smell of him and let him comfort me, as he rubbed my back gently.

"I'll take you home," he said as he ran his hands through my hair. I let him walk me to his dad's truck. He opened the door for me and helped me up inside.

I leaned my head against the window. Chris got in the driver's side and started the engine. He reached over and took my hand in his. "Are you okay?"

"I'm just embarrassed," I said as I looked out the side window. "I don't want to go home yet. Just take me somewhere. Anywhere."

I didn't pay attention to where he was taking me. Honestly, I didn't care. He pulled off into a new housing development that was under construction and parked the truck on one of the side streets.

Chris leaned over and undid my seatbelt. He wrapped his arm around my waist and pulled me closer to him. I leaned my head on his hard chest. I didn't know what to say, but I was thankful that Chris had stood up for me.

"Are you done with him?" he asked.

"Yeah. I've had enough." I was still feeling the embarrassment about what went down.

"Good. He didn't deserve you. You deserve so much better."

"I know," I said without elaborating. It felt nice being wrapped in Chris's arms.

"I would never treat you like that," he said as he rubbed my back. "Give me a chance, Tor. I promise to always treat you good. Please don't tell me no again." He placed a soft kiss on my forehead.

What did I have to lose? I already knew he was a great guy. And the kissing was incredible. I weighed my options, and I couldn't come up with a solid reason to tell him no. The only thing holding me back was my own fear. I had always told myself I wouldn't get in too deep with any guy, but with Chris, I was afraid I was going to fall fast. Fast and hard. And honestly, it scared the shit out of me. "Okay," I whispered. "But promise me... if this doesn't work... I don't want to lose you as a friend."

"It's going to work," Chris said confidently. "I've loved you since seventh grade."

I looked up at him with shock. "You don't mean that. I mean, do we even know what love is?"

"You can call it a crush or infatuation. All I know is that I can't get you out of my head. I've tried, but it always comes back to you. The way I feel when I kiss you... I've never felt that with anyone else."

"Me neither," I admitted.

"I want to kiss you again. It's been too long," he said.

My mind shot back to those stolen kisses we'd shared. "So, kiss me," I said breathlessly.

25

He turned me in his arms and pressed his lips to mine. I opened my mouth and let him in. The fireworks went off and coursed through my body. My panties got wet, and everything tingled. I lay back on the bench seat and brought Chris with me. He hovered over me and ran his hands under my shirt and along my bare stomach. It was electrifying, and I questioned myself as to why I hadn't done this sooner.

I felt his hard dick push into my leg, and I let out a little moan. "Don't do that," he warned with a huskiness in his voice.

"Do what?" I asked.

"Make those sounds. I'm holding on by a thread here and you're not helping," he answered.

"I'm sorry… it's just that…"

"I know. It's so good," he said.

"Yesss," I hissed out.

Chris pulled back and broke our connection. "Let me take you out on a proper date. Tomorrow night."

"Okaaay. What did you have in mind?"

"Dinner and a movie? I know it's kind of cliché, but we've got to start somewhere."

"That actually sounds really nice." It seemed like forever since anyone had taken me somewhere besides a party or to make-out. "What time should I be ready?" I asked.

"How about five? Does that work?"

I bit my lip and nodded. "That sounds perfect."

"I should take you home. I don't want you to be late." Chris scooted back over into the driver's seat and started the engine.

"Chris?"

He turned and looked at me. "Yeah?"

"Thank you for tonight."

Chris picked up my hand and kissed the back of it. "You don't have to thank me. I'll always be there for you."

Chris took me home and walked me up to the door. It was only twelve-thirty, so I'm sure my mom was going to be

26

thrilled I was home early. Chris gave me a quick peck on the cheek and jogged back to his truck.

I opened the door, and my mom was standing there. "That's not who you left with. Who was that?" she asked.

"That's a major upgrade." I smiled. "I got into a fight with Matt and Chris brought me home. You remember him from elementary and middle school, don't you?"

"Yeah. I thought you kind of hated him."

I rolled my eyes. "When I was ten. I'm going out with him tomorrow night if that's all right."

"Just be careful. I don't want you to be one of those girls that gets a reputation," my mom warned.

"Relax, mom. I'm still a virgin. I don't think I'm going to get a reputation." I started up the stairs to my bedroom. "Besides, I have a feeling I'm going to hang onto this one for a while." I smiled to myself.

I went in my room and shut the door. I took out my phone and texted Kyla.

Tori: Guess who I'm going out with tomorrow night?

Kyla: Who?

Tori: Chris

Kyla: It's about time! What happened to Matt?

Tori: I got in a fight with Matt and Chris came to my rescue.

Kyla: I want details tomorrow!

Tori: For sure! Call you in the a.m.

I lay back on my bed and thought about our kiss. Shit... it was soooo good. I couldn't wait until tomorrow night!

Chapter 7
Chris

I didn't know why I was so nervous. This was Tori. It's not like I didn't know her. I was full of anxiety as I got ready for my date.

I took a long hot shower and thought about her as the water sprayed down over me. Fuck! I looked down and my hard-on stared back at me. I couldn't go out on a date with her like this. She would think I was a creep.

I grabbed my dick in my hand. It wasn't the first time I jacked off thinking of Tori, but it was the first time I did it in preparation for going out with her. I leaned one hand against the wall and stroked myself up and down, thinking about her... her tits and her ass, and what she would look like naked... until I felt the built-up tension release from my body. I breathed out a sigh of relief, as I sagged against the wall. I was definitely going to have to try to keep that under control tonight. *No more thinking about her naked*, I promised myself.

I got out of the shower, splashed on a little cologne, and spiked my hair up in the front. I threw on a pair of jeans and went to my closet to search for a shirt to wear. I needed to look good for dinner. I heard my mom walking down the hallway and called out to her, "Mom! Can you come in here for a minute?"

My mom hesitantly pushed open my bedroom door. "What's wrong, sweetheart?" She didn't come in here much since I'd turned into a teenager. I think she was afraid she was going to see something she didn't want to see.

I stood in front of my closet staring at my clothes. "I'm taking Tori out for dinner and a movie tonight, and I don't know what to wear."

My mom smiled. "So, she finally agreed to go out with you, huh?"

"What's that supposed to mean?" I asked.

"I just know you've liked her for a while. When you talk about her, you get this goofy look on your face."

I rolled my eyes. "I do not," I insisted.

"Yeah, you kinda do. And it looks a lot like that," she joked, while pointing at my face. Then she got serious. "Where are you taking her?"

"I made reservations at Brio at Partridge Creek Mall. I figured we could just go to the movies there afterwards."

"That's a nice place." She smiled.

"Yeah, I know. So, what should I wear?"

My mom reached into my closet and pushed the hangers aside, looking at my choices. She pulled out a black short-sleeved button-up. "This shirt looks good on you." She handed it to me. "What do you think?"

"It's perfect. Thanks, Mom," I leaned down and gave her a kiss on the cheek.

"You're welcome, honey. I'm going to leave some money on the kitchen counter for you."

"You don't have to do that. I've got money, Mom."

"I want to. Have fun tonight." She winked at me as she left my room.

I finished getting dressed and raced down the stairs, not wanting to be late. I stopped in the kitchen and saw the money my mom left. Fifty dollars? My mom was awesome! That would at least cover dinner.

I scooped up the money and shoved it in my pocket. I grabbed my dad's truck keys off the hook on the wall and then backtracked. There was a vase full of flowers sitting on the counter. *Should I?* I pulled out a purple rose, her favorite color, and headed out.

On the way over to Tori's house, I must have checked my hair in the mirror ten times. I didn't know why I couldn't shake these nerves!

I pulled up in her driveway and saw the front door open. Tori started out the door, but I wasn't cool with that. I shut the engine off, picked up the single rose and walked up the front sidewalk to the door. Tori was on the porch, waiting for me. "Hey," I said.

"Hey. You ready?" she asked.

"Yeah. This is for you." I handed her the rose and she held it up to her nose, breathing in the scent of it.

"Thank you. This was really sweet." She smiled. "Are you ready to go?"

I leaned down and placed a quick kiss on her cheek. "In a minute. I just wanted to introduce myself to your parents," I informed her.

She rolled her eyes at me. "They already know who you are."

"Yeah, but this is different. I'm taking you out on a date. I want to see them."

Tori's face lit up with a sexy little smile. "They're going to love this!" She opened the door back up and we went inside.

"Mom!" Tori called out. "Chris is here, and he wants to say 'hi'."

Tori's mom came around the corner from the kitchen with a surprised look on her face. I stuck my hand out. "Hi, Mrs. Russo. I know we've met before, but I just wanted to say hello." Tori walked past her and placed the rose in a glass of water.

Mrs. Russo took my outstretched hand and got a little smile on her face. "Hi, Chris. Where are you two off to tonight?"

"I'm taking Tori to Brio and then we're going to see a movie. What time do you want her home?"

Mrs. Russo smiled again. "Around one, will be fine. You two have a good time. And Chris, thank you for coming in."

"Sure thing," I answered. "It was nice seeing you again."

"You too. Have fun." Mrs. Russo walked us to the door, and we headed out to my dad's truck. I opened the door for Tori and helped her up.

I walked around to the driver's side and hopped up into the seat. "Oh, my God!" Tori exclaimed. "I think you just made my mom fall in love with you."

"What do you mean?" I questioned.

"Are you kidding? She's always saying how good manners never go out of style. You just made her night... possibly her year."

I let out a low chuckle. "I take it she's not used to the guys you date actually coming in to meet her."

"Aaah, no," she responded. "So, are we really going to Brio?"

"I made reservations. Is that okay? Or would you rather go somewhere else?" I worried, because finding somewhere else on a Saturday night was going to be tough.

"It's great! So... we're really going to do this?" she questioned. "You're not having second thoughts?"

"None," I answered nervously. "Why? Are you?"

"No. I just was against the idea for so long, that it feels kind of..." she didn't finish but shrugged her shoulders and looked out the side window.

I drove down M-59 to Partridge Creek. "Hey, are you okay?" I asked.

"Yeah. I'm just afraid this is going to change everything between us. I don't want to lose you as a friend."

I reached over and took her hand in mine, pulled it to my lips, and kissed the back of it. "It won't. I promise you. It's going to be good."

Tori and I had a great dinner. We laughed through most of it. Her smile lit up my world and her warm, honey-colored eyes sparkled in the candlelight of the table. Tori didn't wear much makeup. She was naturally beautiful. I don't think she even realized how pretty she was. She wasn't overdone or fake in any way. She was perfect.

After dinner, we walked over to the MJR theater and decided on a movie. It was a hard decision because we weren't old enough to get into the R-rated movies and a lot of the other ones were for kids. We decided on *The Hunger Games*.

Tori and I sat towards the back of the theater, where we could have some privacy. Even though we had just eaten, we still got pop and popcorn, because let's be honest, what was a movie without popcorn? I threw my arm over Tori's shoulder, and she cuddled into my chest. It felt pretty awesome having her in my arms. I had wanted this for so long and now, it was finally happening.

About halfway through the movie, I zoned out. I had no idea what was going on, except there were a lot of people running away from crazy shit. All I could think about was the girl snuggled to my chest. I leaned over and placed a soft kiss on the side of her head. She turned and looked at me. She had lust in her eyes, and it was my undoing.

I put my hand under her chin and raised her face to mine. I pressed my lips to hers and fireworks went off. The electricity between us couldn't be denied. It was a good thing we sat in the back of the theater, because before I knew it, we were full on making out. It was as if everything around us didn't even exist. I was so lost in her kisses, that I barely noticed the movie ended. The overhead lights turned on and we reluctantly pulled apart.

"I think we're going to have to rent this movie when it comes out," she said. "I have no idea how it ended."

"Me neither," I responded.

I took her hand in mine and led her out of the theater. It was only ten o'clock and Tori didn't have to be home until one. "So... what do you want to do now?" I asked.

She scrunched up her nose. "I know this might be silly because it's still summer, but I really want a hot chocolate. I'll buy."

32

I laughed. "If that's what you want, then that's what we'll get." We walked over to the Starbuck's and ordered. We took our hot chocolates to one of the outdoor tables and sat down.

"Thanks for this," she said. She lowered her head and looked up at me through her dark lashes. "I really like kissing you. Since we have time... I thought... well maybe we could go somewhere and do it some more."

My dick twitched in my jeans. "I think that can be arranged."

"It's not too much?" she asked with uncertainty.

"Tori, I don't think it could ever be enough."

Her face broke out into a smile. "I'm still not letting you touch my boobs," she joked.

"We'll see." I waggled my eyebrows at her.

I took her back to that housing development from the night before. I drove deep into the subdivision, parked, and shut the headlights off. I turned the radio down low. Tori undid her seatbelt and slid over towards me. "Thank you for tonight," she said. "I've had a great time."

"The night's not over yet," I reminded her.

She crawled up and straddled my lap. "I know it's not. I haven't finished kissing you yet."

I took her face in my hands and gazed into her eyes. "I've barely started kissing you." I ran my tongue along her bottom lip and sucked in inside. Then I pushed my tongue deep into her mouth and pulled her closer to me. She let out a little moan and pushed herself down onto my hardness. God, she felt good. She leaned her head back and I kissed down her neck, to her collarbone, and along the top of her chest. My hands moved up under her shirt and along the sides of her soft skin.

She was wearing a loose-fitted shirt over the top of a spaghetti strap tank. All I had to do was push the strap down over her shoulder and her tits would be right in front of me. I held onto the little bit of control I had and kissed back up her neck to her lips. "Do you know how tempting you are?" I asked.

"I'm really trying to be a good guy here, but you're making it hard."

"I know," she said as she wiggled her hips into my cock.

"You, soooo don't play fair."

She started unbuttoning my shirt and ran her hands along my chest and over my shoulders. "I just want to touch you."

"You're sitting on my dick. Trust me, you're touching me. Not that I'm complaining," I whispered.

"I want you to touch me too," she whispered in my ear. "I want you to touch my tits."

"Yeah?"

"Yeah."

She didn't have to ask me twice. I slid my hands up her waist and cupped her tits. They were way more than a handful. I squeezed them gently and ran my thumbs over her nipples. The tank she was wearing didn't hide much. "Do you know how long I've waited to get my hands on these?" I asked.

She gave me a seductive little smile. "I'm guessing a while."

"Ever since I kissed you in that closet back in seventh grade." I smiled back at her. "I'm glad you made me wait though, because they're a hell of a lot bigger now."

"Do you want to see them?" she whispered.

That had to be a trick question because what guy would ever say no to that? "I feel like there's not a right answer here. If I say yes, I'm a creep. If I say no, I'm a loser."

She lifted her eyebrows. "There's a right answer," she assured me. "You're not a creep or a loser. You've been wonderful tonight."

"Then I'm going to take a leap of faith here and say yes."

She took off her outer shirt and tossed it to the side. "I don't know why I've been fighting this so long. When I'm with you everything just feels so right," she said.

My fingers fumbled with the strap of her tank, and I slid it down her shoulder. I kissed the swell of her breast that was spilling out the top. "You are so perfect."

Just as I was about to pull the top of her tank down, bright headlights came around the corner. I lifted her off my lap. "We've got company, babe." I started the engine and slowly pulled forward. Tori threw her shirt back on and buckled her seatbelt. As we drove slowly down the street, I realized it was a cop car coming towards us. Just as I thought we were in the clear, he flashed his overhead lights. "Fuck!"

Tori's eyes went wide. "Chris, I'm so sorry. I should have never suggested this."

"You didn't exactly twist my arm. It's going to be okay, Tor. We didn't do anything wrong."

The cop got out of his car and came around to the driver's side. I rolled my window down and he shined his flashlight in my face and then over at Tori. "What are you doing out here?" he asked.

I took a deep breath. "Honestly, I was just trying to spend some time with my girl."

"Have you been drinking?"

"No, sir."

He shined the flashlight around the inside of the truck, as I held my breath. "Get her home. You can't hang out here. I don't want to see you here again. Consider this your warning."

"Thank you, sir. We're leaving right now," I said.

"You do that." He tapped his flashlight on the window and walked back to his car.

I rolled the window up and started out of the subdivision. Tori leaned back against the seat. I reached over and took her hand. "You okay?"

"I'm sorry," she said again.

I kissed the back of her hand. "It's fine. We're fine. I guess this just means we're going to have to find somewhere else to be alone," I smirked at her.

"How come you're so calm? That scared the shit out of me," she said.

"I was nervous, but it's done. No harm, no foul." I rubbed my fingers over hers. "Do you want me to take you home or do you want to drive awhile. We can scout out a new place." I winked at her.

"I don't want to go home," she said.

Chapter 8
Tori

Chris drove us back toward home but went past our houses and continued further north. "Where are you going?" I asked.

He kept driving. "I don't know why I didn't think of this before. I know the perfect spot."

He turned right off the main road onto a dirt trail surrounded by trees. It wound around a little bit and then opened into field. "Where are we?"

"My brother used to bring me out here all the time with his friends. This is where they did all their drinking and smoked their weed. No one ever comes out here. It's totally private and secluded."

I looked out the window. It was really dark. "It's kind of creepy. You sure it's safe?"

"Tori, I wouldn't bring you here if it wasn't safe. I've been here dozens of times."

I looked at Chris and let out a breath. "Okay." I unbuckled my seatbelt and leaned against the door, putting my feet up on the seat. "I was just wondering... do you still smoke weed?"

He turned to me, "Yeah. Not as much as I used to, because of football, but sometimes. Is that going to be problem?"

I shook my head, "No. I do too. I was just wondering."

Chris closed his eyes and let out a sigh. "I thought that was going to be a game changer. I mean...I would quit if you wanted me to."

I scooted a little closer to him. "I don't want you to change for me. I like you just the way you are. I just wanted to get that out in the open. I don't want to have to hide shit from you."

"Does Kyla know you smoke weed?" he asked.

I shook my head. "I don't think that's something I could share with her. I love her, but you know how she is."

"Yeah, she's a little too pure," he said.

"Her parents are really tough on her. She just wants to make them happy. She's so afraid of breaking the rules and disappointing them," I defended.

"Isn't that what being a teenager is all about? Disappointing our parents. Lord knows I haven't been the perfect kid."

"Me neither. My mom has hated every one of my boyfriends."

"What about your dad?" he asked.

"Technically, he's my stepdad, I guess. He adopted me when he and my mom got married. I was four. I never knew my real dad. My mom got pregnant and never told him about me. I think he went off to the military."

"Shit, Tori, I'm sorry. I didn't know," he apologized.

"It's fine. Mike's been the only dad I've ever known. He's great, actually. But he lets my mom handle all the girly stuff with me. I guess he doesn't feel like it's his place. I wouldn't trade him for anything. He's been nothing but good to me."

"Then you lucked out," he said.

"Yeah. He's the one who stands up for me when my mom's being tough. I think she's just worried I'll end up like her. Pregnant and alone." I sighed. "She's cool most of the time though."

"All parents are a pain in the ass. I was lucky I had my brother to break mine in first. He got in a shit load of trouble, so I look like an angel compared to him." He laughed. "Come over here."

I scooted even closer. "I like talking to you," I said. "I don't know why, but I feel like I can tell you anything."

38

Chris ran his fingers through my hair. "That's a good thing, isn't it? I want us to be honest with each other."

I looked him in the eye. "Okay, honest moment?"

"Sure."

"I'm glad we got interrupted by the cops. I shouldn't have let things go that far. I got caught up in you. I mean… what kind of girl shows a guy her boobs on the first date? That was really slutty. And I'm not a slut."

"Tori, I don't think you're a slut. I got caught up too. We can take things slower. But I'm not gonna lie, I was fucking looking forward to it," He let out a husky laugh that sounded more like a groan.

I swatted at him. "I bet you were." I stared down at my hands. "I don't know what I was thinking," I said shaking my head. "I'm not really ready for that. I'm kind of body conscience."

Chris pulled back in surprise. "Why? You've got a great body."

"Oh, please. I've got boobs that are too big for my body and a big ass. I mean, look at Kyla. That girl's got curves in all the right places. I have too many curves."

Chris got a serious look on his face. "Tori, I think you're perfect. I like your boobs and your ass. Neither are too big. That's all in your mind." He ran his hand down my side and squeezed my ass. "You're all I've wanted for a long time. You've got a beautiful body."

"Can we talk about something else now? I'm feeling a little embarrassed here," I said.

"How about we don't talk at all?" Chris pulled me into him and started kissing me. I gave into the feelings and kissed him back. "I can't stop kissing you," he said.

"Then don't. Keep kissing me," I whispered. I wrapped my arms around his shoulders and pulled him down on the seat with me. His kisses were magic. Everything else left my head, but the feeling of his tongue tangled with mine.

"You can still touch me," I said, breathlessly. His hand moved up my side and cupped my breasts. He was gentle, yet firm. Heat pooled between my legs and my panties were soaked. I didn't know what this boy was doing to me, but I felt things with him that I had never felt before. I reached my hand between us and rubbed along the front of his jeans. I could feel him, long and hard, underneath the denim.

He let out a little growl. "You are going to kill me," he said. "Going slow with you, is going to be next to impossible." We continued to touch each other and make out in the front of his dad's truck. Finally, Chris looked at the clock. "It's quarter to one. I've got to get you home."

I reluctantly sat up. "I don't want this night to end."

"Me neither, but your mom thinks I'm a good guy. Let's keep it that way."

"You are a good guy. Thanks for everything tonight."

He slid back over to the driver's seat and started the engine. "Trust me. It was my pleasure." He pulled out of the field, down the curving path, and back onto the main road. We were home in less than 10 minutes.

Chris parked the car and got out. He met me around the front of the truck and reached for my hand. He walked me to the front door and gave me a quick kiss. "Talk to you tomorrow?"

"Definitely," I answered. I opened the door and watched Chris jog back to the truck.

I was lost in my own thoughts. "How was your date?" my mom asked, startling me.

"Great. Really great!" I answered.

"I don't know why you hated him all those years. He seems like a nice guy," my mom said. "And he has manners." She smiled.

"Yeah, he is a nice guy. I'm going up to bed." I leaned over and gave my mom a kiss. "Good night, Mom."

"Good night, sweetie."

Before going upstairs, I grabbed the rose Chris brought me. I went up to my room, shut the door and set the flower on

40

my dresser. I changed into my pajamas and crawled between the cool sheets. I couldn't get Chris off my mind and the ridiculous smile off my face. My phone buzzed on my nightstand. I reached over and saw Chris's name.

> *Chris: Good night, Tori.*
> *Tori: I had a great time with you!*
> *Chris: Me, too! Can I see you tomorrow?*
> *Tori: Yes!*
> *Chris: I'll call you.*
> *Tori: Good night, Chris.* ☺

I fell asleep thinking of Chris's hands on me. He was gentle, yet possessive. He made me feel wanted. He made me feel beautiful. He made me feel like I was falling in love.

The next morning, I met Kyla for breakfast. She was already seated in the booth, and I slid in across from her. She raised her eyebrow at me. "You're glowing," she said. "I guess that means the date went well."

The waitress came over to take our drink orders and hand us menus. I ordered coffee, while Kyla got water. After the waitress walked away, I leaned across the table. "It was great! He was sweet the whole time."

"You two have been dancing around this for so long, I was surprised you agreed to go out with him. What happened with Matt?" she asked.

"Matt's a dickwad. He needed to go. I was sick of his shitty attitude. Honestly, for the last few weeks, he's just been someone to hang out with. I was talking to Trevor at the party on Friday and Matt got all jealous. I pushed him. He pushed me back and called me a bitch. Chris saw it all go down and stepped in. He offered to take me home."

"And you just said you would go out with him?" Kyla asked skeptically.

"Not exactly. We were talking is his truck and he asked me to give him a chance. I decided after what happened with Matt, what did I have to lose? So, I said yes. And then he kissed me, and I swear fireworks went off." I looked at her as I thought about kissing Chris. "That boy makes my panties so wet."

Kyla scrunched up her face. "Oh. Okay. Too much information."

I rolled my eyes at her. "Don't be such a prude. Hasn't any guy ever made your panties wet?"

"Aaah, no. And even if they did, I probably wouldn't tell you about it."

"Well, get used to hearing it, because you're my best friend. Who else am I going to tell?"

Kyla shook her head. "You do realize this is the same guy who stuck French fries up his nose in fifth grade and then ate them?" she asked.

The waitress came back to take our order and then left again. "Yeah, I know. But we were what...ten? He's super sweet." I leaned in really close. "I even let him touch my boobs."

"Tori Arianna Russo!" Kyla scolded.

"I'm a virgin, Kyla. That doesn't mean I haven't done other things. You know I'm not an angel."

"But on the first date?"

I shrugged my shoulders. "I figured he deserved it, since he'd waited so long for me to go out with him."

"But that's it, right? You didn't go further, did you?" she asked. I knew that Kyla had never let a guy touch her, and I think she was secretly getting off on me telling her all of this.

"Almost… but the cops interrupted us."

"What! The cops showed up?"

"You should have seen Chris. He handled it so well. I was scared shitless, but he was totally calm."

"Oh my God! You're crazy, you know that?"

"Yep. And that's why you love me."

42

Chapter 9
Chris

The next morning Jason, from football, came over to workout with me. We hung out in the garage, and I blasted the music. I told him about my date with Tori the night before.

"Tori's cool," he said. "You hit that last night?"

What the fuck? "No! Why would you ask me that?" I asked angrily.

"Chillax, man! It was just a question. She's no angel, you know?"

"What's that supposed to mean?"

Jason looked at me and quirked up his eyebrow. "Nothing. She's hot and she's got a banging bod. I've got classes with Matt. The way he talked, I just assumed she'd put out."

"She's not like that," I defended. "She's a virgin."

"You sure about that?" he asked.

Actually, I wasn't. I had just assumed. But now that I was thinking about it... she had offered for me to see her tits last night. That was kind of forward for a first date. Maybe she wasn't a virgin. Did it really matter? I wasn't. So why did she have to be? My head was reeling. I had this whole idea of Tori in my head, and now doubt was being cast upon it.

"No, I guess I'm not sure. What else did Matt say?"

"I don't know, man. Sounds like she gives one hell of a blow job though."

I didn't want to think about her sucking some other guy's dick. "Well, I wouldn't know, because we didn't do any of that." I started to wonder how far it would have gone if the cops hadn't interrupted us.

"You going out with her again?" he questioned.

"Yeah. I'm supposed to see her today."

"Well, maybe you'll find out. Let me know. If things don't work out… maybe you can send her my way."

"Fuck off, man! I really like her. I wouldn't send her your way. What do think? Because were friends I'm just going to pass her around?" I was getting fucking pissed. "You know what? I'm going to pretend like we didn't just have this conversation. If you still wanna be friends, you'll keep your fucking mouth shut."

"Dude, I'm sorry. I didn't realize you were that into her," Jason apologized.

"Well, I am. I've wanted to date her forever. Just don't talk about her like that. And I'd appreciate it if you didn't say shit like that to anyone else either."

"That's cool."

We finished our workout and didn't talk about Tori anymore.

Everything Jason said earlier was replaying in my head. I don't know why it bothered me. I knew Tori had boyfriends. I'd had girlfriends. I wasn't a virgin anymore. Susie Deluca had seen to that. That girl was a fucking freak in the sheets. And talk about blow jobs… let's just say my hand had a long rest.

What was wrong with me? Why was I setting a double standard? Because this was Tori. She was the one I'd wanted since… well, forever. I didn't want to think of her that way. I wanted to think that I would be her first—if we ever got that far. By the way Jason was talking, it sounded like we would. Sooner than later.

I called her after I took my shower. She didn't pick up but called me right back.

"Hey, Chris."

"Hey. I just wanted to know if you still wanted to hang out today."

"Yeah. What did you have in mind?" she asked.

"I don't know. I could pick you up and maybe we can decide then." I really wanted to take her back to the field where we were last night.

44

"That's cool. What time should I be ready?"

"Be there around two?" I asked.

"I'll be ready," she promised.

I pulled up to her house a few minutes before two. Her mom was out front, working on her flowers. I parked the truck, hopped out, and approached her. "Hi, Mrs. Russo."

She stopped what she was doing and looked up at me with a smile. "Hi, Chris. Tori was getting ready. Just knock on the door. I'm sure she's waiting."

"Thanks, Mrs. Russo." I walked up to the door and barely knocked before the door opened. Tori was standing there in a pair of jean shorts and a sparkly tank top. Her hair was piled on top of her head in some sort of knot. She had on some makeup, but not much. She looked really pretty.

She opened the door and walked out. Her purse ran across her body, the strap right between her tits. I tried not to look, but it was hard. I forced myself to look at her eyes. "You ready?" I asked.

"Yeah," she answered. I reached for her hand and walked her out to the truck. "Bye, Mom."

"Bye, sweetheart. Have fun."

I was starting to feel bad about the thoughts I had about her. I decided that Jason didn't know what he was talking about. I opened the door for her, and she hopped up into the truck. I ran around to the other side and slid into the driver's seat. "So, what do you want to do?" I asked.

"You want to go to Dairy Queen?" she asked. "I'll buy since you took me out last night."

"Sounds good," I answered. I pulled out onto her street and headed toward the Dairy Queen. When we got there, I asked, "Do you want to go in, or do drive-thru?"

45

"Let's do drive-thru," she answered. "Then maybe we can go back to that place from last night."

"It's a plan," I agreed with a smile. I drove to the window and placed our order. When she handed me the money to pay, I felt guilty getting a large Blizzard, especially when she only got a small. "That's all you want?" I asked.

"I'm not an athlete. I have to watch what I eat, or this ass will get out of control."

I rolled my eyes, "I told you, your ass is great."

"Only because I order a small," she answered.

"Whatever." I blew off her comment. I would never understand girls and why they criticized their own bodies. I mean, if I was happy with what I saw, shouldn't that make her happy?

Once we got our ice cream, I headed back towards the field. I pulled in and headed through the trees to the opening. Once I parked, she kicked off her sandals, undid her seatbelt, and leaned against the door. She put her feet up on the seat. Her toes were painted purple with sparkles. I ran my hands over her toes, and she wiggled them. "Your toes look cute," I said lamely. I never really paid attention to a girl's feet before, but I noticed everything about Tori, right down to her sparkly toenails.

"Thanks," she said shyly. "So… what did you do this morning?"

Fuck! That conversation with Jason was creeping into my mind. "Jason and I worked out. Nothing too interesting."

"When does football practice start?" she asked as she took a bite of her Blizzard and ran her tongue along the spoon. I wanted to be that spoon, so bad. I imagined what it would feel like to have her tongue on me like that.

I blinked my eyes and focused on her question. "Actually, it starts tomorrow. It's pretty much every morning until three, five days a week."

"I guess that will keep you busy," she looked disappointed.

46

"What's going on with you the rest of the summer?" I asked.

"I'm going up past Traverse City with my family next week. My parents have a house on Lake Michigan. I'm taking Kyla with me. It's a yearly thing with us."

"That sounds like fun," I said.

"It is. I've been taking Kyla up there with me every summer since we were in third grade. There's not much to do but hang out on the beach."

I started to think about what Tori would look like in a bikini. *Down boy,* I silently told my dick. "Are there a bunch of guys up there?" I asked.

"Not really. It's very private," she answered. She took another bite of her ice cream and then pointed her spoon at me. "Wait! Was that a little jealousy coming out?"

I shrugged my shoulders, "Maybe."

"Like I said, it's really private. It'll just be us girls."

"Good to know," I said. "When do you leave?"

"Not until next Sunday. The traffic going up north isn't bad then because most people are coming back home on Sunday."

"True," I said nodding my head. I reached in my pocket and pulled out a joint. "You wanna hit this with me?"

Tori smiled. "Sure. I thought you didn't smoke during football season."

"The season hasn't really started yet. Besides, I said 'not as much', not 'not at all'."

I opened the door and hopped out of the truck. "Where are you going?" she asked.

"We can't smoke it in the truck. My dad will kill me if he smells it."

She hopped out and followed me over to some logs that were arranged in a circle. "I hadn't thought about that." Tori sat down next to me and looked around. "So, do you guys have bonfires out here?"

"Sometimes, but not usually." I pulled out a lighter, took the joint between my lips and lit it. After taking a long hit, I passed the joint to Tori. She sucked in deep and handed it back to me. I blew out the smoke I was holding. "You're a lot better at that now than you were the first time we did this together," I teased her.

"I've had more practice since then," she replied. "That was almost two years ago."

I nodded. "So… has Matt called you, since your fight on Friday?" I hated to think that our date was just a distraction to her, and that she would go running if he called.

She looked at me questioningly. "No. Why?"

I shrugged and kicked at a rock with the toe of my shoe. "Just wondered. If he does, are you going to go back with him? Would you? Get back with him?"

Her eyes went big, "Wow! You really don't think very highly of me, do you?"

I scrunched up my eyebrows. "What's that supposed to mean?"

"It means that you think I just hop from guy to guy. Yeah, I kissed you on Friday, but only because I'd wanted to for a long time. If you were anyone else, it wouldn't have happened. I thought this was different. I'm not Susie Deluca!"

I knew that she knew I had gone out with Susie. Okay… 'gone out with' was loose terminology. More like I had fucked her. It lasted a few weeks. "I went out with her. Big deal. What are you getting at?"

"Oh, come on, Chris! Everybody knows she's fucked half the football team. You included."

Really? I didn't know that. Talk about an ego-deflator. I also didn't know, that apparently, everybody knew my business. "What are you getting all pissy about?" I asked.

"So, you thought I'd make out with you, let you feel me up, and then go back to Matt? Or were you hoping I was going to give you a blow job first? Is that why you asked me out?" Tori

48

stood up and started to walk toward the path that led to the road. "I knew this was too good to be true," she said.

"Where are you going?" I yelled after her.

She turned and put her hands on her hips. "Home. I thought you really liked me, Chris Capizzio. I guess I was wrong. Now I know what this was all about. You just think I'm easy and were hoping to get your dick wet."

I heard her voice hitch as she finished her rant. Was she crying? Tori Russo did not cry. Ever. Sure, she might cuss you out. But cry? Never. I'd known her since third grade, and I had never seen her cry. I jumped up off the log and ran after her. She had a good head start, but it didn't take me long to catch up to her.

I grabbed her by the shoulders and turned her to face me. Her eyes were all watery. "Are you crying?"

She wiped at her eyes and turned her head away from me. "No!"

"Yes, you are!"

"No! I'm not! I don't cry. Especially not over some guy, who seems to think I'm just an easy lay. What? You saw a vulnerable moment, and figured you'd just slip in while you could? You know what? Fuck you, Chris!" She pulled away from me and kept walking. She was fast, too. She was almost back to the winding road.

"Tori, stop!" She kept walking. "Goddamn it, Tori! Stop walking!"

She stopped in her tracks and stood there. She had her arms crossed over her chest and didn't turn around. I caught back up to her and stood in front of her. Tears were streaming down her cheeks. "What?" she practically shouted.

I cupped her face in my hands. "I'm sorry. I didn't mean to make you cry. I do like you. A lot. I don't think you're easy. Come back and sit with me. I want this to work. I'm sorry if I made you think something else."

She wiped the tears from her face. "I swear, if you tell anyone I cried, I'll chop your dick off."

49

I let out a little laugh. "I won't tell," I promised. "Please, come sit with me." I wrapped my arm around her shoulder and pulled her in tight to my side. I led her back to the circled logs and sat her down next to me. "I only asked because I don't want to lose you. I guess I can't believe that you actually agreed to go out with me. I wanted to see if you were in this for real, or if I was just fooling myself."

"I'm in this for real," she sniffed.

"Me too," I said.

"So, what now?" she asked. "I feel like whatever we do, you'll be judging me."

"I won't judge you. And I'm sure as hell not going to kiss and tell. This is between you and me. Whatever happens… it stays between us."

"Promise?"

"I promise. I don't want to lose you now that you're finally giving me a chance." It was the truth. I'd waited too long to fuck this up.

"You know, I was skeptical. I didn't want this to ruin our friendship, and it almost did," she said.

"I'm not going to let anything break us. I don't care about anything else but us. Trust me."

Chapter 10
Tori

Trust him? That was a hard one. I seriously didn't trust anyone. When I was with Matt and the guys before him, I knew what it was. I didn't give them too much of myself. What it was, was two people messing around and having a good time. Trust? That was a concept I wasn't familiar with.

Did I trust Chris? Now, that was the question. Could I give him my head and heart? If I did, I risked being hurt. I wasn't a fan of risk. I couldn't believe he made me cry. I didn't cry. Ever! It just proved to me that I felt something more for him. I cared about what he thought of me, and I wanted to kick myself for caring. I had shown him the vulnerable side of me, and I hated myself for it.

What do you do when you realize that you're falling in love? That you care? I was a master of turning off my emotions. Emotions were what messed people up. The way I was headed, I was going to be one of those messed up people. Fuck me!

Fuck me, was exactly what I wanted Chris to do. God, I was a slut!

We got through his week of football practice without further incident. I loved hanging out with Chris. Being with him was so easy. Something about us clicked and it was more than the toe-curling kisses we shared.

Sunday, I headed up north with Kyla. She and I drove separate from my parents in my blue VW Beetle. It gave Kyla and me time to talk without my parents around and I desperately needed some girl time.

"What's going on with you and Chris?" she asked. "Is it serious?"

"I'm not sure," I answered honestly. "He says he's in it for real. I'm just not sure I can believe him."

"What does your heart tell you?" she asked.

Why was she asking me that? Kyla had less experience than I did, and she was going to give me advice? "Does it matter?" I asked.

"Yeah, it matters. It matters a lot. Sometimes you need to think with your heart, instead of your head," she answered.

"Oh, yeah? Since when did you get so smart?" I teased her.

She smiled at me cockily. "I've always been smart." Well, that was the truth. "Here's the thing... you know I've only dated a few guys and nothing much has come of it. I dated them because my head told me they were safe, smart...acceptable. But here's the problem. Not one of them has ever made my heart flutter. I never got the butterflies. I want the butterflies. And I think you can only get them when your heart tells you it's right. So... what does your heart tell you?"

"What do the butterflies feel like?" I asked. This was such a weird conversation.

"Since I've never had them, I'm not sure. But I imagine it like this... you wake up and you think about him. You need to see him, talk to him, be with him. When you are with him, there's no other place you'd rather be. And when he kisses you, nothing else exists." Kyla sat back in her seat with a dreamy look on her face. "That's what I think true love is like," she explained.

"God, you're a hopeless romantic. Someday a guy is going to come along and demolish your heart and you're going to be helpless to stop it. And I'm going to have to pick up the pieces. Mark my word on that one."

52

She shrugged her shoulders. "Maybe." Then she narrowed her eyes at me, "You're deflecting. You didn't answer my question. What does your heart tell you?"

I huffed out a breath. "I know that this is going to sound corny, but... I think I love him. I don't know. Maybe it's just a physical thing."

Kyla clapped her hands. "I'm so excited for you. It's time one of us found love."

"Yeah, well, let's keep that little tidbit between the two of us. I'm not ready to let him know yet. Just in case."

Kyla ran her fingers across her lips pretending to zip them shut. "Mums the word. But I have to tell you, I'm rooting for the two of you. You guys are cute together. I think there's been something there for a while. You just weren't ready to admit it."

I rolled my eyes. I figured I should tell her the truth. "You're so right. Did I ever tell you that we kissed at the bonfire last year? And the year before?"

Kyla turned to me with a shocked expression on her face. "After the football games?"

I nodded my head.

"Where the hell was I?"

"Hanging with the other cheerleaders. So, Chris and I hung out some."

Kyla looked at me with regret. "I'm a shitty friend. How did I not even notice you snuck away?"

"You're not a shitty friend. You're the best friend I could ever ask for. You just got carried away with socializing. It's okay. It's not like we're attached at the hip. You're allowed to have other friends."

She shook her head. "Maybe. But even so...that was shitty of me. I'm sorry if you felt left out."

I waved her off. "Are you kidding me? Sneaking off with Chris was amazing. I'll tell you what... that boy can kiss!"

Kyla giggled. "Fireworks?" she asked.

"Like the Fourth of July," I answered.

53

I talked to Chris every night while Kyla and I were away. By Wednesday, I actually missed him. He texted me.

Chris: Wanna Skype?

Tori: OK. Give me a few minutes.

I looked at Kyla sheepishly. "Do you mind going out on the deck and reading for a while? I want to talk to Chris for a few minutes. We're going to Skype."

She grabbed her tablet off the bed and headed toward the door. She got a suspicious look on her face. "This isn't going to be like that one book we read, is it? You know. Where they…well, you know."

I grabbed a pillow off the bed and threw it at her. "God, no! I don't think we're even close to that. All we've done is kiss." She quirked an eyebrow up at me. "Okay! And touched a little bit."

She picked the pillow up off the floor and tossed it back on the bed. "I'll be out back, indulging in my own fantasies. Come get me when you're done." She closed the door behind her and headed downstairs.

I sat on my bed, logged into my Skype account on my laptop, and dialed Chris. He answered immediately, and his face popped up on the screen. Not just his face, but his full naked chest too. He definitely wasn't scrawny anymore. As a matter of fact, his chest was muscular and defined. I wanted to reach through the screen and rub my hands along it.

"You gonna say anything or just look at me?" he asked.

I shook my head. "Sorry. I got distracted. Hi."

He gave me a cocky smile. "Hi. I missed seeing your face."

I immediately became self-conscience. Why hadn't I at least put on some mascara before calling him? I covered my face with my hands. "I probably look like a wreck. I've been out in the sun all day. I didn't think about it before calling you."

"You look perfect the way you are. I don't think you realize how pretty you are."

I felt the redness creeping up my neck. "Thanks. How's practice been?" I asked, trying to move the attention off myself.

"It's fine. Been kicking my ass, but it's all good." One side of his mouth quirked up in a dimpled smile. "I know this might sound crazy, but I've really missed you."

"I've missed you, too. I've kind of gotten used to seeing you every night."

"Me too. I miss kissing you," he said. "When you come home, we'll have to make up for lost time." He waggled his eyebrows at me.

"I think that can be arranged." I uncrossed my legs and laid down on my stomach, propping myself up on my elbows.

"You're killing me right now, you know that?" He groaned.

"What?" I asked innocently.

"Nice boob shot. Can you angle the screen down a little bit?"

I looked down at my chest, and sure enough, my shirt was hanging low, and the tops of my boobs were hanging out. I squeezed them together with my arms, so that they looked even bigger and showed more cleavage. Then I adjusted the screen, so he had a better view. "Does that turn you on?" I teased him.

"More than you know. I'm probably going to have to take another shower after this. When are you coming home?"

"We're leaving Saturday morning so we can miss the traffic. Do you wanna hang out Saturday night?" I asked.

"Do you even need to ask? I can't wait to get my hands on you." He held up his hands and made a grabbing motion with them, like he was squeezing my boobs.

"Oh my, God! Is that all you think about?" I laughed out loud.

55

"I'm a guy. What do you think? I can't help it that you're sexy as hell."

The blush crept into my cheeks. "I'm not."

"You are. And I can't wait to show you."

"You are so bad, Capizzio!"

"And you love every bit of it," he replied.

Oh yeah! I totally did.

Chapter 11
Chris

I spent a lot of time getting ready for my date with Tori. Showered, jacked off again, and even did some manscaping. I'd read online that it makes your dick look bigger.

I was pretty decent in that department, but thought *what the hell?* Every little bit helps, right? Plus, if I did get a blow job, I didn't want her getting a mouthful of hair. Kind of considerate, I thought.

I threw on some cargo shorts and a concert tee with the sleeves cut off. We were just hanging out, so there was no need to dress up. I was a junkie for 70's and 80's rock. There was something classic about it. You just couldn't compete with Mötley Crüe, AC/DC, Ozzy, and a shit ton of others. Today I had chosen Guns N' Roses. Totally classic.

I pulled up in her driveway at five. I quickly got out of the truck and jogged up to the door. When she pulled it open, I had to laugh. She had on a Led Zeppelin tee. It was a V-neck, and her cleavage was showing. "Oh, we were so made for each other," I said. "We gotta go to a concert together." I handed her the single purple rose I bought. I wanted this to be my special thing with her. Something that would separate me from any other guy she had gone out with.

She held the flower to her nose. "I'd be up for that." She smiled as she came out and gave me a quick peck on the lips. "I missed you."

I groaned. "You don't even know how much." I had wanted her for years but having a little taste and then having her go away for a week was pure torture. "Did you eat yet?" I asked.

"Not really," she answered.

"I gotta eat. You cool with Subway?"

After getting our subs, I drove us out to our spot and parked. We sat in the truck while we ate and just bullshitted. I was so starved I practically inhaled my sub, then realized my mistake. Why in the hell did I get peppers and onions on it? My breath was going to kill her.

She finished her six-inch Italian sub and shoved all the garbage in the bag. I watched as she pulled down the mirror on the visor and checked her teeth. While she was looking at herself, I held a hand over my mouth and checked my breath. Fuck! Onion breath at its worst. She flipped the visor back up, reached into her purse, and pulled out some mints. Thank God! She popped one in her mouth and started to put them away.

"Can I have one of those?" I asked.

"Take two," Tori said. "You reek like onions. Did you have peppers on that thing too?" She wrinkled up her nose in disgust.

"Yes. I wasn't thinking," I said shamefully.

"Here. Take them all." She handed me the container of mints.

I popped a few in my mouth. "Hopefully, this will help. Are you still going to kiss me?" I questioned as I handed them back.

Tori shrugged her shoulders. "Maybe. Let's give those mints a chance to work."

"Are you fucking with me right now?" I mean, I knew the onions were bad, but really? I had a hard time believing she would hold back because of it.

She pulled her knees underneath her and crawled like a cat across the bench seat to me. She got a sexy little smirk on her face. "Maybe. I actually really like onions." She leaned forward and captured my lips with hers.

I grabbed the sides of her face and pushed my tongue deep inside her minty mouth. She was a great kisser and I got lost in it. Tori climbed over me and straddled my lap. "You're a little tease. You know that?"

"I'm only a tease, if I don't follow through." She rubbed her hands up under my shirt and along my chest. "I'm not a tease."

"Fuck me," I muttered.

"Not tonight, baby. But we can do other things."

I got hard at her words, and she pushed her center into me. "You're sitting on my dick again," I pointed out.

"Oh, is that what that is?" she chided. "I thought I felt something."

I pushed my hips up into her. "I'll make you feel something, all right."

"I hope so," she moaned, as she moved her hips back and forth over my hard-on. Tori reached for the hem of my shirt, pulled it up over my head, and threw it on the seat next to us. She ran her hands along my chest and up over my shoulders. I was mesmerized as she placed soft kisses along my shoulder and up my neck. I leaned my head back and closed my eyes, as she moved her lips up to my ear and gently took it between her teeth. "What do you want? Other than fucking me?" she whispered.

She was killing me with her words. I got rock hard when she breathed in my car. I wanted her, right now. I grabbed the bottom of her shirt and started pulling it over her head. It got stuck on her boobs and they bounced down in her black bra when her shirt finally released. "Oh my, God. Did I just hurt you?"

She shook her head. "I'm okay. These things are a hazard." Tori got an embarrassed look on her face and turned her head to the side.

I turned her face back toward me. "I think they're beautiful." I cupped her tits in my hands and kissed the swells that spilled out of her bra. I wanted to see them. All of them. I'd seen tits before. Susie Deluca's were kind of small. I'd seen Katie Myers' too. Bigger than Susie, but average, I guess. Tori was way more than average, not obscenely big, just perfect.

I ran my hands down to her tiny waist. "Are you okay?"

Tori lowered her head. "Just embarrassed."

I tipped her head back up. "About what?"

"Getting stuck in my shirt. It's hardly sexy." She looked away again.

"Baby, look at me." She turned her head toward me, and I held her chin. "You're very sexy. I've always thought so. Let me see you and show you how sexy you are." I reached my hands behind her back and reached for the clasp of her bra. I kept feeling along her back but couldn't find it. What was going on here?

She let out a little laugh. "I'm sorry." She covered her mouth with her hand. "It's in the front."

I looked down between her tits and sure enough, there was a clip in the front. I fumbled a bit and finally it gave away. I pushed the cups back and freed her tits. Her nipples were big and dark, the peaks hard. I took her tits in my hands and ran my thumbs over those hard nipples. "You're beautiful," I whispered.

I leaned my head down and kissed the swells again. I poked my tongue out and ran it down one of her tits and circled it around her nipple. She let out a little whimper, and I sucked her nipple into my mouth. God, she was perfection. I worked my way over to the other one and sucked on it. I released her from my mouth and ran my hands over her again. "Don't be embarrassed with me."

60

She buried her head in my neck. "I want to touch you," she whispered.

I ran my hand down over her back, "I want to touch you too."

"We're not having sex," she clarified.

"That's okay. I just want to feel you."

Tori crossed her arm over her chest and climbed off my lap. I didn't want to tell her, but her arm was never going to cover those things. She looked out the window. It was starting to get dark.

"No one's coming back here," I assured her.

"I just feel kind of exposed."

"Trust me. We're alone."

She took a deep breath. "Okay." Tori dropped her arm and reached for the button on my shorts. Her fingers worked quickly as she pulled down the zipper. She looked at me from under her lashes. "Are you sure?"

I nodded my head. "More than sure." I took her hand and placed it at the top of my shorts. Her hand crept down the front and rubbed me on top of my boxer briefs. I took her hand again and moved it down inside. Tori wrapped her small fingers around my dick, and I hissed at the contact. She started to move her hand up and down, applying just the right pressure. She had definitely done this before. She rubbed her thumb up over the head and rubbed the drop of liquid around. She reached her hand down farther and ran her nails along my balls. Her hand twisted up and down along my shaft and I felt myself harden more. It felt fucking fantastic, but I had to stop her. "You gotta stop, Tori."

She released her grip and ran her fingers gently up my dick in a feather-light touch. "Did I do something wrong?" she questioned.

"Not even close. I was ready to come all over your hand," I admitted. "I don't have anything in here to clean up with."

"Well, now I feel bad," she said. "I shouldn't have done that to you. I wasn't thinking."

"Yes, you should have. And trust me, next time I'll be prepared," I assured her. I started kissing her again. It became frantic and animalistic. Our tongues twisted together, and I swear she bit my lip. I squeezed her tits, running my hands all over them. I took them in my mouth again. I couldn't get enough of her, and my dick was throbbing.

Suddenly, she slammed me back against the door of the truck. "Fuck it! I was going to save this for another night, but I want you right now," she said in a raspy voice. Her hands went to the waist of my shorts, and she tried to push them down my hips. I lifted a little and she got them down to my thighs.

I didn't say a damn thing, because I was pretty sure I knew where this was going. And if I was right, I was about to get one hell of a blow job.

Tori's lips locked around my dick and my eyes rolled back into my head. Holy Hell! She worked her hand and mouth in a perfect rhythm, as her tongue swirled up around my head. Watching her bob up and down on me, made me want to touch her. That was my last thought before she sank way down deep, and my mind went blank of everything except one thing…Best. Blow Job. Ever. I felt my dick hit the back of her throat and I thought she was going to choke, but her throat opened and took me deeper. Her throat squeezed me over and over again. She rubbed and tugged and sucked, bringing me to the edge. My balls tightened, and my dick hardened painfully. I couldn't hold back. "Tori, I'm gonna…" but it was too late. I exploded. I threw my head back, "Oh my fucking god!" My body convulsed as I emptied everything into her mouth. There was a blinding light and I swear I heard angels singing. I hoped to God that's what heaven was like because…holy shit, if I died tonight, I'd die happy.

Tori swallowed it all down, then pulled back. She ran her tongue along her lips, then pulled her bottom lip inside, biting it. "Better?" she asked.

"Holy fuck!" I was breathing hard and trying to get my senses back. "Wow… that was…fuck!" The currents of electricity were still zinging through my body.

She let out a little laugh. "That good, huh?"

"You have no idea," I told her. I pulled my shorts back up my hips and tucked myself inside. "I want to touch you. Make you come too."

She shook her head. "Not tonight." She grabbed her bra off the seat and put her arms through it, securing it in the front. Then she searched for her shirt, which had fallen on the floorboards, and pulled it over her head.

This didn't make sense to me. Why would she pass this up? Maybe she was on her period. I didn't know what else to think, so I didn't press the issue. "Are you okay?" I asked. I didn't want her to feel like I had used her. "I didn't expect you to do that. You didn't have to."

"I wanted to. I wanted to make you feel good." She handed me my shirt and I threw it over my head.

"Well, mission accomplished. I don't think I've ever come that hard."

Chapter 12
Tori

I was a slut!

Why did I give him a blow job? I got so fucking turned on, I couldn't help myself. Shame on me! I had promised myself, that I wasn't going to go there with him yet. Matt always liked it, and I figured Chris would too. Was I that desperate for a boyfriend?

Then he wanted to repay the favor. No way in hell that was happening anytime soon. I didn't want him to see my ass. I wasn't blessed with the small, cutesy shape that other girls had. Yeah, I had curves, but they were too much. My boobs were too big... and my ass? Well, I had hips on me for sure. I wasn't fat. My waist was tiny. It was above and below my waist that were the problem. My boobs I could deal with. I mean, what guy didn't like big boobs? But a big ass? That was a whole other story. It wasn't huge or anything, but my hips flared out and most girls our age didn't have hips like mine yet.

Besides, I knew he wanted to try to make me come. I had never been able to with a guy. Matt tried, and I had to fake it. I didn't know what was wrong with me. I could get myself off, but I wouldn't suffer the humiliation of faking it again. I mean... I guess I would have to, eventually, but I wasn't ready for it tonight. I didn't want to have to fake it with Chris.

Guys expected girls to get off as easily as they did. My body just didn't work that way. I didn't want Chris to think he wasn't enough for me. Honestly, I didn't want him to think I wasn't enough for him. I knew he was more experienced than me. Shit... I didn't want to think about him with Susie Deluca, but I knew the truth about them. For all I knew, Susie wasn't the only one. Maybe there were others.

I laid in bed that night and tried not to think about it. Chris had invited me to his house tomorrow night to have dinner. Apparently, his mom and dad wanted to meet me. I had seen them at school events over the years, but I didn't really know them.

I didn't even know what to wear. I asked Kyla and she suggested the cute dress I bought when we were up north. I wasn't a dress person. If I was being honest, it was an impulse buy. But Kyla was right, it did look good on me. My ass didn't look that big, and that, in itself, was a bonus.

I spent extra time doing my hair and makeup, then threw the dress on with some cute strappy sandals. "You look really nice," Kyla said. "You should wear dresses more often."

I rolled my eyes at her. "I feel awkward. Dresses aren't my thing."

"Trust me," she said. "Chris is going to love it!"

"You think so?" I asked.

"I know so. You look gorgeous. I wish I had your curves. And your height," she said with envy.

"You don't think they're too much?" I asked, letting my insecurities show. At five-foot five I wasn't tall, but I felt like a giant next to Kyla. She was so petite.

"No. You're beautiful. You worry too much. He's going to love it!"

I gave her a tight hug. "Thank you for helping me. I promise, one day I'll repay the favor." I knew she had been hoping to fall in love. I felt a little guilty that she was spending her time helping me, when I knew she wished it was her that had found someone.

"You don't owe me a thing. It'll happen for me someday. When the time is right," she insisted. "I hope this all works out for you, because I think you two are super cute together." She looked at her phone. "It's time for me to skedaddle. I don't want to be here when Chris shows up." She gave me a final hug. "Have fun, but not too much fun!"

She bounced down the stairs and ran out to her car. I looked in the mirror one last time. Kyla was right, I did look pretty.

Chris showed up promptly at five-thirty to pick me up. I let my mom open the door and smiled when I heard them talking. My mom liked Chris and that was a good thing. I listened for a little bit, then made my way down the stairs. My mom could barely contain her smile when she saw me, and I knew she approved of my outfit. She was always trying to get me to dress more girly, and I was always against it. For once, I agreed that going with a dress was the right move.

Chris walked me out to the truck and helped me inside. I was sure he got a great view of my ass. I ran my hand along the back of the dress and tried to slip in without giving him a show. Chris ran around to the driver's side and hopped up into the truck. He took my hand in his. "You look really pretty tonight."

"Thank you." I wasn't used to compliments and felt uncomfortable.

"I like you in a dress. Your legs look sexy. Plus, I'm thinking easy access for later." He lifted his eyebrow at me.

I playfully swatted at his arm. "Get your head out of the gutter, we're going to have dinner with your parents."

"They're going to love you," he assured me. "Are you nervous?"

"A little bit. I've never gone to meet a guy's parents before."

"Don't be nervous. They're cool. My mom is about the sweetest thing you'll ever meet."

It was an innocent comment, but I don't think most guys would refer to their mom that way. It was endearing, and I knew Chris had a vulnerable, soft side to him.

We pulled up to his house a few minutes later. Chris ran around to help me out of the truck. He held my hand and put one arm around my waist. It was a sweet gesture that I appreciated.

We walked into the kitchen, where his mom was making dinner. "We're here," Chris announced. Then he walked over and gave her a kiss on the cheek.

Mrs. Capizzio wiped her hands on a dish towel. "Hi, sweetie. This must be Tori." She came over and gave me a hug, taking me by surprise.

"Hi, Mrs. Capizzio. It's nice to meet you."

"I've heard so much about you, and I wanted to finally meet the girl who has my son all smiles lately."

"Mom!" Chris exclaimed.

She smacked him with the dishtowel. "Well, it's true."

I couldn't help but smile at their banter.

Chris's dad walked in a few moments later. "So, are you going to introduce me to this pretty girl, or what?"

Chris rolled his eyes. "Dad, this is Tori. Tori, my dad."

I gave him a little wave. "Hi, Mr. Capizzio." He was a big man. He was at least six-foot three with wide shoulders. I wasn't sure what to make of him. Chris wasn't short, probably about five-eleven, but seeing his dad made me think he was probably going to grow a couple more inches.

"Chris, why don't you come out and help me with the grill? Let your mom and Tori talk."

I got a little panicky. I didn't want to be left alone with his mom yet.

"Yeah, okay," Chris agreed. He gave me an apologetic look, asking if I was all right.

I just gave him a shrug as he backed out the door. I turned to Chris's mom, determined to make the best of the situation. "Can I help you with anything?" I asked. My mom was a horrible cook, so I didn't know how to do jack shit. However, it only seemed polite to at least offer.

67

"Oh, no. Everything is just about ready. Just have a seat. Can I get you something to drink?" Relief swept through me that I wasn't expected to do anything.

"Umm… water is fine." I felt really awkward. "I can set the table if you'd like," I offered.

She smiled at me. "That would be great." Mrs. Capizzio started to take out the plates and silverware and set them on the counter. I quickly scooped them up and placed them around the table. I figured if I kept busy, it would make things less awkward. But setting the table didn't take long.

I sat at the table, searching my mind for something else to say or do. "Thank you for inviting me for dinner."

"Oh, it was my pleasure. I had to meet you. I haven't seen Chris this happy in a long time."

I wasn't sure what to say. "I'm sure that has to do with football season starting. I know he's excited about it," I said.

She cocked her head to the side. "Maybe, but I think there's more to it than that. Do you go to the games?" she asked.

"Yeah. I mean… yes. I'm on yearbook. I'm usually there taking pictures. And my best friend, Kyla, is on the cheer squad."

"Do you like photography?" she asked.

"I love it, but mostly I just take pictures for the yearbook. I'd like to buy a really nice camera of my own, but they're very expensive. So, until I can afford one, I'll have to settle for taking pictures with my phone or the school camera." I shrugged. "I'm still trying to figure out what I want to go to college for. I'm thinking photography or journalism, but I'm not sure yet." I realized I was rambling and shut my mouth.

"Well, you have plenty of time to figure it out. Chris is going into engineering. His dad works for General Motors, so that will help him find a job when the time comes."

"I didn't realize he'd already decided," I stated. I felt like maybe I should already have a plan too, but honestly, I hadn't given it that much thought. We had two more years of high school. I always figured I had plenty of time to decide.

The slider opened, and Chris came in carrying a plate of chicken. *Are you okay?* He mouthed to me.

I nodded my head. We all sat down to eat, and Chris was right, his mom was about the sweetest thing I had ever met. His dad, on the other hand, rubbed me the wrong way. I found him to be kind of scary. He didn't do anything wrong. He was just gruff and very no nonsense... and big.

After dinner, I offered to help clear the table and do the dishes. Chris's mom wouldn't hear of it. She shooed us off and we made our way out to the backyard.

It was a great yard. It was big with a lot of trees. I looked out far onto the property. "Is that a treehouse?" I asked.

"Yep. My dad helped my brother and me build it when I was about eight. Wanna see it?"

"Sure," I agreed. Chris took my hand, and we walked out to the back of the property. There was a ladder nailed to the trunk that led up to the treehouse.

"Climb up," he said.

I narrowed my eyes at him. "I don't think so. I'm wearing a dress and you're not getting a show. You go up first. I'll be right behind you."

He laughed. "Can't blame me for trying." He grabbed the first rung and started up the ladder.

I followed behind him. When I got to the top, Chris took my hand and helped me up. It was bigger inside than I thought it would be. There was a make-shift table in the center with overturned crates around it. The windows had shutters on them, and it was decorated with posters of rock bands. "This is really cool," I said.

"We used to have bean bag chairs and stuff in here, but no one ever uses it anymore, so we cleaned almost everything out," he said. Then he stepped closer to me and wrapped his arms around my waist. "I've been waiting to do this all night." He lowered his head to mine and gave me a long, passionate kiss. It was sweet and soft. I opened my mouth, and he kissed me deeper, twisting his tongue with mine. "Did I tell you how pretty you look and how good you made me feel last night?"

I smirked at him. "You might have mentioned it."

"Tori?"

"Hmmm?"

"I want to make you feel as good as you made me feel. Did I do something wrong last night?" He took my dark hair and pushed it out of my face and over my shoulder.

I bit my lip and shook my head. I didn't want to have this conversation. "You didn't do anything wrong."

He cocked his head to the side. "Then why wouldn't you let me touch you? Is it…you know…that time?"

This was embarrassing. "No, it's not that."

"Then what's the problem?" I didn't answer him. "Tori, talk to me. What's the problem?"

I didn't think that not letting him touch me would cause this big of an issue. I figured as long as I made him happy, that would be the end of it. I felt the stress rise up inside me. When in doubt… be a bitch. It was my classic go-to. I raised my voice out of frustration. "What do you want from me?" I turned away from him and crossed my arms over my chest.

Chris was totally unaffected by my outburst. Instead of getting pissed, he wrapped his arms around me, so that my back was against his chest. "I want you to be honest with me," he said softly.

I pulled myself from his embrace and sat down on one of the crates. I had hoped to avoid this. Now it was truth time. "I didn't want you to see me! Okay?" I buried my face in my hands.

He kneeled in front of me. "What? Why?"

"I don't want to talk about it." A tear ran down the side of my face. All my insecurities came to the surface, and they were ugly. And embarrassing. It wasn't that I didn't want Chris to touch me. I did. More than anything. But my mind was trumping my body, and I couldn't let it go.

Chris wiped it away with his thumb. "That's the second time I've made you cry. I'm not very good at this boyfriend thing." He wrapped his arms around me and held me to his chest. It felt nice. He was warm and strong. And he smelled good. I snuggled into his warmth.

I closed my eyes and summoned up my courage. "Chris, I like you. A lot. I'm just not ready for you to see all of me yet."

He held my face in his hands. "Tori, you're beautiful. Seeing all of you is not going to make me change my mind about that. I don't know why you feel this way. I love your curves." Then he thought for a moment. "Would you let me touch you, if you didn't have to let me see you?"

"What do you mean?" I asked.

"Well, you are wearing a dress." He smirked. His hand crept up under the hem and onto my thigh. "I really want to touch you."

I took a deep breath. "I want you to. I wanted you to, last night."

"Then let me." He pressed his lips to mine and kissed me deeply. Then he lifted me off the crate and laid me on the floor. I wrapped my arms around his neck and returned the kiss. It became feverish and frantic. His hand crept up my thigh and reached around to cup my ass. He squeezed it and then moved his hand to the front of my panties. He rubbed along the fabric, but never stopped kissing me. His hand moved down between my legs. He ran his fingers along the edge of my panties, and he pulled them aside. I wanted him to touch me so bad. He slipped a long finger inside me, and I gasped.

"You're so fucking wet," he moaned. Chris pulled his hand back and inserted two fingers. He slowly began to pump them in and out of me.

"Chris, I don't think…." But the thought died off. The intrusion was wonderful. I closed my eyes and savored the feeling of his touch. "Oh, my god," I gasped. He curled his fingers inside me and hit a spot that felt oh so good. I wasn't going to come from it, but the pleasure was still there. I let it consume me, and gasps of ecstasy escaped me. Never had I felt this way before. But I was greedy, and I wanted more. I wanted him to do what no one else ever had. I wanted him to make me come. "Rub my clit, Chris," I begged. "Please… I need more."

He pulled his hand back and rubbed my wetness over my clit. He used his thumb to rub small circles on my most sensitive area. I could feel myself climbing and my thighs clenched. I was soooo close. I had never felt this way before with a guy. He whispered in my ear, "Come for me, Tori."

My eyes rolled back into my head, and I could feel myself on the edge. A few more strokes and lights flashed behind my eyes as my hips lifted from the floor. "Oh, my God! That's…wow!" He stuck his fingers back inside me and pumped me hard. The shock waves zipped through my body and when I came down, I was sure my body had turned to jello.

I opened my eyes and Chris was staring down at me, just inches from my face. "That's what I wanted to do to you last night."

I was still trying to catch my breath. "I've never… that was a first," I stuttered.

Chris narrowed his eyes in confusion. "You've never come before?"

My embarrassment set in again. "No… I have. Just not like that. You know… from someone else. I've never been able to… I'm just going to shut up now." I tucked my head into his shoulder.

"No one has ever made you come before?" he asked.

I shook my head. "Just myself. That was soooo much better." I couldn't erase the silly grin from my face. "I think you have magic hands."

He held up his hand and wiggled his fingers. "Who knew?" He let out a low laugh, then pulled me up into a sitting position and I smoothed my dress down over my legs.

"What are you doing to me, Chris Capizzio? I knew you could kiss, but that was… amazing."

"I aim to please." He leaned down and kissed me hard. His hands ran over my breasts and cupped them. "I love your body. You make me want you so bad."

"Slow down, magic man. We're not going there yet." I smirked at him. "Besides, I think we better get back to the house. I don't want your parents thinking I'm one of those girls."

He stood up and reached his hand down for me to hold. I grabbed it, and he pulled me to my feet. "They won't," he assured me. Chris led me back to the ladder and I went down first. When Chris got to the bottom, he took my hand in his and we walked back up to the house.

The wall I kept up around my heart and emotions was starting to crumble. I was falling for this boy, and I was helpless to stop it.

Chapter 13
Chris

I took Tori home and walked her to the door. I was falling for this girl. Hard. Shit, who was I kidding? I had fallen for her years ago, but spending time with her and touching her was better than I ever imagined.

I went right to my room when I got home and laid on my bed thinking about Tori. I couldn't believe that no one had ever made her come before. It felt good knowing I was the first. I still wondered about what Jason said. Was she a virgin? The way she gave a blow job, I highly doubted it. But the fact that no one had ever made her come before, gave me hope that maybe she was. I didn't want to think about her with another guy. I'd heard that sometimes girls faked it. Could she have faked it tonight? Was it all an act? No. I felt her clench my fingers. I was pretty sure it was the real deal.

My phone buzzed, and I grabbed it off the bed next to me. It was a text from Tori.

Tori: Thanx for 2nite. Listening to Heart "Magic Man" and thinking of you!

I laughed out loud and texted her back.

Chris: So cool that you know that song.
Tori: You earned the title tonight.
Chris: I'll try to live up to it!
Tori: Don't think that will be a problem.
Chris: See you tomorrow?
Tori: Definitely!!!

I went to football practice in the morning. Coach had us running our asses off and it was grueling. As it got closer to the start of the season, he was pushing us harder.

When we finally got a break, Jason sidled up next to me. "So how are things going with Tori?" he asked.

I'm sure my face gave everything away. "Good. Really good."

"So, is she or not?" he questioned.

That kind of pissed me off. He was way too interested in my girl. "Not your business, man," I replied.

He held up his hands in surrender. "Just wondering. I went out with Susie this weekend. Man, that girl rocked my world."

"Been there, done that. I think she's rocked half this team. Ain't nothing special."

"Oh, and Tori is?" he questioned.

"Yeah, she is! That's all I'm saying. The rest isn't your concern," I answered.

"You must really like her. It's not like you to get hung up on some girl."

"What the fuck is that supposed to mean?" I asked.

"It means, you're getting whipped. Pussy must be good."

I didn't even think. I cocked my fist back and plowed my fist into his face. The fucker didn't go down, so I hit him again. Blood spurted from his nose. He held his face in his hand "What the fuck, man!"

I stood over the top of him. "I warned you! Don't talk about her that way!"

Next thing I knew I was being hauled back by my shoulders. "Take a walk, Capizzio!" coach shouted at me. I pulled out of his grasp and walked away with my hands on my head. I couldn't believe I just punched one of my best friends. Fucker pissed me off! Next thing I knew, coach was in my face. "I don't know what's going on and I don't want to know. Take the rest of the day off! And if you pull that shit again, you're sitting the bench the first game!"

I stalked off the field. It was only 10:30. I needed to keep my cool. I didn't want to sit the bench, but that fucker totally deserved what he got.

My mom had dropped me off at practice. I didn't have a way to get home, so I started walking. I pulled out my phone and called Tori. It rang twice, and she picked up.

"Hey. I thought you were at practice."

"I was. But I'm walking home. I'll explain later. Do you think you could pick me up?" I asked.

"Yeah. Where are you? I'm leaving right now," she said.

"I'm walking down 25 Mile Road. I'll meet you at the gas station at the corner."

"Okay. I'm on my way. Are you alright?"

"Not really, but I will be when I see you," I confessed.

"See you in a few," she said and hung up.

I was so fucking pissed. What the hell? I warned that asshole. No one was going to talk about my girl like that and get away with it. I threw my phone into my duffle bag and kept walking. My dad could not know about this. I would get my ass reamed. He didn't put up with this kind of shit. I knew better, but I just couldn't help myself.

I walked up to the gas station and sat down on the curb outside. Five minutes later Tori pulled up in her old blue beetle. It was the perfect car for her, and I couldn't keep the smile from my face. Whenever I saw her, everything else just seemed to melt away.

I walked up to her car, threw my stuff in the backseat, and slid in beside her. I leaned over and kissed her. Hard. "Are you alright?" she questioned.

"I am now."

"Want to talk about it?"

"Not really. Can you take me home? I need to shower and change. And I need to cool down. Coach sent me home."

"Oh," was all she said. She turned forward and drove out of the gas station parking lot. She pulled into my driveway a few minutes later. "Do you want me to wait for you or would you rather be alone?" she asked.

"I don't want you to leave. Come in and wait. I won't be long."

Tori got out of the car and followed me into the house. I grabbed her hand and led her up to my bedroom. "Make yourself comfortable," I said as I grabbed some clothes and headed toward the shower.

"What if your parents come home? I don't think I should be in here."

"They're not coming home," I assured her. "I'll be quick and then we can get out of here."

Tori nodded her head as I went off to shower. I tried to be quick. I couldn't get what that fucker said out of my head. I fucking warned him. When it came to Tori, I would protect her any way I could. I could see myself with her years from now. This wasn't like Susie or any of the other girls I had been with. I was falling in love with her. And nobody would disrespect her!

When I got back to my room, Tori was laying on my bed, texting on her phone. I liked the way she looked on my bed. She was totally fuckable. I pushed it all down and pulled it together. "You ready to get out of here, baby?" I asked.

"Sure. Where do you want to go?"

"Anywhere. I need to call my mom and tell her practice ended early. Obviously, she won't need to pick me up today."

"You gonna tell me what happened or pretend like nothing did?"

"I don't want to talk about it. I lost my cool and coach sent me home. Not much more to say," I answered.

"I don't believe you, but it's okay. You don't need to tell me," Tori said.

I appreciated the fact that she wasn't going to push the issue. I didn't have the heart to tell her why I popped Jason in the face. She didn't need to know. I sat down on the bed next to her and took her hand. "I fucked up, Tor. That's all I'll say."

77

She ran her fingers along the side of my face. "I'm sure you had your reasons."

"I did," I assured her.

Tori sat up and took my face in her hands. "Let's get out of here. Want to go to the beach?"

I rubbed my face along her soft hands. "That sounds great. Did I totally screw your day?"

"You made my day one hundred percent better." Tori pressed her lips to mine.

I lowered her back to the bed. My hands caressed her soft curves, and I devoured her lips with mine, taking in all the sweetness that was her. The repercussions of what I had done today would be worth it. She was worth it.

I wanted to crawl under the covers and keep her here with me all day. I wanted to feel her soft skin against mine. I wanted to push into her and hear her scream my name. It would happen eventually. I just had to be patient. I would wait for her.

I pulled Tori to her feet. "We better get going."

We spent the day holding hands and walking barefoot through the sand along Lake St. Clair. We laughed and talked as we sat in the sand looking out over the lake. I wrapped my arm around her shoulder and Tori snuggled into my chest. We fit together perfectly. I leaned over and kissed the side of her head. "Thank you for today. I really needed this. You turned a shit day into something great."

Tori looked up at me with her honey-colored eyes, "I didn't do anything special. I'm just me."

"I know, but it's everything." I lifted her head to meet mine and kissed her deeply. "You're everything." The alarm went off on my phone and I looked at the time. "We need to get going. I want to get home before my dad does."

"Is he going to be mad about today?" she asked.

"I don't plan on telling him, but if he finds out, he won't be happy."

"Well, let's go. I don't want you getting in trouble." We walked back to Tori's car and made the quick trip home.

78

My heart sank when we pulled up to the house. My dad's truck was already in the driveway. "Fuck," I muttered.

Tori squeezed my hand. "It'll be okay. Call me later and let me know how everything goes."

I leaned over and gave her a quick kiss. "I will," I promised.

I jogged up to the house and tried to act cool, taking the stairs two at a time up to my room. "Where the hell have you been all day?" I turned and looked down the stairs, where my dad stood. He looked pissed.

"Umm... I went to the beach. I called mom and told her practice ended early today."

"Want to try again?" He folded his arms across his chest. I had no choice but to go down and face him. "In my office. Now!" he bellowed.

I followed him into his office and sat down in the chair across from his desk. I felt like I was ten years old again. "I messed up," I said without making eye contact.

My dad leaned against the desk, sitting on the edge in front of me. "Yeah, I got that part when your coach called me."

My eyes popped up. "Coach called?"

He nodded his head. "He said you got into a fight at practice." He looked me up and down. "You look fine. What does the other guy look like?"

I hesitated. "Broken nose, I think. I'm not sure."

My dad ran his hand over his face. "Jesus, Chris. Do you want to sit the bench? You've worked too hard for this."

"It won't happen again. I just...ugh...he pissed me off!"

My dad threw his arms out to the sides. "About what? What would make you punch your teammate in the face?"

I shook my head. "You wouldn't understand. It doesn't matter."

"Obviously, it does. So, what was it?"

I looked him in the eye with all the conviction I could muster. "Jason was talking shit about Tori. I wasn't going to let him get away with that."

My dad let out a huff. "So, this was all about a girl? She worth getting kicked off the team for?"

"Yeah, she is! I knew you wouldn't understand." I got up and turned to leave, storming out of the room.

"Chris, wait!" I stopped and faced him. "You've had other girlfriends. What makes this one so special?"

It was my turn to throw my arms out. "Everything! She's everything to me! I'm not going to stand by and let someone disrespect her! I'll always protect her! Because you know what? I love her!"

My dad looked shocked as he stood there and looked at me. "Wow! You've only been dating her for a few weeks."

"I've loved her since seventh grade. I don't know what it is. All I know is that when I'm with her, nothing else seems to matter."

He pointed at me and then to the chair. "Come sit back down." It wasn't a request. It was an order.

I walked back to the chair and plopped down. I didn't want to listen to whatever he was going to say. I just wanted to find out what my punishment was and go up to my room.

He put his hand on my knee. "Actually, I do understand. I'm proud of you."

My eyes snapped to his. That wasn't what I was expecting.

"If she means that much to you, I wouldn't want you to let someone disrespect her. Your mom and I liked her. It's your job to protect her. You do what you have to do, just don't get kicked off the team in the process."

"Really?" I asked incredulously.

He nodded his head. "I didn't raise you to be a coward. The fact that you stood up to your friend and to me today, proves that you're not." He looked up at the ceiling, like he was thinking, and then looked back at me. "I'm going to ask you a question and I want you to be honest with me."

I wasn't sure what was coming. "Okaaay."

"Are you having sex with her?"

I swallowed the lump in my throat and answered honestly. "No."

"But you want to?" he questioned further.

I felt like everything was written all over my face. There was no way I would be able to hide the truth from him. "Eventually. She's not ready for that yet."

"But you are? Are you still a virgin?"

I dropped my head. How in the fuck did me punching Jason in the face lead to this conversation? I hadn't prepared for this.

"I'll take that as a 'no'. Is she?" he asked.

I blew out a breath. "Honestly, I don't know. We haven't talked about it."

"Well, you should. I know whatever I say won't stop you from having sex. I remember being sixteen. Just be safe. I'm not ready to be a grandpa yet, but if you get in trouble you can come to me. I won't judge you. I don't want you to have to hide shit from me. We'll handle it."

"Why are you being so cool?" I questioned. "You've always been a hard ass with me."

My dad laughed. "It was being a hard ass that taught you not to be a coward. Did you know that your mom and I dated in high school?" I shook my head. "Yeah, I messed it up pretty good, but she took me back. I believe you when you say that you love her. Or at least you think you do. Time will tell. And I know you wouldn't risk getting benched for just anyone. Are you seeing her tonight?"

"I guess I assumed I would be grounded. Can I see her tonight?" I asked.

My dad smiled at me. "Yeah, you can see her."

"Thanks, dad!" I was ready to jump out of the chair.

My dad stopped me. "One more thing. I think we should get you a car. You should be able to drive your girl around. And not in my truck."

I was in shock. "Are you serious?"

"It was your mother's idea. You can thank her. We'll go tomorrow night and look at the dealership."

I jumped up. "Thank you! I'm gonna go find mom."

"You're welcome. Have fun tonight. Take my truck."

I couldn't believe my dad was so cool. He was always busting my balls about something. I called Tori and arranged to pick her up after dinner. After the conversation, I'd had with my dad, I put a condom in my wallet, just in case. He was right though; I did need to find out if she was a virgin or not. I didn't know how to ask her without making her feel like shit. All I knew, is that I needed to be prepared, because I didn't know where this was heading.

I picked her up and we headed to our usual place. I unbuckled my seatbelt and sat sideways on the seat. Then I pulled Tori over to sit between my legs. I wrapped my arms around her, and she rested her head back on my shoulder.

"So... I guess things went okay with your dad?" she questioned.

"He was pissed at first, but actually he was really cool."

"That's good. I didn't think I would be seeing you for a while. I figured you'd be grounded. Your dad scares me a little bit," she admitted.

"My dad is a hard ass, but he's a good guy. He's pretty no nonsense about stuff. He didn't want me to get kicked off the team. I mean... I don't either. I just gotta keep my cool at practice." I ran my hand along the side of her face.

She looked up at me. "That's probably a good idea."

"Tor?"

"Yeah?"

"I didn't push you too far last night, did I?"

She shook her head. "No. You were perfect. I know you think I'm ridiculous. You know... about not wanting you to see me."

"You know what I think? I think you're beautiful. I love all your curves. I've loved them for years. There's nothing you could show me that would make me change my mind." I leaned down and captured her lips with mine. I wanted to tell her that I loved her, but I didn't think she would believe me. So instead, I showed her by devouring her mouth with mine.

She broke the kiss first. "You made me feel so good last night. I didn't think you would be able to, but you did. Thank you."

"Are you seriously thanking me for making you come?" I spoke softly in her ear. "Tor, I want to do everything with you. This isn't one-sided. I want you to enjoy it as much as I do. I loved seeing you like that."

"Chris? What are we doing here? It feels like everything is moving so fast, and I'm helpless to stop it."

"Do you want to stop it?" I asked.

"No. I want to be with you. Everything just feels too perfect right now."

"Maybe that's because it is." All I could think about was that condom in my wallet and how much I wanted to use it tonight. I had a feeling it wasn't going to happen, but a guy could wish. I turned so that I could move Tori on my lap. She sat on her knees straddling my waist, her center pushing into my hardness. I couldn't control it around her. She wrapped her arms around my neck, and I held her face in my hands. "Being with you is the best decision I've ever made," I told her.

"What about Susie?" she asked with a bit of jealousy in her voice.

"Nothing compared to you," I answered honestly.

"Was she your first?" she prodded. I didn't want to talk about this with Tori. Especially with her sitting on my lap. But I couldn't lie to her either.

"Yeah," I answered. "What about Matt? Was he your first?"

She turned her head to the side. "No."

She wasn't a virgin. Matt hadn't been her first. How many had there been? I couldn't think about it. I didn't want to picture her with anyone else. I let it drop and kissed her instead.

83

Chapter 14
Tori

What the hell was wrong with me? Chris basically asked me if I was a virgin, and I led him to believe I wasn't. I don't know why I did that. Okay, yes, I did. The truth was, I didn't want him to know how inexperienced I was. Sure, I'd given hand jobs and blow jobs, but that was the extent of it. I was sure when I was ready to have sex with Chris... and let's be honest, I wanted to... that I could fake it. I mean how hard could it be? It wasn't brain surgery.

That Thursday, Kyla came over to spend the night. Since Chris and I started dating, we hadn't spent much time together. We were laying on my bed watching *Game of Thrones* on Netflix. There was a lot of sex and it felt like we were watching porn. All I could think about was having sex with Chris.

I paused the show and blurted, "I'm thinking about having sex with Chris." I held my breath and waited for her response.

Kyla's eyes went big, and she let out a sigh. "Are you ready for that?"

I rolled on my back and put my hands over my face. "I don't know," I answered. "It's just that when I'm with him... I don't know," I repeated.

"Do you love him? I mean, like really love him. Not a crush."

I couldn't keep the smile from creeping onto my face. "I think I do."

Kyla pushed on my shoulder. "You should see your face right now. You totally do!" she exclaimed.

"Okay, I do. I didn't want to, but it just happened. Remember when you told me about the butterflies? It's like that.

When I'm not with him, I wish I was. And when I am, nothing else seems to matter."

"What if things don't work out? Will you regret it? You only get one first time." Then Kyla scrunched her eyebrows at me. "This would be the first time, right?"

I rolled my eyes at her. "Yes. You're my best friend. You should know that."

"Just checking." Kyla started picking at her nails. "You do know about Susie, right?"

For someone who was so innocent, Kyla certainly wasn't naïve. She knew what was going on, even if she pretended not to. "I know."

"How do you feel about that? Knowing you won't be his first?"

"Honestly?" I blew out a breath. "I'm trying not to think about it. In a perfect world, I would be his first, too. But I won't. I can't change the past. Do I hold that against him? You don't think he'd do me and walk away do you?"

"All I know is you two have been dancing around this for a while. I think he really cares about you. You just need to prepare yourself for whatever might happen. I'd like to think he's not that kind of guy. But still, he's a guy. And an experienced one at that."

I grabbed the pillow off the bed and held it over my face. I let out a frustrated scream. Why was this so hard? I had to make a decision. I pulled the pillow from my face, "I'm gonna do it!" I declared.

Kyla sighed. "Just be careful. And call me afterward if you need moral support. I'll always be here for you."

Friday night, Chris and I were going to dinner. I dressed in a cute jean skirt and a black sleeveless blouse. Kyla and I went to Victoria's Secret during the day, and I bought a lacy black thong and matching bra. Thongs really weren't my thing. They were uncomfortable as hell. Who wanted a piece of string riding up between their ass cheeks? But I wanted something sexy for my date, just in case. Also, I figured a thong could easily be pushed to the side without having to take my underwear off. Huge Bonus!

I spent extra time in the shower and shaved everything. After watching Game of Thrones, it seemed like the right thing to do. I knew this might be the last night of my virginity. I was excited, but nervous. Like Kyla said, you only got one first time.

Chris pulled up in his dad's truck at six. I was nervous as we walked out to the truck, and he helped me in. He jumped into the driver's seat and crinkled his eyebrows at me. "Are you alright?"

I let out an anxious breath and plastered on a smile. "I'm fine. Where are we going for dinner?"

He took my hand and squeezed it. "I thought we could go to Outback."

"Oh, I love those breaded mushrooms they have." As if on cue, my stomach rumbled. I hadn't eaten all day. I knew we would be having a big dinner and my nerves were out of control.

Chris let out a little laugh. "Well, let's get you fed." He picked up my hand and kissed the back of it. "You're wearing a skirt tonight." It was a statement and I wondered what he was thinking.

"I thought since we were going out to dinner, I should dress nice." It was a lame excuse for an answer, and I knew it. The truth was, if we were going to have sex, I wouldn't have to take it off.

"Is that all?" he asked. Damn him. I felt like he was in my head and my intentions were transparent.

"What do you mean?" I asked innocently.

He stared out the front windshield with a smirk on his face. "Yeah, okay. If that's the way you want to play it."

I quickly changed the subject. "When are you getting your new car?"

"Truck," he corrected. "My dad is going with me to pick it up tomorrow morning. The payment was higher than he wanted to spend, but I promised I'd get a job after football season to help make up the difference. I can't wait for you to see it. It's an all-black Chevy Silverado. It's fucking cool."

I smiled at his enthusiasm. "Are we taking it to the bonfire tomorrow night?"

"Hell, yeah!" Chris parked the truck, and we walked hand in hand into the restaurant. He had called ahead so we didn't have to wait long.

We'd just ordered our appetizers when I saw her over Chris's shoulder. I let out a groan. "Really?"

Chris looked over his shoulder and Susie was waving frantically at him, pulling Jason along behind her. "Hey, you two!" she exclaimed excitedly.

Chris smiled. "Hey, Susie." Then he looked at Jason and nodded an acknowledgment.

Weird. I thought they were friends. I ignored Susie and looked up at Jason. His nose and under his eyes were all bruised. "What happened to you?" I asked.

His eyes darted to Chris and back to me. "Someone punched me in the fucking face."

Chris chuckled and muttered, "You probably deserved it."

What was going on here? I looked at Chris suspiciously and turned back to Jason. "I'm sorry that happened. Is your nose broken?"

"Yeah. Hurts like a bitch, too." He pulled Susie by the hand. "We need to get going. It was good seeing you, Tori." He didn't say anything to Chris. It was obvious there was some tension there.

I watched as they walked away, then gave Chris a glare. "Did you do that to him?" He just stared at me without answering, "I thought he was your friend."

Chris huffed. "*Was* being the keyword. That guy's a dick."

"Okaaay. Care to explain?" I wondered if it had to do with Jason dating Susie. Maybe Chris was still hung up on her.

"No." His answer was short, and I knew he wasn't going to tell me.

"Is that why you got sent home from practice on Monday?"

"Maybe. I don't want to talk about it," he answered. I couldn't help but wonder why.

The conversation ended when our waitress showed up with our mushrooms. I didn't want to press him for details, but there was definitely something he wasn't telling me. I let the issue drop and we finished our dinner without any further discussion about it.

After dinner, we went to Partridge Creek Mall and walked around a bit. It was a warm night and we sat on one of the benches by a big fountain. Chris pointed to another bench, not far from ours. "See that lady over there?"

I looked at where he was pointing and started to laugh. "The one with the dog? She's here like all the time. Just sitting there with that little dog."

"I know. It's kind of weird, right?"

"I think she's just lonely. Maybe her husband died, and she needs to get out of the house."

"Maybe." Chris looked around and then nudged me. "Okay, smarty pants, what's their story?"

I turned in the direction he was looking and started to giggle. A very large woman was walking with a very tiny man. He was carrying all her bags and she was grumbling at him. "Oh, he's her sex slave. I'm pretty sure she's a dominatrix. She likes leather, whips, and chains."

"Oh my God! I think I just threw up in my mouth. That's so gross!"

I shrugged my shoulders. "I call 'em the way I see 'em." I looked around at all the people walking by and saw a woman who looked a little haggard as she pushed a stroller and had two other small children in tow. "Your turn. What's her story?"

"My guess would be that her husband works long hours, or at least that's what he tells her. He's probably got a girl on the side, and she wonders what happened to her life. If she were to have a night out by herself, I think she'd be wild and get stinking drunk."

I frowned. "That's so sad, but you're probably right. I hope I never end up that way."

Chris grabbed my hand and kissed it. "You won't." Then he kissed the side of my head. "You're more likely to be the dominatrix."

I pulled back in shock. "Seriously?"

Chris held up his hands in surrender. "What? You'd look good in leather."

I took that as a compliment and pondered the chance that maybe one day, I'd dress in leather for him.

Later that night we were back at our favorite spot. I was nervous again because I knew tonight might be the night. I wanted it to be the night. Kind of like ripping off the band-aid. Once it was out there, I wouldn't have to be afraid of it anymore. Yeah, I was scared. Freaked out, if I was being honest.

I wanted Chris. I couldn't deny that. I wanted him to be my first. From what he'd shown me so far, I was sure he wouldn't make me sorry. I mean... he cared about me. He had for a long time. Surely, he would try to make this special for me.

Once we were parked, it became hot and heavy fast. That damn steering wheel kept getting in the way, so we moved to the back seat. I straddled Chris's lap. He kissed along my neck, down to my chest and between the buttons on my shirt. His fingers quickly worked the buttons and opened my blouse. I leaned my head back and moaned as he kissed the swell of my breasts. He ran his fingers over the lace and my hardened nipples, "I love this bra. It looks amazing on you."

My arms were around his neck, and I needed to get out of this blouse. I unwrapped my arms and went to shrug out of my blouse. He zigged when I zagged and the next thing I knew, my elbow was in his eye. And not a gentle bump, like a full-on collision. His head bumped back against the seat and now I felt awkward and shitty. "Oh, my god. I'm so sorry."

He bounced back like nothing happened, "So you like it rough, huh? I'm down with that." His lips collided with mine and I forgot that my elbow had just been in his eye socket. He sucked on my bottom lip and pulled it into his mouth. I returned the kiss with as much eagerness as him. His hands reached behind my back and released the clasp of my bra. The straps slid down my shoulders and he pulled it away from my body. "I fuckin' want you, Tori." His voice was deep and needy. God, it turned me on.

I felt my panties, if you could call them that, getting soaked as he latched onto my nipple and sucked me hard. The skirt I was wearing was gathered around my hips and my thong pressed into his erection beneath his jeans. "I want you, too." It was the only thing that came to my pleasure-fogged mind. It was the truth. I wanted him inside me so bad. I needed to feel him push up into me. I didn't know what it would feel like, but it was sex. Everybody loved sex, so it would have to feel good.

His mouth moved to my other nipple and my hand went to the button on his jeans. My fingers were quick and before I knew it, I had him unbuttoned and unzipped. I reached inside his pants and began to stroke him.

His head dropped back against the seat. "Are you sure about this?" he questioned.

I wasn't sure. My head was telling me 'no', but my body was telling me 'yes'. "I'm sure," I answered.

He reached for his wallet and pulled out a condom. He slid his jeans down over his hips and his cock sprang free. I took it in my hands and rubbed him up and down. He groaned, then ripped the condom open with his teeth.

This was it! He rolled the condom over his long length, and I pushed my thong to the side. I raised up on my knees and positioned him at my entrance. I closed my eyes and sank down, just a little. He was big, and he stretched me. I sank a little further.

"I've wanted you for so long, Tori. You're so fucking tight and wet. Fuck me," he gasped.

I slid all the way down and pain ripped from between my legs. I closed my eyes again and threw my head back to hide the grimace from my face. I was no longer a virgin. I let the pain recede and concentrated on the feeling of him inside me. I felt full. Stretched. I raised up on my knees and sank back down. His hands grabbed my hips and guided me up and down. We were moving at a frantic pace, and I waited for the ecstasy to come. But it never did. It felt good, don't get me wrong, but I thought the feelings I had felt when he made me come, would be there. They weren't.

"Fuck, baby!" The words tore from his lips, and I knew he was enjoying it. I kept waiting for the bliss I was sure was coming. The muscles in his neck tightened and I felt his body shuddered beneath me as he came. I hoped it was good for him. Because for me… not so much.

I moved off his lap and he removed the condom. He reached over the seat and searched the glovebox for a napkin. He wrapped it up and set it in the front seat. He leaned back in the seat and kissed my cheek, "You don't know how long I've waited for that."

I didn't know what to say, so I just kissed him and said nothing. I looked at the clock. "You need to take me home. I don't want to be late," I said, trying to keep the disappointment out of my voice. I could have given two fucks if I was late. I just wanted to go home. I wanted to get away from him. I wanted to crawl under my sheets, cover my head, and cry.

I grabbed my bra and put it on and then my blouse. I opened the door and moved to the front seat. I eyed the used condom sitting there. It was a reminder of what I had just given up.

Chris hopped in the front and started the truck. He eased us onto the main road, and we were back at my house in no time. He walked me to the door and wrapped his arms around my waist. "I'll call you tomorrow. We're still on for the bonfire, right?"

"Of course," I smiled. We so weren't. I gave him a quick peck and watched as he pulled out of the driveway.

I made my way up to my bedroom and crashed down on the bed. "What the fuck was I thinking?" I whispered to myself. I grabbed my pajamas and made my way to the bathroom. I needed to shower. I felt dirty and used. It wasn't his fault. It was mine. I should have been honest to begin with. I was filled with self-hate and shame. I couldn't believe I had saved myself for *that*.

I didn't want to see Chris again. Ever! I was done. Whatever we had, was gone. I stepped into the scalding shower and let the water wash over my body as the tears I'd been holding back streamed down my face. I was so fucking stupid!

Chapter 15
Chris

As I was driving home, I couldn't get the nagging feeling out of my head that I fucked up. She seemed distant after we fucked. I asked her if she was sure, and she said 'yes'. But then afterwards, she was in a hurry to get home. Something was not right.

She felt so tight around my dick and God it felt good. I should have made her come first, but I got so caught up in the moment that all I could think about was myself. So stupid! Next time, I would make sure she came first.

I got home and made my way up to my room. I changed out of my clothes and grabbed a clean pair of underwear. I was sliding them on when I noticed there was blood on my balls. What the fuck? Where did that come from? Maybe she was getting ready to start her period and that was why she acted so weird. That had to be it. I didn't give a shit about that. All I knew was that I couldn't wait to be inside my girl again.

The next morning, I went with my dad to get my new truck. It was a thing of beauty. I wouldn't have to depend on my parents anymore. I had my own ride. I called Tori on the way home. I wanted to show her my new truck. The phone just rang and rang until her voicemail came on. I left a message, "Hey, Tor. I just picked up my new truck and wanted to show you. Call me when you get this."

When I got home, I decided to work out in the garage. I put my headphones on and worked my body into a good sweat. When I was finished, I checked my phone. Hmmm? Tori hadn't called back.

I went for a run and got lost in the music that blasted in my ears. Why hadn't Tori called? Last night, the memory of being buried deep inside her, made my dick hard. It wasn't ideal for running, but it couldn't be helped.

I got back and took a shower. Afterwards, I checked my phone and still nothing. I texted her.

Chris: Where are u? I wanted to show u my new truck.

I waited for a reply, but still nothing. I went and made myself a sandwich, then flicked on the T.V. and watched an episode of *Criminal Minds*. When it ended, I turned off the T.V. and my phone buzzed.

Tori: Sorry. Been busy.

I texted her back.

Chris: No problem. R we still on 4 2nite?
Tori: Can't. Not feeling well.

I frowned. Well, that was a bummer! Maybe she had cramps or something. I texted back.

Chris: Hope u feel better. Want me to come over?
Tori: No. Go have fun!
Chris: I'll miss u!

She didn't text back. That should have been my first clue.

That night I went to the bonfire without her. I knew a bunch of the guys from the team would be there. I backed my truck into the circle surrounding the pit and cut the engine. Before I even got out of the truck, Trevor was at my door. "Hey, man! What's up?" He clapped me on the back. "Where's Tori?"

"She wasn't feeling well," I answered. I walked over to another one of the trucks and grabbed a beer out of the cooler in the bed.

"I'm glad you and Tori are together, man," Trevor said. "That guy, Matt, was a total fucking dick. You two are good together."

"Thanks, Trev. I think we are too." Trevor and I sat on the tailgate of my new truck and downed a couple of beers. Our first game was next weekend and this bonding time with my teammates was so needed.

Trevor and I sat there bullshitting when Kyla walked up to me. "Where's Tori?" she asked. That was weird. Seemed like she would know that her best friend wasn't feeling good and had stayed home.

"She said she didn't feel good. She stayed home," I answered.

Kyla scrunched up her face. "What the fuck did you do?" she questioned.

I wasn't expecting that. Kyla was always easy going and this was a side I wasn't used to seeing. "Nothing!"

"Really? Is that why she hasn't answered any of my calls today?"

So, she hadn't just been avoiding me. She was avoiding everyone. That should have been my second clue. "You'll have to ask her. Everything is good between us." Now, I was wondering if it was. Fuck! Something was not right.

"Trust me, I will!" She huffed as she walked off.

"What the hell was that all about?" Trevor asked.

"Hell, if I know. Girls are fucking crazy."

"Ain't that the truth," Trevor answered, shaking his head.

The night went on and all I could think about was Tori. Was she avoiding me? And if she was, why was she avoiding Kyla too? This was not right. Something was very wrong, I just wasn't sure what it was. I should have left and went to her house, but I didn't. Instead, I grabbed another beer.

Trevor and I hung out for most of the night. We were standing next to the fire when Matt showed up. He was stumbling drunk, and I wondered what Tori ever saw in him.

He walked right up to me and patted me on the back. "Hey, Chris! How's Tori?"

I scowled at him. "Why do you fucking care?" I asked.

"Just wondering. I fucking miss that bitch. She gives one hell of a blow job and I miss her lips around my dick. She open her legs to you yet?"

"What the fuck, man? Don't talk about her like that! She's my girl, asshole!" I threw my beer to the side and lunged after him. Trevor grabbed my shoulders to hold me back.

"Be cool, man," Trevor hissed in my ear. We were attracting a crowd.

"Don't get all pissy. It's not personal. She's got a great mouth." Matt laughed. "But she held on to that virgin shit, like it was some kind of badge of honor. She let you in yet?" That was my third clue, but with the rage I felt, I didn't even realize it.

I wanted to fucking pummel his face. I lunged at him again and tried to take a swing, but I was being held back. I could feel the rage building inside me, and I tried to pull loose. "Not your fucking business, asshole!" I screamed in his face.

"Whatever! Guess that means she's locked you out too. Good luck!" He flipped me off, as he walked away with a shit-eating grin on his face.

"Fuck you, Matt! Tori was too good for you! Walk away now while you can because this isn't over!"

Trevor pulled me back over to my truck. "He's just trying to get you riled up. The fucker's jealous," he said.

I fell back against the tailgate, processing what Matt had said. *She held on to that virgin shit, like it was some kind of badge of honor. She let you in yet?* I turned to Trevor as realization hit, and everything made sense. My eyes went wide. "I fucked up!"

"What are you talking about?" he questioned.

I looked back toward the fire. Kyla was staring me down and shook her head in disappointment. "Oh. My. God!" I threw the tailgate up and ran around to the driver's side of my truck. "I have to go see her now!" I shouted. "I'm so fucking stupid!"

I got in my truck and pulled out onto the main road headed for Tori's house. I texted and called her with no response. She gave me her virginity and I acted like it was just another fuck. No wonder she wouldn't talk to me. She thought I used her.

96

I pulled up to her house a few minutes later. I looked at the clock. It was almost 12:30. All the lights were off in the house. What the hell was I going to do now? I certainly hadn't thought this out very well. I looked at her house. I didn't even know which bedroom was hers.

I stopped and tried to think. This house was similar to mine. My parents' bedroom was in the front and mine was in the back. Hers must be too. I walked around the back of the house and stared at the two windows. I picked up a hand full of pea gravel from beneath the picnic table and looked at the two windows. Eeny, meeny, miny, moe... I tossed the first pebble at the window. It bounced off the glass and I sent another one sailing. At least a dozen had hit before I saw some movement. The window slid open, and her stepdad appeared. I quickly dropped the rocks in my hands. "Hi, Mr. Russo." I gave him a little wave and he did NOT look amused.

"Wrong window, Chris." He scowled at me. "I assume you want to talk to Tori."

I nodded my head, not knowing what to say. He disappeared, and the light in the next room turned on. Tori's hair was all disheveled when she appeared in the window. "Chris, it's late. Go home!"

"I can't," I said. "I need to talk to you."

"We don't have anything to talk about. Go home!" She turned away from the window.

"Tori! Stop! Please talk to me. I'm not leaving!"

She faced me again and huffed. "Fine! I'll be out in a minute."

The light turned off and I sat on the picnic table and waited. It seemed like forever before the back slider slid open. "What are you doing here? Are you drunk?" she questioned.

"I'm not drunk," I stated.

"Why are you here?"

"I saw Matt tonight," I explained.

"Well, good for you. Did you two compare notes?" Her arms were folded across her chest and her tits were pushed up.

"Kind of," I admitted.

"Well, again, good for you! Now you can both have a laugh. Go fucking home, Chris!"

She turned to walk away, but I couldn't let it go this way. I grabbed her arm and spun her back toward me. "Why didn't you tell me?"

"Tell you what?" She growled. Like, actually growled from deep in her chest.

"You know what," I said.

"I don't know what you're talking about. Please, go home," she pleaded. She tried to keep up her tough façade, but I could see through it.

I wasn't going to let her get off that easily. I loved her. I knew I fucked up, but she had some responsibility too. I pulled her back to me and whispered in her ear, "Why didn't you tell me you were a virgin?"

Her eyes went big, a look of hurt crossed her face, and then she was back to being the Tori I knew. The one who didn't take shit from anyone, including me. "Like it mattered. I'm over it. You popped my cherry. Good for you! You got what you wanted, now move on!" She stormed back toward the house.

Her words stung. I hated that after the time we spent together, she would think I used her. There had to be a way to fix this. "So that's it? That's what you think I wanted? You know what I want? A do-over."

She stopped and looked over her shoulder. "There are some things you can't get back. I learned that the hard way." She sighed, then said softly, "I'm done. We're over. Go home." She opened the slider and went back into the house, leaving me in the dark all alone.

Chapter 16
Tori

I crept back up the stairs and Mike was standing there at the top. "Is everything all right, sweetheart?"

"Not really, but it's okay," I answered.

He reached out and pulled me into a hug. "Do you want to talk about it?"

A tear rolled down my cheek and I quickly wiped it away. "I'm fine, but thanks for offering."

He lifted my chin and searched my eyes. I wasn't very good at hiding my feelings right now and I knew he could see the sadness. "I don't know what happened, but I do know that boy is in love with you." I didn't believe it for a second. He got what he wanted, tomorrow he would move on to someone else. "You might want to cut him a break. Boys are stupid, and they do a lot of stupid things. Lord knows I did." Then he let out a little laugh. "Shit...I still do. But your mom loves me anyway, because she knows I'm not perfect and sometimes I'm gonna mess up. Just think about it because I think you really care about him too."

I gave him a weak smile. "I'll try." It was the best I could do. I would try to forget him. I would try to forget that I loved him. I would try to forget the way he made me feel.

I went back to my room and looked at my phone. I had another text from Chris.

Chris: You're wrong.

I sighed and put my phone back on the nightstand. Maybe I was wrong, but those weren't the words I wanted to hear from him. *I'm sorry* would have been nice. Or *I love you.* Something that would've made me think he cared.

I crawled back between the sheets and let silent tears fall down my face. The thing was, I knew he cared and if I was being honest, I wasn't mad at him. Disappointed would have been a better word. I just thought that after that night in the treehouse, he would have taken better care of me. My heart ached. This was why I didn't get emotionally attached. I had never wanted to be *that* girl. I gave him a huge part of myself, and it wasn't appreciated. I couldn't get that part of myself back. Chris would always have my virginity.

Maybe I had watched too many movies and I had unrealistic ideas of what our first time should have been like. I had just expected…more. I should have insisted on it. I should have never jumped on his dick in the back seat. That was on me. If I was mad at anyone, it was myself. Chris was just a reminder of how stupid I was. I knew I wouldn't be able to avoid him with school starting soon. I just didn't know how I would be able to look at him without feeling regret.

"You look like shit." I woke to Kyla sitting on my bed.

I cracked one eye at her. "Thanks. I kind of feel like shit."

"Want to talk about it? I missed you last night."

"You went to the bonfire without me? How was it?" I asked. I had assumed that if I didn't go, she wouldn't either.

Kyla pushed me over and crawled under the sheets with me. She laid with her hand propped up under her head and stared down at me. "Interesting."

"What do you mean it was interesting? What did I miss?"

"Chris and Matt got in a screaming match. I thought Chris was going to take him out."

"They got in a fight? About what?"

Kyla rolled her eyes. "You."

100

"Really?"

Kyla nodded. "Matt said some shitty things and Chris was right there to defend you. He would have beat Matt's ass if it weren't for Trevor holding him back. Afterwards, he left in a rush." She shook her head. "You had sex with him, didn't you?"

I picked up the sheets and pulled them over my head. "Yeah." My voice came out muffled.

Kyla pulled the sheets back from my face. "Why didn't you tell him? He didn't know. You should have seen his face." She looked down at me with sadness and disappointment. "What happened?"

I blew out a breath, "Things got hot and heavy in the back of his dad's truck. Next thing I knew, I hiked up my skirt and he was inside me. It wasn't anything like what I expected my first time to be."

"Is that all his fault? You didn't exactly tell him no."

"I know. He came by here last night. He said he wants a do-over. How do you give your virginity away twice? It was kind of a one-time deal."

"What did you tell him?" Kyla asked.

"I told him to go home. That we were over."

"Wow! I thought you loved him?"

"I do. I guess I'm kind of embarrassed. We can't go back. I know I hurt him too by not being honest. It's better if we pretend it never happened. I just need to move on."

"Who are you punishing? Him? Or yourself?" Kyla asked. She was insightful in a way I didn't expect.

"Both of us," I answered honestly.

I hadn't heard from Chris all week. It was killing me. He had left the ball in my court, and I hadn't made a move yet. Our first football game was tonight, and I knew I would see him. I just didn't know how I was going to manage avoiding him.

I watched the game through the lens of my camera. I snapped pictures for the yearbook, getting some good ones of the guys, the cheerleaders, and the crowd. I couldn't help but watch Chris, and he looked hot in his uniform. I was so screwed.

After the game, I drove over to the field with Kyla. Before we got out of the car, Kyla took my hand. "Are you sure you want to be here? I can take you home."

"No. I have to face this. School starts on Tuesday and we're going to see each other."

"If you change your mind, let me know. I'll take you home. Okay?"

I nodded. "Thanks. Let's go have some fun." I didn't want to see Chris, but it was inevitable. We always had classes together. I just wanted to get this over with. The sooner we dealt with it, the better. Then we could both move on.

The bonfire was just getting started. I grabbed a beer out of a cooler and popped the top. Kyla and I walked over to talk to some of the other girls from the cheer squad. We were there for about twenty minutes when I felt it. The tingles that ran up and down my spine. Damn him! I wasn't going to turn around. I could ignore it. And I did… for about thirty seconds.

His breath was warm as he whispered in my ear, "Hey, Tor. I've missed you."

I swallowed down the lump in my throat. "Hey."

"Come walk with me."

I shook my head. "I can't." The smell of his cologne surrounded me, and I felt my resolve slipping. I had to be stronger than that.

"Yes, you can," he said softly. "I need to talk to you. And I've got a joint. Come smoke it with me."

Well, shit! "Okay." I tapped Kyla on the shoulder, to let her know I was going with Chris.

She gave me a stern look. "Be nice."

I rolled my eyes at her, then followed Chris. He reached for my hand, and I wrapped my arms around myself. Touching him would not be a good idea. We walked over to the trees and

102

sat down on the rocks, just like we had done a few years ago. I didn't say anything. This was a disaster waiting to happen, and I had front row seats.

Chris pulled the joint out of his pocket and lit the end. He took a deep drag and then passed it to me. I did the same and passed it back. Chris bumped his leg into mine. "I'm sorry. I didn't use you. I hate that you think I did."

I drew lines in the dirt with the toe of my shoe, then admitted what the real problem was. "I know. It's more about me, than you. I guess I thought it was going to be different."

He stared out into the woods. "It should have been." I could hear the regret in his voice.

I put my hand on his knee. "It was what it was. Let's just forget it ever happened. Go back to being friends." Yeah. Like that was a possibility.

Chris took another hit off the joint and passed it to me. I pulled in the smoke and let it relax me. I rested my head on his shoulder and he wrapped his arm around me. He felt warm and safe. And damn it… he smelled good too.

"I can't just be your friend, Tori. I don't want to forget it happened," he whispered. "I don't want to take it back. The only thing I want to change is how it happened. I got carried away, I wasn't thinking."

I huffed out a breath. "We both did. I should have told you the truth from the beginning."

"You should have." Then he looked at me with sadness. "Did I hurt you? I mean, down there?"

"It wasn't the best thing I've ever felt," I admitted.

"I'm sorry. I should have been gentle with you. I should have made it special. Even if you weren't a virgin, our first time shouldn't have been like that."

I sighed. "That's on both of us. We should have just stayed friends. Whatever we thought we had… it's gone. It was fun while it lasted, but let's just move on." I went to stand up. "I should get going."

103

Chris grabbed my hand. "Kiss me first. If you don't feel anything, you're free to go. But if you do, if the sparks are still there, give us another chance."

I pulled away from him. "This is just silly. There's too much regret, too many hurt feelings. We can't go back. You know this can't work now." I started to walk away.

Chris shouted to me, "Why can't it work? What are you afraid of? I thought you were tougher than that."

I stopped in my tracks. Son of a bitch! Fucker was gonna call me out. I stomped back over to him. He had a cocky smirk on his face that I wanted to slap off. "Fine, I'll kiss you and you'll see... it's gone."

"Prove it," he challenged me.

I wrapped my arms around his neck and pulled his lips down to mine roughly. I kissed him hard, trying to prove that there was nothing left between the two of us. Chris ran his tongue along my bottom lip and nipped at it. I opened my mouth and let his tongue push deep inside. My hands reached up and ran through his hair. His hands cupped my ass, squeezing and kneading.

Fireworks exploded between the two of us. We were a mess of tongue and teeth and groping hands. We devoured each other. He grabbed my right thigh, and I wrapped it around his body. He pushed his hardness into me, and I gasped. When we finally broke apart to breathe, he let go of my leg and dropped it back down. "You were right," he said. "Nothing."

I put my hands on his chest. "You're an asshole."

"What? Did you feel something?" One side of his mouth quirked up, showing off an adorable dimple.

"Not a thing!" I spat at him and tried to walk away.

Chris grabbed my hand. "You're a horrible liar. Come back here and kiss me again."

He gave me a little tug and I collided with his chest. "Okay." I smirked. "I might have felt something."

"Let's get out of here. I want to be alone with you."

"Fine," I huffed, "but we're not having sex."

"Of course, we're not. What do you think? That I'm easy?" he joked. Then he caressed the side of my face. "The next time we have sex, isn't going to be in the back of a car. I'll make it special for you. I promise." He gently pushed my hair behind my ear. "I love you, Tori. I don't care if you don't say it back, but you need to know how I feel. This past week was torture without you."

"I missed you," I said softly. "I was embarrassed."

"I told you before, you don't have to be embarrassed with me. Come on, we can talk more in the truck." Chris laced his fingers with mine and led me out toward his truck.

"I need to grab my purse from Kyla's car. I'll be back in a minute." I quickly found Kyla and sidled up next to her.

"Well? Is he still alive?" she asked, lifting her eyebrow.

"Yeah, he's alive," I assured her. "You won't be mad if I go hang with him, will you? We're working things out."

She smiled at me. "Go." Then she leaned in close to me. "Be nice, just don't have sex with him tonight. Be smart."

"Yeah, I don't think that will be happening again anytime soon. I need to get my purse from your car. Chris is going to take me home."

We walked to Kyla's car, and she grabbed my purse for me. "Tori, I'm serious though, be nice to him. He likes you. And you like him too. Don't let your pride get in the way of something that could be really good."

"I won't. I don't want to mess this up again." I looked down at the ground and then got a little smile on my face. "He said he loves me."

Kyla pulled me into a hug. "I knew it! Did you say it back?"

I shook my head. "Not yet."

"Well, go tell him." She turned me around and gave me a little shove.

"When did you get so pushy?" I asked.

"When you started acting dumb. Now go!"

"I'll call you tomorrow. Thanks, for being understanding. Love ya, girlfriend."

"I already know that. Now go tell him. I'll talk to you tomorrow."

Chris drove us out to our secret place so we could be alone. He parked his new truck and fiddled with the radio. "I know this is cheesy, but this song really made me think about you." He pushed play, and the cab of the truck filled with Buckcherry's "Sorry". Chris pulled me between his legs and held me as the song played. I rested my head back on his shoulder and listened to the words. This guy, for being so tough on the outside, was a big mush ball. And I liked it. I liked it a lot.

As the song ended, Chris whispered in my ear, "I'm sorry, baby. I'm going to do better. Say that you forgive me, and you'll give us another chance."

I turned my head, so that I could kiss him while being wrapped in his strong arms. "I forgive you," I said. "I've never said this to anyone before and I'm not saying it just because you did." I paused, then took a deep breath. "I love you too. I have for a while."

He smiled down at me. "I've loved you forever, Tori. I've wanted this for us for so long. Now that I have you, I don't want to lose you."

I closed my eyes and took a deep breath. "I'm sorry I shut you out. I was embarrassed."

"Why? Because you were a virgin?" he asked.

I moved out of his arms and leaned against the door on the other side of the truck. I hated telling him all of this but hiding the truth hadn't worked out so well for us. So, I decided to lay it all out there. "Not just that. I knew you had more experience than me and I wanted to be enough for you." I stared down at my hands. "I tried to be something I wasn't. And then I ended up regretting it and I didn't know how to face you," I admitted.

Chris reached over and took my hand in his. "I'm sorry I made you feel that way. It didn't matter to me if you were a

106

virgin or not. It wasn't going to change the way I felt about you. I'm sorry that you regret what we did. That makes me feel bad."

"I don't regret giving you my virginity. I had already decided before that night, that I wanted to give it you. I regret that I didn't tell you the truth. I regret the way it happened. I didn't think I was going to care about how it happened, but then afterward, I did. That's not your fault. It's mine. I had unrealistic expectations as to what it would be like." I dropped my head. I couldn't believe I had just told him all of that. I wasn't used to being so honest with my feelings. Something about Chris, had me spilling everything.

He lifted my chin with his hand and gazed into my eyes. "I doubt your expectations were unrealistic. I know you said we can't have a do-over and you're right, you only lose your virginity once. But if you give us another chance, I'll make sure your second, third, fourth, and all the times after that are so much better. The next time we have sex will be in a soft bed where I can take my time with you."

I looked up at him from under my lashes. "That sounds really nice."

"And while we're on the topic, I need to tell you one more thing."

"What's that?" I asked.

"The next time we have sex, I want you totally naked. I love your body. I know you're insecure about it, but don't be. Not with me. Your curves are so damn sexy. I want to run my hands and tongue over every inch of you."

I felt my panties getting wet, as his words sent heat right to my core. "Yeah?"

"Oh, yeah." He leaned in and captured my lips with his. I opened to him and let our tongues tangle together. There was no way I could let him go. He lit a fire inside of me that consumed me. I felt like I couldn't get enough of him.

Our kiss became primal. I bent my head back to give him access to my neck and I slid down in the seat. Chris hovered over me, caging me in. I reached my arms around his neck and pulled him down on top of me. He pushed his hips into me. His hardness rubbed against my center, and I moaned. "Oh, god... touch me."

He pulled back and stared into my eyes. "This is how we got in trouble last time. Are you sure? Like really sure?"

"No sex, but I need to feel your hands on me. I wanna feel like you made me feel in the treehouse. I want you to make me come. Please," I begged.

"I want to feel you. I want to slide my fingers deep inside your pussy. I want to feel you come around my fingers."

His words sent shivers down my spine. No one had ever talked to me like that before. It turned me on more than I wanted to admit. "Please... do it. Make me come, Chris." My voice was breathless and needy, and I couldn't have cared less. I just needed the release I knew he could give me. I untangled my arms from around his neck and started to unbutton my jeans.

Chris pulled on the zipper. "You're going to have to pull these down."

I took a deep breath, "I know." I lifted my hips and Chris slid my jeans down, leaving my panties in place.

"God, you're beautiful. I want to take these off, too." He hooked his fingers in the sides of my panties. "Let me see you."

I nodded. Chris slipped my panties, along with my jeans, down to my ankles. Even though it was dark, I knew I was on full display for him. And I didn't care. He slipped my shoes off and slid my jeans over my feet.

He ran his hands over my hips and down to my core. "You are perfect. I love you, Tori." He slipped a finger inside of me, and God it felt so good. He pulled it back and sank two fingers in. "You're so fucking wet, baby. I'm gonna make you come so hard." He pumped and curled his fingers inside of me. I wanted more. I needed more. I wanted what I knew he could provide.

My back arched off the seat. "More...please!" I gasped. He slipped his fingers out and spread the wetness over my clit. He moved his fingers in deep slow circles over my most sensitive parts. I started to feel it. That feeling from the treehouse. It started as a slow burn and got more intense. "Fuck! Chris… that's so good!"

"Come for me, Tor. Just let go." His fingers worked me relentlessly. They were in me pumping hard and curling. Hitting that magic spot. His thumb pressed hard into my clit, using my own wetness to glide over every last nerve ending. This was way more intense than the last time. So much better, if that was possible.

I clenched my muscles, and it kept building. I lifted my hips into his hand and arched up, dropping my head back. I felt like I was being wound so tight that I could snap at any moment. And then I fell over the edge, and I was gone. My body convulsed, as my head swam with the feeling of bliss. I couldn't think of anything but the intense pleasure. Chris continued to pump me hard with his fingers, while stroking my clit with his thumb. Ecstasy took over my body. "Oh, my god, Chris!" I screamed out. "Harder…please!" He slammed his fingers in and out of me, bruising me in the best way. When I finally came down, he slipped his fingers from me. I watched as he stuck each one in his mouth and sucked it clean. Holy fuck, that was hot! "What are you doing?" I asked, breathlessly.

"Finding out if you taste as good as I thought you did." He licked his lips. "Better than I thought."

"That was kind of hot."

"No. Hot was watching you come and hearing my name on your lips."

Reaching down, I grabbed my panties off the floorboard and slipped them back on. I wrapped myself around Chris and buried my head in his neck. "That was amazing. I love how you make me feel."

"Tori, I want this to work between us. I really do love you. I want to give you a million orgasms like that. I love knowing I'm the only one to have ever made you feel like that." Chris untangled me from around his neck. He stared into my eyes and pushed my hair over my shoulder. "Does this mean you're giving us another chance?"

"If I say *no*, does that mean you'll stop giving me orgasms like that?" I asked. Chris squinted his eyes at me and pursed his lips. I rolled my eyes at him. "Okay! Yes! I want to try this again."

"I'm not going to promise you that I won't ever want to have sex with you in the back of a car again, because honestly, I have a hard time controlling myself around you. But I promise that our next time will be better, and I'll make it special. I'm leaving the when up to you. You let me know when you're ready. Just don't take too long or I may die of blue balls," he said.

I laughed at him. "Now you're being dramatic. I don't think you can actually die from that. Besides, I know of another cure," I said, licking my lips.

"You are so fucking bad…and I love it."

Chapter 17
Chris

Disaster averted! Thank God I convinced Tori to try again. I knew once she got another taste of what we had, she wouldn't be able to say 'no'. I gotta admit though, she had me sweating it. This past week had fucking sucked. I couldn't stand that she wouldn't talk to me.

I loved that she challenged me. And I think she liked that I challenged her, too. She didn't take shit from anyone, and that was a fucking turn on. She might be hard on the outside, but for some reason I could crack that tough outer shell and get to the soft side underneath. She wouldn't be happy if I told anyone what was under that tough exterior. And honestly, I wanted to keep that secret all to myself.

I went to her house for dinner on Saturday night. Her mom and stepdad were super cool. After dinner, I watched the Michigan State game with Mike on T.V. Tori sat against the arm of the couch with her legs across my lap. She was reading on her tablet, occasionally sneaking peaks at the game. She came to all the games, but wasn't sure if she actually liked football, or just came for the social part of it. She seemed way more into the book she was reading, than the game. Sometimes when I looked over at her, she had this little smile on her face. What the hell what she reading?

When the game ended, her stepdad went upstairs, leaving us alone. I snatched her tablet from her hands. "Hey, give that back!" she exclaimed.

"No. I want to see what you're reading." She reached for the tablet, but I kept it from her reach. "This must be way more interesting than me," I teased her.

"I'm serious. Give it back!" she demanded. "Now that the game is over, I'm done reading." She reached over me and tried to grab it from my hands.

"Why? What's the big deal?" I laughed. "I just want to check it out."

"It's nothing," she insisted. "Just a silly romance novel. It wouldn't interest you."

I jumped up off the couch and went out back to the picnic table, taking her tablet with me. I started to read the page she had left-off on. Holy fuck!

Tori stood before me with wide eyes. "Please give it back," she pleaded.

I kept her back with one arm and continued reading. "You dirty little girl." I couldn't help my smirk from sneaking out. I whispered, "You're reading porn."

"Shhh! It's not porn," she whispered back.

"The fuck it isn't." I started to read aloud from the page in front of me, "*I bent her over my motorcycle and pulled her skirt up. I ripped her panties off and stuck my hard dick into her wet pussy. I slammed into her over and over again. She was so tight and wet. I fucked her relentlessly, each thrust bringing me closer. My dick hardened, and I knew I was going to come. At the last minute, I pulled my cock out of her pussy and came all over her ass.* Do I need to go on?" I asked. "This is definitely porn."

"Keep your voice down," she scolded me. "I don't want my mom to know."

"Relax. It'll be our little secret. You and I will be the only ones that know," I assured her. It kind of turned me on that she was reading this shit.

Tori scrunched up her face and covered it with her hands. "Yeah… you, me, and Kyla. She's reading the same book."

"What?" I exclaimed. Then I lowered my voice. "Are you fucking with me?"

Tori shook her head. "No, it's kind of our thing."

112

I was shocked. "I never would have guessed. You...maybe. Kyla...never!"

"Yeah, once that girl gets over her fear of...well, everything...," she stuttered. "I don't want to talk about her, but we've been reading this stuff all summer," Tori admitted.

I wrapped my arms around her waist and pulled her between my legs. "Read anything you wanna do?" I asked. "Cuz I'll do anything with you. I want to fuck you senseless, 'til you can't remember your own name."

She melted into my arms and leaned down close my ear. "I've fantasized about all kinds of things with you. I want to try everything. Eventually, we're going to do it all." Her voice was breathless and needy.

"Fuck, Tori. You're making my dick so hard."

"You wanna get out of here? I can take care of that for you."

She didn't have to ask twice.

School started on Tuesday. I really wanted to drive Tori to school, but she didn't want to abandon Kyla. I respected her for that. She was a loyal friend. So instead, we decided to meet in the parking lot.

I sat in my truck and waited for her little blue beetle to pull up. She parked next to me, and I quickly jumped out of the truck, wrapping her in my arms. "Good morning, beautiful." I kissed her deeply and slid my tongue into her mouth. She surprised me by returning the kiss with just as much enthusiasm. I got lost in her. Everything else faded into the background.

I heard a throat clear and snapped back to reality. "Yeah, I'm still here," Kyla teased. "Good morning."

"Hey, Kyla. Sorry about that," I apologized.

"No, you're not, but it's okay. You two are cute together. Looks like you've got all your issues resolved."

I smiled at my girl. "We're working on it."

I grabbed Tori's backpack and we walked into the school. Kyla and Tori promised to meet at lunch time and then went their separate ways. They didn't have any classes together. Kyla took mostly advanced classes, while Tori and I stuck with classes for non-brainiacs. Tori and I had been in several classes together over the last two years and this year was no different. We had three out of six classes that were the same. It would give us an excuse to study together.

We stopped at her locker, and I handed her the backpack I was carrying. She unzipped the front pocket and pulled out a picture. "Hey, let me see that." I swiped it from her hand. It was a picture of us she'd taken with her phone over the weekend. I looked at the two of us in the picture. We made a good-looking couple. We both had an Italian heritage that gave us the same complexion and dark hair. My eyes were dark and her were a lighter honey-colored brown. We were smiling and looked happy. "Can you make me a copy of this?" I asked.

"Yeah, I'll do it after school." Tori took the picture and attached it to the inside of her locker with a magnet. "What time do you get out of practice?"

"Not 'til 4:30. Do you wanna meet up after dinner?"

"Do you think your parents will be cool with that? I know with practice it'll leave you less time for homework."

I lifted her chin and placed a gentle kiss on her lips. "I don't think we'll have homework tonight. It's the first day of school. Plus, we can always study together."

"Hey, Chris. How was your summer?" I cringed. I knew that voice. She stopped right next to us and ignored Tori. This was awkward.

"Hi, Susie. It was fine. Yours?" I was trying to keep it short without being rude.

"Great! I'll see you around. Maybe I'll see you in class." She eyed Tori with disdain. "We can talk later." She winked at me and walked away with a sway in her hips.

Tori let out a huff. "God, I hate her!"

I rolled my eyes. "She's harmless, Tor."

Tori squinted her eyes at me. "She wants to get you back in her pants. Trust me on that. I'm a girl. I know these things."

"I think you're reading too much into this," I said. I didn't know where this jealousy was coming from. I thought I had proved to Tori that I was only interested in her. That no one else mattered.

She put her hand on my chest. "Please, just stay away from her. For me."

I crossed my chest with an X. "Cross my heart. I promise. She's nothing to me. Do you trust me?"

"You, I trust. Her... not so much. I mean, wasn't she just with Jason last weekend? Now, she's flirting with you."

That was true. "You've got nothing to worry about, baby. You're the one I love." I leaned down and gave her a peck on the cheek. "Come on. Let's get to class."

After school, I had football practice. Susie was on the cheer squad with Kyla. The girls practiced on the track while we practiced on the field, and Susie eyed me as we ran drills. Maybe Tori was right about her. I needed to make sure I didn't do anything to encourage her, because if Kyla saw anything suspicious, there was no doubt she would tell Tori. That was a headache I didn't want to deal with.

I stayed focused on my team, running hard and sweating my ass off. I thought about my girl, and I thought about Susie. There was no way I was going to let anything come between Tori and me. She was giving me a second chance. I wasn't going to blow it. Especially on someone like Susie.

Don't get me wrong, Susie was pretty. Blond hair and blue eyes. I thought she had liked me when we started dating. We had sex on the second date, and I felt like a king. Three weeks later, she was riding some other guy's dick. It crushed my ego. She didn't have a genuine bone in her body, everything was for show. I would never leave Tori for that.

Tori was the real deal. She wasn't fake. What you saw was what you got. She told it the way it was, and I loved that about her. But over the last month, I learned there were more layers to her than I had initially thought. I had managed to peel them back one at a time. Inside, she was soft and insecure. Most people would never know that about her.

When practice ended, I walked toward the locker room. Jason jogged up next to me. His face looked better, but there was still some slight bruising under his left eye.

"Chris! Can I talk to you for a minute?"

I kept walking. "I don't have anything to say to you, man."

He stepped in front of me, and I tried to control my temper. I sidestepped him. "Don't push me. I'm not in the mood," I spat out.

"I'm sorry!" That stopped me. I turned and glared at him. "I'm sorry for what I said about Tori. I deserved it."

"Yeah, you fucking did," I confirmed.

"I'm trying to apologize here. I saw you and Tori this morning. I can tell you're really into her and I shouldn't have said that shit."

I threw my arms up. "I don't know what you want me to say. I'm not sorry I hit you and I'm not going to tell you what you did was okay."

"I know. But we're teammates and I want to put his behind us. I was a dick and I'm sorry." He looked over to the girls, who were still practicing. "You were right about Susie, too. She already dropped me. I think she's on the hunt again."

I had to at least appreciate his honesty. I'm sure it wasn't easy to for him to admit he was wrong, but I wasn't going to let him get off that easy though. "I accept your apology. But, if I ever hear you say another thing about Tori, you'll wish I only broke your nose. And that's a promise." I wasn't fucking around, and he needed to know that.

116

"That's cool. I don't wanna fight with you."

I eyed him up and down. I had a couple of inches on him and more muscle. "No, you don't." I walked into the locker room, leaving him standing there.

After dinner, I headed to Tori's. She was sitting out back talking to Kyla on the phone. Those two were tight. Always had been, probably always would be. When I started dating Tori, Kyla kind of came along as part of the package deal. It was cool though. She gave Tori and me our space.

I slid into the chair as Tori ended her call. "How was practice?" she asked.

"Fine." The shit with Susie was really weighing on my mind. "Tor?"

She quirked her eye at me. "I don't like the look on your face right now. What's going on?"

I pulled her over to my lap and kissed the side of her head. "I don't want you to worry about Susie. Okay? I never had feelings for her like I do for you. You're it for me. Understand?"

She nodded. "I still don't like her. She's everything I'm not. She's popular, pretty, has a great body and I can't compete with that. I don't like thinking of you two together. I don't like knowing you slept with her. I felt like she was throwing it in my face today."

I lifted her chin. "I know, but I can't change that. I'm with you now. And I think you're much prettier and your curves... I love them." I kissed her deeply, running my hands up and down the sides of her body, then pulled back. "I don't like thinking about you with Matt, but it's something I have to deal with."

"I didn't sleep with Matt. It's not the same," she defended.

"But you did other things. It's kind of the same," I answered. "None of it matters though. It's just you and me." I brushed her hair over her shoulder and pulled her face to mine. "I love you, Tori. Always have." Then I whispered in her ear, "Let's get out of here. I want to make you come all over my fingers. Make you forget about everything but me. I want to show you how much I love you."

"Such a smooth talker," she teased. "How am I supposed to say no to that?"

"You're not. Let me take care of you." I lifted her off my lap and took her hand. I led her out to my truck, where I tried to erase every thought she had. Except for me.

Chapter 18
Tori

A couple of weeks later, after the next home football game, Kyla and I went to the field. We usually got there before the guys since they had to shower. We walked over to the bonfire that was already started and took a seat on some of the logs that had been strategically placed around it.

"I really need to find a date for Homecoming." Kyla sighed. "It's going to be here before we know it, and I don't want to miss out. I wish Trevor would ask me, but I don't think that's going to happen," she said dejectedly.

"Why wouldn't he ask you? You're cute and sweet," I asked.

"Because just like all the other guys around here, he just sees me as a good friend. Maybe if I hiked my skirt up and pushed my boobs out like Susie, I'd have a better chance. I just don't have it in me."

"Please! Do not use that bitch's name around me. Trust me. You do not want to be like Susie," I said.

"You're right. I don't want to be like her, but it would be nice to get noticed once in a while."

"Kyla, everybody likes you. You're super popular."

"Then how come no one wants to date me? What's wrong with me?"

I hugged her tight. "Nothing is wrong with you. You're perfect just the way you are. One day, a guy will come along who will appreciate everything you have to offer. I promise you. It'll happen." I didn't want to tell her that she needed to loosen up a little bit. She was so tightly wound, sometimes I was afraid that she was going to snap.

"Yeah, I'm sure it will. You and Chris look so happy. No offense, but it makes me a little jealous." She picked up a stick and started poking at the ground with it. "So, what's your beef with Susie?"

I cringed. "She's a slut."

"That's nothing new. Does this have to do with her and Chris? I thought she was with Jason now?" she asked.

I rolled my eyes. "She was. That's over. I think she wants Chris back. Or at least she wants his dick."

Kyla scrunched up her nose. "Really? Why do you think that?"

"You should see her." I imitated her sickeningly sweet voice, "*Hi, Chris. I wore this short little skirt for you. Wanna stick your hand up under it? Wanna touch my tits?* Wink, wink." I stuck my finger down my throat and pretended to gag.

Kyla laughed out loud. "It can't possibly be that bad."

"Okay, maybe I'm exaggerating a little bit. But seriously, I want her to stay away from my man."

"I don't think you have anything to worry about. That boy only has eyes for you." She looked over my shoulder. "He's on his way over here now."

Kyla and I both watched as he walked toward us, looking confident and sexy. Out of nowhere, Susie was on his arm. Even though the night air was cold, she hadn't changed out of her cheer skirt. We could hear her shrill voice from where we were sitting. "Hey, Chris. Great game tonight! You're looking so good out there, I can barely keep my eyes off you."

Chris looked uncomfortable. He was trying not to be rude, but you could tell the attention was unwelcome.

"Go save him." Kyla gave me a little shove. "Go claim your man."

"Fuck right, I will!" I stood with determination and strode over to him.

Chris's eyes went big when he saw me approaching. He probably thought I was going to go ballistic. I wasn't. I so had this. I pushed Susie to the side with my hip and wrapped my arms around Chris's neck. "Hey, baby," I said in a sultry voice.

Then I pulled his head down to mine and stuck my tongue in his mouth.

Once his shock wore off, his mouth moved with mine, deepening the kiss. His hands reached down and grabbed my ass. He pulled me into him, and we kissed as if no one were watching. I pulled back from the kiss and turned my head to where the bitch was standing, "Oh, hi, Susie. I didn't see you there."

"Whatever," she huffed. "See you later, Chris," she flirted with a wink.

"Get a clue, bitch," I said under my breath.

"Come here, you." Chris picked me up and spun me in a circle. He lifted me like I weighed nothing. At five foot-five, I wasn't petite, but he acted as if I was. "You got a little devil coming out." He waggled his eyebrows at me. "I like it."

"Seriously, how fucking clueless can she be?"

We walked over and sat down by Kyla. "Hey, girl." Chris bumped her with his shoulder.

"Hey, Chris. Good game tonight." She smiled.

"Thanks."

"Do you know if Trevor has a date for Homecoming?" she asked sheepishly.

"Yeah. I think he's going with Crystal."

"Oh," she said quietly. "You know what? I think I'm going to get out of here. Can you drive Tori home?"

"Of course. Are you okay?" Chris asked with concern.

Kyla waved him off. "I'm good." She stood and leaned down to hug me. "I'll see you guys later." I felt bad for her as she walked toward her car.

"What's going on with her?" Chris asked.

"She's just going through some stuff. She was hoping Trevor would ask her to Homecoming." I shrugged my shoulders. "She'll be all right."

"You want me to see if I can snag us a couple of beers?" Chris asked.

"Sure." I needed a drink after dealing with Little Miss Hoebag.

Chris gave me a quick peck and then went in search of our drinks. I sat and stared at the fire, wondering how long it was going to take for Susie to get the message. I couldn't believe how aggressive she was. It was obvious that Chris and I were together.

"Hey, Lips!" That voice made me tense up.

I turned and glared at Matt. "What the fuck are you doing here? I thought you hated jock parties." Not only did I have to deal with Susie tonight, but now Matt. This night was going nowhere good, and fast.

"Where's your man? Didn't last long when you wouldn't open your legs?"

I stood and faced him. "Fuck you, Matt!"

"I tried that, remember? At least your mouth worked." He smirked, enjoying messing with me.

I didn't think. I hauled my hand back and slapped him across the face. It was a stupid move, but I was fucking pissed. "You're a fucking asshole. I don't know why I ever dated you."

He grabbed my wrist as I pulled it back to slap him again. "Watch it, bitch!" he warned me. "You know we had a good time. You liked me down your throat. Admit it." He took my hand and put it on his cock. "You miss this, don't you?"

I tried to pull away, but he had my wrist tight. "Let go of me!"

Next thing I knew, Chris had his hand on Matt's shoulder and spun him around. "I warned you, fucker!" Chris's arm cocked back and caught Matt in the side of the face. Matt didn't go down, so Chris hit him again. This time he fell to the ground, holding the side of his face.

I'd never seen Chris hit anyone before. My eyes were wide, and I grabbed his arm. "That's enough. I think he got the message." He had fire in his eyes.

Chris stepped on Matt's dick. "Stay down, fucker." He pushed a little harder with his foot. "And leave my girl alone. Next time I won't be so nice."

We had attracted a crowd. "Show's over!" he announced. "Come on, babe." He draped his arm over my shoulder and led me to his truck. "What'd he say to you?"

"Nothing. He was just being a dick." I didn't want to tell him what Matt said.

"I doubt it was nothing. I saw you slap him." He didn't push the issue though and I appreciated that. "Did he hurt you?"

I shook my head. "He just grabbed my wrist." Chris opened the truck door, and the overhead light came on. He pushed my sleeve up and inspected my wrist. It was a little red, but I would survive. He kissed my wrist and then helped me up into the truck. "You didn't have to hit him," I said cautiously. I didn't want Chris to think I was defending Matt.

"Yeah, I did. Nobody's going to disrespect my girl. I wouldn't be a good boyfriend if I let him get away with that."

"Who knew tonight was going to turn into such a dramafest?" I blew out a breath. "First Susie, then Matt. What the hell?" I wrapped my arm around his bicep and curled into him, resting my head on his chest. "I just want to be alone with you."

Chris kissed my forehead. "Me, too."

I didn't slide back to my seat. I stayed wrapped around Chris and breathed in the scent of him mixed with the smell of soap from his recent shower. It relaxed me, and all my stress from the night's events washed away. I loved the boy beside me. He'd shown me tonight that he would protect me. I never felt the need to be protected before. I always took care of myself, but it was nice to know I didn't have to. Chris would always have my back.

It was in that moment that I knew I was ready to have sex with him again. I wanted… no needed… to feel closer to him. I wanted to feel him inside me. And I knew that this time it would be different. That he would take care of me.

But right now, I wanted to take care of him. I slid my hand up his thigh and between his legs. I rubbed him through his jeans and felt him harden under my hand. Chris groaned, "Jesus, baby."

I undid the button on his jeans and slowly slid the zipper down. I reached my hand inside and rubbed his hard length over his boxer briefs. "What are you doing?"

"Just focus on driving the truck, I'm going to focus on driving you," I said sweetly. I pulled the fabric away from him and freed his cock. I rubbed him up and down with my hand, then lowered my head, taking all of him in my mouth. I moved up and down at a slow, leisurely pace, pleasing him with both my hand and my mouth.

Chris's hips bucked up off the seat. "Jesus Christ, you're going to get us in an accident." I thought he wanted me to stop, but then his hand pressed on the back on my head, pushing me deeper. "That feels so fucking good, Tor." I felt the truck make a quick right and slam to a stop. Now that he wasn't driving, I picked up the pace and squeezed him tighter with my hand. I took him all the way to the back of my throat and swallowed him down.

That was the thing about Chris and me. We both gave unselfishly. I would please him, not expecting anything in return and he was the same way. I couldn't even count the number of times he'd made me come and got nothing in return. He was just happy making me happy.

Chris pushed down on my head again and lifted his hips into me. I took all of him. Rubbed him harder, sucked him deeper, made sure he'd forget his own name. I felt him tense and then he emptied everything into my mouth.

He relaxed back into the seat and ran his fingers through my hair. I stroked him a few more times with my lips and tongue and then tucked him back into his boxers. I pulled my legs up onto the seat, tucking them in close, and laid my head on his lap as he caressed the side of my face. "I love you, Tori," he said softly.

I laid there and soaked in the feelings of the moment. "I'm ready," I said quietly, almost a whisper. "I'm ready to have sex with you again." He continued to caress my face and the feeling put me in a state of complete calm. "I don't want you to fuck me though. I want you to make love to me. I wanna feel you slow and deep inside me. I want to feel the weight of you on top of me. I wanna look into your eyes while you love me."

When he didn't say anything, I started to regret my words. I had laid it all out there and now I was starting to feel embarrassed. I started to pull away, but he didn't let me get far. He cupped my face with both hands and locked eyes with me. "I want that, too. I wanna lay under the sheets with you and rub my hands over every inch of your body. And when we're done making love, I want to fall asleep holding you in my arms."

"That sounds nice. The sooner the better. I don't want to wait."

Chapter 19
Chris

I needed a plan, and I needed it fast. I promised Tori it would be different this time, and I intended to keep that promise.

One major problem… where the hell was I going to take her? It wasn't like I could ask my parents to leave for the night. I laughed as I pictured how that conversation would go. *Hey, dad, think you could take mom out for the night so I can have sex with Tori. I wanna give her multiple orgasms and fuck her brains out. Would you mind?*

I only had one choice, so I swallowed my pride and made the call.

"Hey, little bro. What's up?"

"Hey, Jim. I ummm…I need a major favor."

"What's that?"

"You know I started dating Tori?" I asked.

"Finally! You've been crushing on her for years." He laughed.

"No, I haven't," I lied. Did everybody in my family know this?

He kept laughing. "Whatever! You suck at lying. So, what's the favor?"

"I need somewhere to be alone with her. Like alone-alone if you know what I mean?" I said hesitantly.

"You mean sex. What's wrong with that new truck of yours?" he asked.

"Already did that. Didn't work out so well. I wanna be able to spend the night with her. I wanna do it right. She's not just any girl. She's THE girl," I emphasized. "I wanna make it special for her."

"Sooo…you want me to help you get your dick off. Oh, baby bro…you're growing up so fast. Is that thing even big enough to get inside her?" he teased.

"Fuck you, Jim! Forget it! I thought I could count on you, but obviously, I was wrong. I'll figure it out." I hung up on him. Throwing my phone down, I laid back on my bed. Now what? I didn't want to let Tori down. I pounded the heels of my hands against my forehead. *Think. Think. Think. What can I do?*

My phone buzzed next to me. Jim was calling me back. "What?" I answered impatiently.

"I'm sorry, Chris. I didn't realize you were that serious about her," he apologized.

"I am, but if you don't want to help me, that's cool." It wasn't. I had covered for him many times over the years. He owed me this.

I heard my brother sigh on the other end. "What can I do?"

"Can you get me a hotel room? Not some sleazebag place either, but something nice. It doesn't have to be expensive, just decent."

"She must be something special," he said.

"She is. Will you help me or not?"

"Yeah, I'll help you."

Jim and I figured out a plan and then I called Tori.

"Hey, baby," she answered. I loved when she called me that. It made me feel all warm inside.

"I want to take you out tonight," I said.

"I kind of assumed we'd be together, so yeah."

"No, I mean, all night. Do you think you can tell your parents you're spending the night with Kyla?"

"Ummm… yeah, I guess so. What's going on?" she asked curiously.

"I wanna make good on my promise. I'm gonna treat you right tonight."

"Oh." I could almost picture the look on her face. "We're spending the night together?"

"I want to take my time with you. Are you all right with that?" I had assumed she would be onboard with staying the night together. But maybe I was wrong.

"Yeah. I mean, yes. I'm more than all right. But how are we going to do that?"

I smiled to myself. "You worry about making a cover story for tonight and I'll worry about the details. I've got it all handled. I'll call you back in an hour. And Tori?"

"Yes?"

"I'm looking forward to tonight."

My brother went to Oakland University, majoring in engineering, and stayed in the dorms there. It was only about a half hour away. He stopped by the house and slipped me the key card for our room, then put on a big show in front of my parents and invited me to stay in the dorms with him for the night.

Of course, I said yes. I rushed up the stairs to "pack a bag". I grabbed the bag I had already packed and called Tori. I told her where to meet me and ran back down the stairs. My parents were so happy that Jim and I were spending time together that they didn't even blink.

Jim and I walked out to our cars. He threw his arm around my shoulder. Jim was a couple of inches taller than me, but I was catching him fast.

"I can't tell you how much I appreciate this," I said. "Thanks for being cool."

He winked at me. "Sorry I gave you a hard time. You've got more game than I did at your age. I already checked in, so you can go through the side door."

"Thanks, man. How much is this night costing me anyway?"

He waved me off. "It's on me. I probably owe you. Have fun tonight." Then he grabbed me around the neck with his arm.

I squirmed to get away, but he was still stronger than me. "Don't forget to wrap your shit. I don't want to be an uncle yet."

"Very funny. Trust me. I'm more than prepared."

He high fived me. "I guess being a Boy Scout was good for something." He laughed.

I jumped in my truck, and he got in his. I followed him out of the subdivision, but when we got to the main road, I went my way, and he went his.

I pulled into the Coney Island down the road from the hotel and waited for Tori. Her blue beetle pulled in a few minutes later. I hopped out of my truck and walked over to her car. She rolled down the window, and I leaned inside and handed her a purple rose. She snapped the end and tucked it in her hair, behind her ear. I placed a gentle kiss on her lips. "Do you want to leave your car here tonight or leave it at the hotel?"

"You got us a hotel room?" she asked, eyes wide.

I nodded. I kept her in the dark purposely, so that I could see her face when I told her. It was worth it, because after her surprise wore off, she got a wicked little smile on her face.

"I'll follow you," she said. "This car is one of a kind. I don't want to leave it anywhere."

I kissed her again and then hopped back in my truck. We went right to the hotel and drove around to the side entrance. She parked next to me and grabbed her bag from the back of her car. "I can't believe you did this! How in the world were you able to manage this?"

I wrapped my arm around her shoulder and led her to the door. "Let's just say, it's good to have a brother four years older who owes you big time."

I swiped the key over the sensor on the door and it clicked, letting us in. We took the stairs to the second floor and found our room. I opened the door and Tori walked in before me. I closed the door, making sure to put the "Do Not Disturb" sign on the handle and deadbolt it. I didn't want any distractions. Just Tori and me, and the king-sized bed in front of us.

She put her bag on the dresser and I placed mine next to hers. She surveyed the room. "This is just...wow!" Tori let out a big sigh.

"There's no pressure," I told her. "If you change your mind, it's fine. I'd be happy just holding you all night." That was a lie. I couldn't wait to be inside of her, but I needed to let her make that decision.

"Are you fucking with me right now?" she said, giving me her classic Tori face.

She had thrown my own words back at me. I loved it when she was sassy and oh sooo bad. I shook my head. "Nope. This is all you. It'll be whatever you want it to be." I nuzzled into her neck, and she smelled good. She usually didn't wear perfume, but tonight she wore a light floral and vanilla scent that had my dick standing at attention.

"I'm kind of nervous," she admitted. "The first time was lust fueled. This just seems like... so much more."

"This is how it should have been the first time," I answered her. "It's our do-over."

"Yeah?"

"Yeah."

"Give me just a minute." She disappeared into the bathroom and shut the door behind her.

I pulled out my phone and clicked on my playlist for tonight. REO Speedwagon's "Can't Fight This Feeling" played softly. I'd put a lot of thought into this, and I wanted it to be perfect. Then I reached into my bag and pulled out the box of condoms I bought. I didn't know how many I was going to need, but I'd gotten the big box just in case. I ripped off three and placed them on the nightstand. That should be enough to get started.

I'd never admit it to anyone. Only me and my computer knew... but I even Googled some shit. I was pretty damn sure I knew how to please her. According to *Maxim* consistency and persistence were the key. I knew where her hot button was. Now I just needed to prove it to her and myself, that my mouth was just as magic as my fingers. When I went down on her…a first for me…she would be screaming my name.

I pulled back the comforter and folded it at the end of the bed. I'd seen a special on *60 Minutes* that highlighted all the nasty-ass stuff found on hotel comforters. The thought of it grossed me out. I slipped off my shoes and laid back on the sheets, waiting for Tori.

She came out a minute later and eyed the comforter at the bottom of the bed. "Did you see that special on *60 Minutes*…" she started.

I threw my hands over my face and stopped her. "Yes! Don't talk about it. It grosses me out!"

Tori started laughing so hard that she snorted. She threw her hand up over her mouth in embarrassment and fell into another fit of laughter. I grabbed her around the waist and pulled her down on top of me. It was perfect. All the awkwardness dissolved in a heartbeat.

We started kissing, and the fireworks between us exploded. She rubbed her softness into my hardness. It was like the appetizer before a five-star steak dinner. I wanted her so bad.

Tori shifted so that she was straddling my waist. She stared at me with lust in her eyes. Her hands slid up under my shirt and rubbed along my chest and abs. I couldn't wait to have her nails scratching down my back. I had no doubt they would be.

I put my hands on her hips and then reached under her shirt to feel the soft skin of her tiny waist. Her hands went to the hem of her shirt. She lifted it up and over her head in one fluid motion. She was wearing a sexy black bra. It pushed her tits up and gave her incredible cleavage. I ran my finger between her breasts, down to her belly button, then wrapped my arms around her waist and quickly flipped her over. I wanted to be on top for this.

I quickly removed my shirt, and she giggled underneath me. It was a sight to see. Because Tori giggling, was a rare sight indeed. "I love you," she said. "I love every little piece of you. Thank you for last night... and for tonight."

I leaned down and kissed her plump lips. "I think I should be the one thanking you for last night. I thought I was going to crash my new truck. But even if I did, it would have been totally worth it."

I reached down, undid the button of her jeans, and started to unzip them. I'd seen every part of her, although usually it was dark. What I hadn't seen, was all of her at the same time.

She grabbed my wrist. "Wait!"

I gently removed her hand from my wrist. "No more waiting. I told you, I want all of you. Naked. You are nothing but beautiful."

She blushed, and it was so damn cute. Not a word most people would equate with Tori's rough exterior, but damn she was cute when she got shy. She nodded her agreement, and I slid her jeans down her legs. Tori was wearing lacy, black boy shorts under those jeans, and the sight of her set me off. My dick became painfully hard.

I quickly removed my own jeans and laid on the bed next to her. I had my head propped up on my hand. "I don't want you to be shy or embarrassed with me. I already love you and I love your body. You're perfect." I leaned forward and captured her lips with mine. Kissing her was like nothing I had ever felt before. The chemistry between us was so strong. I felt it back in seventh grade and I felt it now. It was undeniable.

I pulled back and ran my finger over her swollen lips. "Are you sure about this? You can change your mind at any time. I'd never get mad at you for that."

"I'm sure." She sucked my finger into her mouth. "I want you to make love to me." She bit her lip, and I knew she was nervous. I had never made love before, all I had done was fucked. But I was going to do my best. She deserved it. I planned on making her feel so good, that her nerves would be the last thing she was thinking about.

132

I rolled on top of her, straddling her hips, and moved the straps of her bra down off her shoulders. She arched her back and I slid my hands behind her to release the clasp. It gave away, and I moved the straps further down her arms, gently lifting it from her body. Her tits were beautiful. I ran my hands up her ribs and ran feather-like fingers along the outside edges of her breasts. My mouth pressed soft kisses to her skin and my hands cupped her tits, gently massaging them. Quiet moans of pleasure escaped her lips, encouraging me to please her like no one had ever done before. Her nipples were hard, begging me to suck on them. I leaned down and ran my tongue over one of her hard peaks. I looked up at her and she was watching me as my tongue swirled and flicked her. I sucked her nipple into my mouth. She threw her head back and let out a straggled moan. The sounds she made, turned me on even more. I sucked her hard, then moved to her other tit.

With her still in my mouth, I moved to lay beside her. I ran my hand down the flat of her stomach and under the lace of her panties. All I felt was bare skin. I slid my fingers through her folds and down to her sweet pussy. She was soaked. "You're so fucking wet, baby." I gently slid one finger into her and then another.

"I can't help what you do to me," she said breathlessly.

"Trust me. I'm not complaining. I love knowing I make you like this. Do you like my fingers in your pussy?"

Tori's body trembled. "Yes," she gasped.

"I think I know something you'll like even more." I stared at her hungrily, as I continued to work my fingers in and out of her.

"What's that?" she gasped.

"Close your eyes."

"Why?"

"For once, don't argue with me," I said softly. "Do you trust me?"

"You know I do."

"Then lay back, close your eyes, and relax. Let me take care of you."

Tori took a deep breath and closed her eyes.

"No peeking," I teased her.

"I'm not peeking," she whispered.

I slid my fingers in the sides of her panties and eased them down her legs. Her breath hitched, and her body tensed. "Relax, baby. I got you."

I slid her panties the rest of the way down her legs, as her body relaxed into the mattress. This was the first time I had seen all of her. She was laid out before me. I imagined what she looked like, but nothing could compare to the real thing. Yes, she was curvier than most girls our age, but I loved every single curve of her body. I ran my hands up from her ankles to her knees, and gently pushed them apart, so that she was on full display for me. I unconsciously ran my tongue over my lips.

I moved between her legs, rubbed up her thighs, to her hips and squeezed her ass. "You are beautiful. I love every inch of you. Every curve is perfect." I wanted her to feel beautiful. I wanted to ease her insecurities. I needed her with me one hundred percent, before I made my next move. "Are you still with me?" I asked.

She barely nodded her head, "Yes." It came out soft and breathless and it was sexy as fuck! Her eyes were still closed, proving that she trusted me.

I kissed one leg from her ankle to the sensitive spot behind her knee, running my tongue over the soft skin. Then did the same to her other leg. Her back arched up and I pressed her back to the bed. She was already so responsive. "I wanna make you come so hard, baby. Do you think you can do that for me, Tor? Are you gonna come for me tonight?"

"Yesss…please. Touch me, Chris. Make me come. Need it so bad," she whimpered.

I moved my hands down the insides of her hips and used my thumbs to open her folds to me. I leaned forward and used my tongue to make the first swipe across her clit. She shuddered

134

beneath me, and I continued to stroke her clit with my tongue. I sucked it into my mouth and her hips raised off the mattress. Her hand went to the back of my head and pushed me into her pussy. It encouraged me. I must have been doing something right. All I wanted to do was bring her pleasure. I swiped the underside of my tongue over her clit in a back and forth motion, using my fingers to apply pressure to the base of it with a gentle squeeze.

Tori threw her head back, "It's too much… I can't take any more. It's so intense!"

"Tor, relax and enjoy it. Ride it out, baby. I promise it will be worth it. Now come for me! Come for me, Tori!" I pushed my fingers back into her, pumping them in and out and continued to assault her with my tongue. Her thighs tightened around my head, and I knew she was close.

"Oh, my god!" Her breath came in quick, short gasps. "Chris!" My name left her lips as she came around my fingers. Her head thrashed, and she fisted the sheets, trying to find something to ground her. Her thighs squeezed my head and her body quaked. She was panting hard. I did a mental fist pump. Thank you, Google!

She began to come down and a satisfied grin crossed my face. I crawled up on her and kissed her lips. "You can open your eyes now," I said.

She did. I peered into her honey-colored eyes. "Now, I want to make love to you. I need to be inside of you. I need to feel you wrapped tight around my dick."

"Yes," was all she could say.

I quickly stripped off my boxer briefs and grabbed a condom off the nightstand. I rolled it onto my hard length and settled between her legs. "This is the way it should have been."

I lined myself up and pushed in, just a little bit. I pulled back and pushed in a little deeper. She was so tight. I fought the desire to thrust in hard and fast, instead using long, slow strokes. Her arms went around my shoulders and her nails dug into my back. One final push and I was deep inside her. "Are you okay?"

"I'm more than okay. Keep going. I need to feel you move inside me."

It was all I needed to hear. I controlled myself and pushed into her slow and hard. What I really wanted to do was screw her senseless. *All in good time*, I told myself. I pushed into her over and over again. It was sweet torture. She felt so tight around me, yet so wet. I kept the slow pace, feeling her slide along my dick. Tori lifted her legs and wrapped them around my waist, using her heels to push me in deeper, as she pushed her hips up into me. "You feel so good, Tor. I'm not going to last long," I gasped out.

Our eyes locked. The look on her face was pure ecstasy. "I'm going to come again. More! I love you, Chris. Faster...please...I need to feel you!" Her words were desperate. Pleading. I wanted nothing more than to please her. I picked up the pace and thrust into her harder. I felt her pussy squeezing my dick as she came around me. I slammed into her, searching for my own release. "Yes... fuck yes!" she screamed.

Her words pushed me over the edge, and I came. Long and hard. Liquid fire shot through my veins and coursed through my body. "Fuck, Tori!" I collapsed on top of her, then pushed up on my elbows.

"That's what I imagined our first time would be like," she gasped out.

"Let's not dwell on that. Our second time was pretty great," I told her. I looked at the clock next to the bed. "It's only seven o'clock. We've got all night to do whatever you want."

A little smile spread across her face. "I can think of a few things I'd like to do." She shrugged her shoulders. "If you think you can handle it," she challenged.

"I'm a sixteen-year-old guy. I can pretty much go all night." To prove my point, I pulled out of her and switched out the condom for another one.

"Is that right?" she asked.

"Oh, yeah. You're in trouble now because I want to fuck you every which way I can."

136

"Promises, promises," she laughed.

I pushed back into her hard and her breath hitched. "I don't break promises. Your pussy is going to be wrapped around my dick all night."

Chapter 20
Tori

It was amazing! So much better than the first time. I was glad I gave Chris a second chance, because he really did make it special for me. When he went down on me, I got nervous. But the way he worked my body, had me aching for more. And he thought my body was beautiful. I had worried over nothing.

After we made love the second time, I laid in his arms, feeling totally content. My head rested on his chest and the sheet was pulled up over us. "Chris?"

"Yeah, baby?"

"I love you. Thank you for tonight. Everything was perfect."

"It was perfect, wasn't it? You and me...we were meant to be. We're perfect together."

"We are, aren't we?"

Chris kissed the top of my head, "Yes." He tilted my head up, so he could look at me. "Are you sore?" he asked with concern.

"A little...but only in the best way. If you're asking If I'm too sore to do it again, the answer is no."

Chris got a sexy little smirk. "What have I done to you? You're going to be insatiable, aren't you?"

"I'm pretty sure I'm addicted to you."

He laughed, "You're addicted to my dick?"

"Yeah, but I'm addicted to the rest of you too. You know those smutty romance novels I read?"

"You mean the porn?" he questioned with a slight laugh.

I slapped at his chest. "It's not porn!"

"I know what I read. Anyway, what about it?"

"I wanna do all that stuff with you. I want us to try everything together," I said.

Chris kissed my lips hard. He ran his fingers up and down along my back and goosebumps broke out over my skin. "What did you have in mind?" he asked.

I closed my eyes and told him the truth. "To start, and I know it's gonna sound lame, but I want to be on top, but different than before."

"Everything about this is different than before."

"I love making love to you, but I wanna fuck you too," I confessed. I wanted to explore this with him. I knew I was safe with Chris.

"I love your dirty mind and your dirty mouth. And hearing you say you want to fuck me is making my dick hard again. I wanna be untamed with you. No overthinking. Just doing. Just feeling."

I put my chin on his chest and peered up at him. "You don't happen to own a motorcycle, do you?" I smirked.

Chris started laughing, "I don't. But my brother has a Kawasaki Ninja and I know how to drive it. Why? Do you want to be bent over it?"

"Yeah, I want you to take me for a ride."

"I think that can be arranged, but first…you're going to ride me." He reached down between my legs and rubbed his fingers along my opening. "You're still fucking wet."

"I'm lying in bed naked with you. What did you expect?"

He took my hand and placed it on his cock. It was thick and hard under my palm. "I think we're both ready." He pulled the sheet back and I took in the sight of him. God, he had a great body. And if he looked like this at sixteen, I could only imagine what he would look like at twenty. Definitely something to look forward to.

I leaned across Chris and reached over to the nightstand. I swiped another condom and started to rip it open with my teeth. I placed it over the tip of his dick and rolled it down, Chris's hands covered mine, guiding me. Once it was properly in place, I straddled his waist. His hands went to my hips and gently squeezed. I lined my pussy up with his dick and slowly slid down. I half expected the pain I had felt last time, but it never came. All I felt was full and stretched in the most fantastic way.

I raised up on my knees a little and then slid back down "Oh, my god!" I exclaimed. "I never knew it could be this good." I lifted myself and lowered down on him over and over again. I shifted my hips forward and rubbed my clit along his dick. It rubbed me in just the right way. Fuck that felt good! I became shameless as I searched for my own release again. Before I knew it, I was grinding into him.

I ran my hands up and down the hard muscles of his chest, as I moved my hips in a continuous rhythm. Chris palmed my tits and ran his thumbs over my hard nipples. I leaned further forward, and he captured one in his mouth. His tongue swirled around the tip and then gently sucked on it. I was so overstimulated. My senses went into overdrive, and I soaked in the bliss as he continued to please me.

I didn't realize I had closed my eyes. When I opened them, I gazed into his chocolate-brown eyes, that were staring back at me. "Fuck me, baby," he said breathlessly. "I want you to get off on my dick, because once you do, I'm going to flip you over and fuck you relentlessly." His words encouraged me to rub my clit on him even more. His dick buried deep in my pussy, no space between us at all. It was like we were one. I couldn't tell where he ended, and I began.

The pressure built inside me. I moved my hips with desperation, pushing me further and further towards the edge. I felt like I was going to shatter. And when I finally did, the sparks coursed through me from my head to my toes. I fell on top of Chris. Breathless. He wrapped his arms around me and quickly flipped me over. He pushed my legs up to my chest and thrust into me hard and deep. Nothing could compare to the pleasure he brought me.

When he came, he released my legs. "Fuck! I can't get enough of you!"

"I feel the same way." I held Chris as he collapsed on top of me.

He rolled to the side and pulled me to his chest. It was early, but the sheer exhaustion of everything we had done started to take its toll. I tangled my legs with his and rested my head on his muscular chest. I fell asleep in his arms, feeling safe and warm and blissful.

It was still dark outside when I woke, but my sex drive was out of control. I rubbed my hand up and down his leg, then stroked his dick, bringing it to life. I thought he was still sleeping, but his hand reached out and grabbed my wrist. "Unless you want me to piss all over your hand that probably isn't a good idea."

I giggled. "Go. But we still have a few hours left. I'm not ready to let you go yet," I confessed.

He kissed my forehead and headed towards the bathroom. I went in after him, handled my business and brushed my teeth. I was sore, but in a good way. I didn't know if I would ever be able to recover from the night we had spent together. Sleeping with him exceeded all my expectations. I knew that tonight I would be in my own bed. Alone. That thought was depressing.

I crawled back in bed with him and cuddled into his chest. "I love you, Chris. This has been the best night of my life. I don't want it to end."

"Me neither. I'm going to owe my brother big time for this."

"We can do it again. I'll chip in for the room. I'd hate to think this is the only time we'll have together like this," I said.

"Tori, I don't want this to be a one and done. We'll never be the same. No matter what happens, I'll love you forever." Chris proclaimed his love for me. "We'll do this again. I promise. And I always keep my promises." He began kissing me. His lips were soft and gentle. His tongue ran along my bottom lip, and I opened for him. Our tongues twisted together in a slow dance. Everything about it was perfect. Chris's hand slid down my side, over the small of my back, and down to caress my ass. He gave it a gentle squeeze.

"I love your ass," he whispered in my ear. A shiver ran down my spine. "I want to do you while you're on your knees, bent over in front of me. I want to see your ass, while I push deep inside you."

"I don't think you really want to see that," I whispered back. My insecurities were creeping back in. I wasn't sure I wanted him to have that kind of view. There would be no hiding my imperfections.

"Yeah, I really do," he answered. "I've been looking at your ass for years. It's fucking sexy, Tor. I just want to try it. If you don't like it or it's uncomfortable, we'll stop."

I wasn't sure. This is what I got for being a big talker about that stupid book. But I did want to do all those things with him. I would have to get over my insecurities sooner or later. "Okay," I said hesitantly.

"I'll be gentle. I promise." And I knew he would be. Chris pulled the sheet back and went to his bag for another condom. I wondered how many he had in there. We'd used quite a few last night. I pulled the sheet back up and covered myself.

Chris shook his head at me. "You're still shy? I've already seen every inch of you, and trust me, I'm not complaining." I released my death grip on the sheet and Chris pulled it down, exposing me. "Roll over, baby." I did as he asked. His fingertips ran down my naked back and over my rear with the lightest feather touch. "Now pull up on your knees." His voice was like velvet, soothing me. It was a complete turn on listening to his demands. In that moment, I was submissive and wanted nothing more than to make him happy. It was so not me, but I liked it. I liked him in control.

I raised to my knees and arched my back, pushing my breasts out. "Fucking hell, Tori," he swore. "I'm gonna blow my load before I ever get inside you. You look perfect like this." Chris ran his hand from my neck, over the arch of my back, and down the crack of my ass. "Spread your legs for me. I want to

142

see your pussy. Make sure you're good and wet." He didn't have to worry about that. I could feel my own wetness pooling between my legs. His seductive tone had me following his every command. I spread my knees, knowing I was showing him everything.

Chris's hand went between my legs, and he slipped his fingers inside me. He moved them in and out in a slow rhythm. "I can't wait any longer," I gasped. "Stick your dick inside me and fuck me."

I heard the foil of the condom rip and then Chris was kneeling behind me. "I want you so bad, Tor. I can't wait to get my dick inside your wet pussy."

"Then stop wasting time and fuck me already," I whispered.

He let out a little laugh. "Always so damn bossy." His hands grabbed my hips as he slid into me. "That better, baby?"

A contented sigh escaped my lips. "Much better." Chris started to move, slowly pushing in and out of me.

"Fuck, baby you feel so good like this. So tight around my dick."

"It feels so good. Faster," I demanded. Chris picked up the pace, but it wasn't enough. "Harder, Chris. Fuck me harder." And he did. He pushed into me hard and fast, and without thinking I started pushing back into him. Everything about this was erotic. I didn't think. I just let my body take control and enjoyed the pleasure it was bringing me.

I reached between my legs and started rubbing my clit. It didn't take long. I was so turned on. Within seconds, I felt the pressure rising inside me. I clenched my muscles and fell over the edge. Wave after wave coursed through me, as Chris continued to pound me from behind, "Fuck, baby. You're squeezing me so tight." Incomprehensible sounds came from my throat and my eyes rolled back into my head. The orgasm ripped through my body and blinded me. With one final thrust, Chris emptied everything inside me, and I fell onto my elbows in exhaustion. I slid my arms forward and stretched out like a cat as

143

Chris draped himself over the top of me. His warm breath was at my neck. "That was so fucking good, Tor. I love you. I love you and I can't get enough of you."

I turned my head to kiss him, "I love you, too," I said breathlessly. Everything about this moment was perfect.

Chris and I both took quick showers and then went back to the Coney Island for breakfast. I knew we were young, but I couldn't see myself with anyone else. Ever. Chris was the perfect combination of soft, sweet, bad, rough, and sexy as fuck.

I reached over the table and took his hand in mine. "Promise you're not going to break my heart."

Chris looked at me in confusion. "Why would you say that?"

I bit my lip and let the honesty flow. "Because I never wanted to fall in love. It destroyed my mom when she was young. I never wanted that to be me. I never wanted to let anyone in. It's why I told you no so many times. I was afraid of completely falling for you." I took a deep breath and continued, "Now that I have, I'll never be the same. Last night was perfect. You were perfect. It's going to destroy me when this ends."

Chris took my other hand. "I don't have any intentions of this ending. I've wanted you for so long and now that I have you…I'm not letting you go. This thing that's between us… it's real. I'm sure we'll have our ups and downs but you're everything I want or need. I love you. I promise not to break your heart." He leaned forward and gave me a soft kiss.

"Thank you. Thank you for everything," I smiled at him.

"You don't have to thank me. Being with you is enough." He was still holding my hands over the table. "I think this is a formality at this point, but…will you be my date for Homecoming?"

I teased him, "I'll have to check my calendar, but I think I'll be available on that night."

He laughed. "You think you'll be available? You're not going to make me come and kidnap you, are you?"

"Do I have to wear a fancy dress and high heels?"

"Absolutely! I don't think I've ever seen you in heels," he said.

"That's because I don't like dresses. I never have. But for you, I'll make an exception," I winked at him.

"I don't know why," Chris said. "The few times I've seen you in a dress or skirt, you looked hot. You've got nice legs." Then he shook his head and laughed, like he knew some private joke.

"What's so funny?" I asked.

"I was just remembering the first time I met you. You had pigtails and a dress on. You were so mad your mom made you wear it because you wanted to go on the monkey bars."

I looked at him incredulously. "I remember that dress. It was awful."

"It wasn't awful, but boy, were you pissed."

"How did you know about the monkey bars?" I asked. I had forgotten all about that.

"I was listening to you talk to Kyla. Why do you think I hung out by the playscape at recess?" He quirked an eyebrow at me.

"So, you were a perv back then too, huh?" I laughed.

"I wasn't a perv," he defended. "But I wasn't going to pass up the chance at getting to see your underwear."

I dropped my head to the table in mortification, "Oh, my god!"

He lifted my chin with one finger, "So is that a yes on Homecoming?"

I smiled up at him, "It's a yes. I'll wear a fancy dress with heels and everything."

I drove from the Coney Island straight to Kyla's house. I opened the door and went right in. They didn't expect me to knock anymore, since I was practically their second daughter.

Kyla's mom was sitting in the kitchen. I popped my head in. "Hi, Mrs. O'Malley."

"Hi, Tori. Kyla's up in her room."

"Thanks!" I gave her a little wave and bound up the stairs two at a time. I burst through Kyla's door and flopped down on the bed next to her.

Kyla jumped up in surprise, "Jesus, Tori! You scared the crap out of me!"

I gave her a big hug. "Sorry."

"You certainly are in a good mood." She went to shut the door and laid down next to me. "So, how was your night?"

"Phenomenal!" I couldn't contain the smile that spread across my face. "Kyla, it was so perfect. He had his brother get us a hotel room. We spent the whole night together. I'm never going to be the same."

Kyla laughed. "You should see your face right now! I've never seen you like this. You're all giddy."

"I can't help it! I'm so in love with that boy. Thanks for covering for me last night. I owe you big time!"

Kyla pursed her lips and looked at the ceiling. "You can start by helping me find a Homecoming dress."

"You got a date?" I asked.

"Yeah." She didn't seem very excited about it.

"What's wrong?" I asked with concern. "Why aren't you happier about this?"

Kyla shrugged her shoulders. "It's just a date. Chad from my bio class asked me and I said yes. He's kind of cute, I guess. But beyond that, I don't see it going anywhere." She looked down at her hands and picked at her nails. "I wish Trevor had asked me instead of Crystal."

"Oh, sweetie, forget about Trevor. You're too good for him anyway. I promise you, the right guy will come along. And when he does, he's going to sweep you off your feet."

146

"Maybe," she shrugged again. "It's fine," she waved me off. "So, do you want to go dress shopping?"

"UGH! I don't want to wear a dress. And heels!"

Kyla laughed, "One, you have to wear a dress for Homecoming. And two, you're a knockout. You're going to blow Chris away. That, in itself, should be worth it."

"Yeah, yeah. Keep talking. You know how I feel about dresses," I complained.

Later that day Kyla and I stood in the dress shop, searching through the racks. Kyla had a great body, but she was conservative. I had way more curves and I didn't want anything that would make me look slutty. Some of the skirts were so short, I was sure I would be giving a show if I barely leaned over. Dress shopping was a pain. Especially when my heart wasn't in it.

After a lot of searching, Kyla and I both pulled dresses from the racks, holding them up for each other. She had picked one for me and I had picked one for her. "How about this?" we both said at the same time. We started laughing, traded dresses, and headed toward the dressing room.

God, I hated this. I slid my jeans off and slipped the black dress on. It was cut into a V in the front and tied behind my neck. Once I had everything in place, I turned and looked in the mirror. It fit me perfectly. The top was embellished with sequins and showed just enough cleavage without being slutty. It was fitted through the waist and flared out at the hips. The skirt came just a few inches above my knees. I turned in the mirror, to admire it from every angle. I felt like Marilyn Monroe in her famous subway grate scene. The dress was very similar, only black. She was a curvy woman who embraced her body, maybe I should too. I did a silly twirl and watched the skirt billow around me. I let out a little giggle, covering my mouth with my hand to silence it. I looked pretty. I felt pretty. Who would've thought?

"Are you going to come out and show me or what?" Kyla shouted through the door.

I took a deep breath and slowly opened the door. "Well?" I asked.

Kyla stared at me and shook her head. She looked me up and down. "Twirl," she said, motioning with her finger. I spun around and showed her the back, which was mostly open. I turned back to face her.

Kyla still hadn't said anything. "Well?" I asked again.

"You look gorgeous. That dress is amazing. It accentuates your curves perfectly. I think we found a winner!" She clapped her hands happily. "I'm thinking...hair up with crystal drop earrings. Now, we just have to find you the perfect shoes."

"Really? You like it?" I questioned.

"I love it!"

I finally let the smile I'd been holding back, break free. "Me too!" I said excitedly. "Now stand back so I can see your dress." It was a turquoise and black cocktail dress with spaghetti straps. It was form-fitting and, of course, looked fantastic on her petite frame. "Looks like we both found winners. That looks great on you!"

We changed back into our regular clothes and made our way to the registers. The shrill voice that echoed through the store was like nails on a chalkboard. "Hi, Kyla!"

Susie sauntered up to us, completely ignoring me. "Are you shopping for Homecoming?" she asked.

"Yeah," Kyla replied. "Tori and I both found perfect dresses."

Susie quirked her eyebrow at me, "You're going to wear a dress? Hmmm…"

I plastered on a smile. "Of course! It's Homecoming. Chris loves me in dresses." Then I added in a whisper, "You know, easy access. He just can't get enough." I finished with a catty wink to drive home my point.

Susie pulled back in shock. "Oh!" Her face started to turn red. "Well, you girls have fun shopping. I'll see you later, Kyla." Then she disappeared between the racks.

Kyla smacked me on the shoulder. "You are so bad!"

I flinched back. "She's a bitch. She needs to get the hint and quit chasing after my man." I pointed to my head. "She's thick. Subtleties don't work with her."

Kyla covered her mouth to keep from laughing out loud. "You're totally right."

Our next stop was the shoe store. High heels scared me more than dresses. Mostly because I didn't have any experience wearing them. I didn't want to look like a baby deer on ice… all wobbly and unsure.

Kyla picked up a strappy pair of black heels. They were tall, probably about three inches. "These would look perfect with your dress." She handed the shoes to me. I inspected them, while she looked through the shelf for my size. They were pretty, and Kyla was right they would look great with the dress. I just wondered if I would be able to walk in them.

Kyla pulled a size seven from the shelf and shoved them toward me. "Try them on," she insisted. I sat down on the bench with a huff and started taking off my Converse. I slipped my feet into the shoes and fastened the straps around my ankles. I looked at Kyla with worry on my face. "Stand up." I hesitantly stood. "Now, walk around," she instructed. I took a cautious step. The heels weren't too spikey and had more support than I expected. I took a few more cautious steps around the store. *I could do this.* I took another step and my foot wobbled.

"I don't know if I can wear these," I admitted.

"Sure, you can," Kyla encouraged. "We've got three weeks until Homecoming. Wear them around the house and practice. You just need to get comfortable. Trust me, it's not that hard."

"Okay, I'll try. But, if I end up breaking my ankle, I'm blaming you."

She waved me off. "You won't."

Chapter 21
Chris

My night with Tori had exceeded all my expectations. Now that she had gotten comfortable with us having sex, she was a little wild cat. I think at some points, she enjoyed it more than me, if that was possible. I could only imagine all the things we would do down the road. I wanted to have wild, crazy monkey sex with her. Everything about her was sexy as fuck!

I called my brother on the way home to thank him.

He answered the phone, sounding a little groggy. "What's up, little man?"

I rolled my eyes even though he couldn't see me. "Hey, Jim. I just wanted to thank you again for hooking me up. Everything was great."

"No problem. How's your girl?" he asked.

"Amazing!" I answered.

"So… is she a freak in the sheets?" he laughed.

That kind of pissed me off, but he was my brother. I expected it. "Not that it's any of your business, but yeah. I'm not gonna give you all the details."

"Trust me, I don't want them. I'm having a hard time picturing my baby brother having sex. It just seems wrong," he said.

"One… I'm gonna be seventeen in a couple of months. You were having sex at my age if I remember correctly. Two… then why the fuck did you ask?"

Jim started laughing. "Yeah, I was having sex at your age. And I asked just to get a rise out of you."

"You can be an asshole sometimes, you know that?" I should have known. He never passed up a chance to razz me. It was okay though because he was still a cool brother.

"Yep," he answered. "And that's why you love me."

"Whatever, man. I just wanted to say thanks. And maybe you could hook us up again in a few months." I wanted to throw that out there to see how he'd react.

"Sure thing. But next time, it's on your dime."

"That's cool. I'm almost home. I gotta let you go. I'll talk to you later."

"Later, bro," he said and hung up.

No matter how much he liked to get my goat, he'd always been cool with me. He always included me, even when I was just a little shit. He never made me feel like I was crashing his party. I was lucky to have him as my brother.

Later that night I got a text from Tori.

Tori: I got a dress. U owe me.

Chris: Cool! What color?

Tori: Black

Chris: Shoes too?

Tori: Yes! If I break my ankle, I'm blaming U and Kyla.

Chris: LOL! You're going 2 look hot!

Tori: You'll have 2 carry my books if I end up on crutches!

Chris: I already carry your books.

Tori: True. Can't wait to see u tomorrow!

Chris: Ditto! Luv U!

Tori: Luv U 2!

I was getting a kick out of all her bitching. She hated dresses, but seriously, how bad could it be? I had rarely ever seen her dressed up. Maybe in elementary school for our music concerts, but that was a long time ago. Come to think of it, the dress she wore to my house for dinner was one of the few times I'd seen her not wearing shorts or jeans. And there was the night she wore a jean skirt. The night I took her virginity. I cringed at the thought. That night was more than a little tainted.

152

The next Saturday, I decided to surprise my girl. I drove over to her house and knocked on the door. Tori answered wearing shorts and a T-shirt. She smiled at me and I was reminded once again how lucky I was.

I shook my head. "This will never do," I said motioning to her outfit.

Tori looked down at what she was wearing. "Why? What's wrong with what I'm wearing?" she asked nervously while staring down at her bare feet.

"Don't get me wrong, you look beautiful, but it's all wrong for this date," I said cryptically.

"What should I be wearing?" she asked, clearly confused.

"Jeans, tennis shoes, and your leather jacket." I ticked off her proper apparel on my fingers. "You should probably braid your hair too."

"Okaaay. Can I ask why?"

I winked at her. "You'll see."

Tori shrugged her shoulders and bounded up the stairs. She came down a few minutes later wearing a pair of jeans with a hole in the knee, a Pink Floyd concert tee, and her Converse. Her hair was braided over her shoulder and a few loose strands framed her face. "Better?"

"Better," I assured her. She looked cute as can be. "Where's your jacket?"

"Oh, I don't think I'll need it. It's pretty warm out," she answered.

"You'll need it."

Tori went to the hall closet, pulled out her leather jacket, and hung it over her arm. We stepped out on the porch, and she looked around. "Where's your truck?"

I pulled her forward around to the front of the garage. "We're not taking my truck."

I knew when Tori finally saw the bike. "Are you serious?" She walked over to the sport bike and ran her hand along the seat. "I've never been on a motorcycle before."

"Are you up for it?" I asked.

"Hell yeah! This is going to be so much fun!" She jumped up and down, clapping her hands. She was like a little kid on Christmas morning. This was yet another thing I was going to have to thank Jim for.

Tori quickly slipped on her jacket, and I handed her the helmet. She tried to fasten the strap under her chin but fumbled with the buckle. "Here, let me help you." I grabbed the ends and secured it under her chin, gave her a kiss, and then pulled the visor down. "Now you're ready. Go ahead and get on." She climbed up like a pro and I showed her where to put her feet.

I put on my own helmet and straddled the bike in front of her. I wrapped her arms around my waist. "Hold on tight and don't let go," I instructed.

"I won't," she promised.

I started the bike and turned us around. "Are you ready?"

"Uh huh!"

I pulled down the visor on my own helmet. I pulled out my phone and pressed play. "Slow Ride" pumped through our Bluetooth helmets. Not too loud, but loud enough. I eased down the driveway and out of the subdivision. I took the Van Dyke Expressway to 23 Mile Road and headed east towards the lake.

Twenty minutes later we were driving along Anchor Bay, listening to "Stranglehold" by good old Uncle Ted. The ride was relaxing, and it felt good having Tori wrapped around me. She took the turns like a pro, leaning naturally with the bike. The bay to our right shimmered in the sunlight and you could see all the boats out on the water. Another twenty minutes and we would be at our final destination.

When we finally got to Algonac, I parked along the boardwalk. Tori and I removed our helmets, and we climbed off the bike. I watched Tori as she stretched out her muscles from the long ride. "I haven't been here in years. We used to come here to watch the fireworks on the Fourth of July. My mom would bring blankets and a ton of snacks. We would campout all evening waiting for it to get dark. And then the fireworks would start."

I placed our helmets on the seat of the bike and took ahold of her hand. "I thought we could walk along the boardwalk and watch the freighters go up and down the river."

"This is perfect," she exclaimed. "Thank you for bringing me here."

We walked down the boardwalk to the end, where Tori sat down and hung her legs over the edge of the seawall. I sat next to her, wrapping my arm around her waist. She rested her head on my shoulder. "So, was this a good surprise?" I asked.

"Yes, I love it. It's relaxing and peaceful." The seagulls flew overhead, searching the water for their dinner. Tori watched them carefully, "I hate those damn birds though. I'm always worried one of them is going to poop on me."

I laughed. "Who? That little guy?" I pointed to one walking along the boardwalk, stopping about five feet from us. It cocked its head at us, as if asking if we had food.

"They're so damn bold. And God help you if you have french fries." Tori waved her hands at the seagull. "Shoo bird, shoo!"

I laughed at her. "If you chase that one away, two more will take its place."

She laughed too. "I know, right?" Tori looked across the St. Clair River to the houses on the Canadian side. "I love those houses. They're so big. It would be so cool to live in one of them."

"Then you'd have to worry about the seagulls pooping on you," I pointed out.

"True," she laughed as a huge freighter went by blocking our view of the houses.

"Are you hungry? There's a little restaurant across the street where we can sit on the patio."

"I'm starving," she answered.

155

I stood up and offered her my hand. I pulled her to her feet, and she collided with my chest. She wrapped her arms around me, reached up on her toes, and kissed me. It was soft and gentle, but I quickly forgot we were out in public. I stuck my tongue in her mouth and we shared our own fireworks. After our tongues had tangled, she pulled back. "I love this day. I loved the ride. I love being by the river. I love being with you!"

"I love being with you too. I love what we have, Tor. I've never felt this way before. I knew we would be good together, but this has exceeded all my expectations."

"I'm sorry I waited so long to say yes," she apologized.

"Don't be sorry. I think it only made this better." I grabbed her hand and pulled her across the street to the little bar and grill. We sat at a table out on the patio under an umbrella.

"What are you getting?" she said, holding the menu out in front of her.

"I thought maybe we could share something. You know like in the movies where they get one milkshake with two straws."

Tori smirked at me. "Do the guys on the football team know you're such a mush ball?"

"Shhh! That's only with you." I took her hand and kissed the top of it. "Since I punched Jason in the face, the guys think I'm a badass with a bad attitude. I like it that way. Keeps anyone else from thinking about flirting with you. I want to keep you all to myself."

"You don't have anything to worry about." Tori blushed. "I can't see myself with anyone, but you." She scanned over the menu. "Oooh! How about the loaded nachos? It comes with onions and peppers." She smirked.

"Ha ha, funny girl. I'm not making that mistake again." After the Subway incident, I was conscience of what I ate when I planned on kissing her.

She pouted. "Don't be so sensitive. I kissed you, even though you reeked of onions. And peppers," she added, raising her eyebrows. "But this time, we'll reek together. So, what could be better?" She shrugged as if sharing onion breath would be the best thing in the world.

Since she put it that way and let's face it, nachos are awesome, I agreed. The waitress showed up to get our order, and I closed my menu. "We'll get the loaded nachos with two plates." I smiled. "Also, a regular Coke and a diet Coke."

"I'll have that right up," she said as she walked away.

Tori shrugged out of her leather jacket and hung it on the back of her chair. All I could focus on was her tits. Her T-shirt was cut low into a V in the front and her cleavage was showing. "It's so nice out today. This is a perfect day for coming here and sitting by the water."

I barely heard her and apparently, I was more than a little obvious. "Uhh, Chris? Up here." She pointed at her face.

I shook my head and focused on her face. "Sorry. It's just that…"

"You love them. I know," she laughed. "You've made that abundantly clear."

"Don't get me wrong, I love all of you. They're just an added bonus." The waitress returned with our drinks and set them on the table. "So, tell me about your dress for Homecoming."

She tapped her fingernails on the table. "I'd rather not. I want it to be a surprise. All I'll say is that I really love it. So much so, that I don't even mind wearing a dress. I think you'll love it too."

I was sure I would. Tori was sexy as hell. All I could think about was her in a sexy dress and high heels. Hello boner!

Chapter 22
Tori

The waitress brought our nachos, and I wasn't shy about digging in. I grabbed a chip covered in goodness off the plate and lifted it to my mouth. The cheese pulled into a long string, still attached to the plate. It finally snapped when I put the nacho in my mouth and stuck to my chin. I quickly used my finger to get the cheese off my chin and sucked it into my mouth. "Oh, my god! These are delicious!"

"They're nachos. What's not to like?" Chris answered while popping a chip into his own mouth. He quickly grabbed his Coke and took a big drink. "Whoa! That was fucking hot. I think I swallowed a whole jalapeño."

"Don't be a pussy. The hotter the better!" I teased him.

Chris pulled back and gave me an offended look. He pointed at himself in the chest. "Did you just call me a pussy?"

"It's okay. Not everyone can handle the hot factor. I happen to love this stuff," I said nonchalantly, popping another nacho into my mouth.

He squinted at me. "I can handle hot."

I waved my hand at him. "It's nothing to be embarrassed about. Some guys can handle it, some can't." I loved teasing him because he was adorable.

Chris signaled to the waitress and called her over to our table. "Could we get a side of extra jalapeños," he asked.

"Sure thing, sweetie." She smiled and headed back to the kitchen.

"Challenge accepted." He eyed me. "I won't be called a pussy. If you can handle it, so can I."

"You don't have anything to prove. I already love you, despite your inability to stomach hot peppers." I kept it up, just to get a rise out of him.

A few minutes later, the waitress returned with a small bowl filled with jalapeños. Chris picked it up and poured it over the top of our nachos. "Now we'll see who's a pussy."

We continued to devour the plate of nachos and judging by how many refills we had on our drinks, I would bet both of us had pushed our limits. "My mouth is on fire," I whispered over the table to him.

"Oh, thank god. Mine is too." He laughed. "I didn't want to admit it, so I'm glad you did first."

"Think we're going to regret this later?" I asked.

"Probably. Should we start heading back?"

I didn't want this day to end, but then again, I didn't want to be too far from home when the peppers won the battle with my stomach. "That's probably a good idea."

Chris quickly paid our bill while I put my jacket on. He grabbed me by the hand and led me across the street to the boardwalk. Our fingers were laced together, swinging between us as we made our way back to the motorcycle.

When we finally got there, Chris helped me put my helmet on and I hopped on the back. He put his helmet on and got on the bike in front of me. I scooted myself as close as I could and wrapped my arms around his waist. Chris made me feel safe and I trusted him implicitly. He grabbed my hands and pulled me even closer.

He turned on some music and "All Along the Watchtower" filled my ears. My mom and Mike were music junkies, so I grew up listening to this stuff. I loved it. And I loved that Chris loved it too.

We made it back home in what seemed like record time. I wasn't ready for our time together to end. And neither was he. Chris took the bike home and came back a few hours later. We snuggled up on the couch together and watched a movie. It was the perfect ending to a perfect day.

I sat on the edge of my bed, staring at my shoes for Homecoming. They intimidated the hell out of me. Kyla had suggested wearing them around the house to get used to wearing heels. I had been avoiding them like the plague for almost two weeks.

I took a deep breath and unfastened the straps on the sparkly shoes. "Here goes nothing," I said to myself. I put them on my feet and stood in front of my floor length mirror. Wearing shorts, I slightly resembled a hooker. But I did have to say that they made my legs look longer. It was probably why hookers wore heels with shorts, I concluded.

Sunday was cleaning day, and as long I could remember, my mom and I tackled the chores together. I walked down the stairs, holding tightly to the rail to begin my dusting and vacuuming. I finally made it down and teetered on wobbly feet to the kitchen.

My mom busted up laughing at the sight of me in my sparkly heels and shorts. "You know it's cleaning day, right?" she asked, pointing at my feet.

I collapsed into the chair. These shoes already hurt my poor virgin heel-wearing feet. "I know. But these are the shoes I'm wearing to the dance and Kyla said I should practice while walking in the house. I'm running out of time and figured if I could clean the house in them, I could dance in them," I explained.

"That's a good plan. Better turn on some music, so you can get your groove on," she teased.

"That's a great idea." I went over to the stereo and cranked the music up. I tried to do little dance moves while dusting but kept wobbling all over the place. I kept at it, determined not to be beaten by the vicious killer heels. They could fuck off, I was going to win this battle.

By the time I started vacuuming, I think I had learned the trick. Keep your weight on the front of the shoes, the heels were just for balance. Before I knew it, I was rocking those bitches. I swung my hips to the music as I pushed the vacuum along the carpet. I was lost in the music and my newfound love of heels. When AC/DC's "You Shook Me all Night Long" came on, I abandoned the vacuum completely. I did a sexy little turn, kicked my leg up, hooked it at my knee, and threw my head back,

"What in the hell is going on in here?" Mike asked. He was clearly confused. He looked at me like I had truly gone over the edge.

Startled to be caught dancing, I stumbled, but caught myself before I fell over the side of the couch and face planted. "I'm practicing for the dance," I said matter-of-factly.

He quirked an eyebrow up at me. "You're going to dance like that?"

I was a little embarrassed Mike had witnessed my porn star moves. I shrugged my shoulders. "I'm experimenting."

"Try something else, you look like you should be dancing on a pole."

I gave him a thumbs up. "Right. Thanks for the advice." I stood up from the couch and grabbed the vacuum. Pushing it back and forth across the carpet, I swayed my hips and sang along with the music. A few more days of practice and I would be ready to rock these shoes.

Kyla and I walked down the hallway a few days before the dance. "I've mastered the heels," I told her. "I'm ninety percent sure I'll get through the night without humiliating myself. Do you want to come over to get ready for the dance?" I asked her.

She hugged her books tightly to her chest. "Nah. I'll get ready at home."

I stopped and turned her by the shoulders. "What's wrong? You seem kinda sad."

Kyla shrugged her shoulders. "Honestly, I wish I never told Chad I'd go to the dance with him. He's acting all creepy now, like we're a couple or something."

"What do you mean *creepy*? Creepy like I need to have Chris take him out?" If this guy was freaking her out, we were going to have a big problem.

"No, no." Kyla held her hand up. "It's just that I feel like I'm leading him on when I don't have interest in him like that. He wants to put his arm around me and stuff. I try to politely scoot away, but…"

"You're too nice and don't want to hurt his feelings," I finished for her.

"Exactly. I mean, he's a nice guy, but not the guy for me. I'm afraid after this date he's going to think it's more. And I sure hope he doesn't try to kiss me." She scrunched up her shoulders and made a disgusted face.

"Don't be so dramatic. It can't be that bad." I laughed.

"It could be worse," she admitted. "I have no desire to kiss him. What if he tries to grope my ass while we're dancing?"

"We are talking about Chad Finkle, right?" Kyla nodded. "There's no way that guy is going to try to grope your ass. He's a total nerd, albeit a cute nerd, but still."

"Have you ever seen *Revenge of the Nerds*?" I shook my head. "Well, I have. Nerds are total twisted sex freaks."

I couldn't contain my laughter at her ludicrousy. "So, you think Chad is a twisted sex freak?"

Kyla threw one hand up in the air while still clutching her book with the other. "Hell, I don't know. I just know it's the quiet ones you've got to worry about. Why did I ever agree to this?"

I wrapped her in a hug. "It's going to be fine. I'm sure he's not a sex freak. Come over and I'll do your hair and makeup. It'll be fun girl time."

"Okay," she agreed. "But don't make me look too sexy. Sweet and innocent. That's what I'm going for."

"Can I tell you a secret?" Kyla nodded, and I leaned towards her ear. "You are sweet and innocent."

"Thanks, girlie."

"One more thing. If he does try to grope your ass, knee him in the balls."

Chapter 23
Chris

Tori and I had become inseparable. We spent almost all our free time together. Whether it was studying or making out in my truck, every moment I spent with her, I fell deeper in love. We just clicked.

She could infuriate me one minute and have me on my knees the next. She was a dangerous mix of sinner and saint. Tori was a little bit of everything, all rolled in to one irresistible package. What she portrayed to other people wasn't who she really was. She reminded me of the song "Bitch". So tough on the outside, telling the world to fuck off with a single look. Even when Matt acted like an asshole to her, my girl held her own. She may have been hurt on the inside, but she wouldn't let him, or anyone else, get that satisfaction. Tori still wouldn't tell me what he had said. She was shielding me. I would undoubtedly lose my shit if I knew the truth. She was as fiercely protective of me, as I was of her.

Beneath all that hard exterior, Tori had a softer side. The way she made love to me—she gave everything so freely. The way she could be rough and dirty, or soft and sweet. She'd tell me to fuck her harder and then finish with *I love you* and a gentle kiss. She held my heart in the palm of her hand and I trusted her completely with it. She would do anything for the people she cared about. She was loyal to a fault. I saw it with her mom and Mike. I saw it in her relationship with Kyla. I saw it when she had finally let her walls down and let me in. I wasn't proud the first time I'd made her cry, but at that moment, I knew she was all in. She'd opened her heart to me and left it raw and exposed, trusting me to keep it safe. I wouldn't take that for granted.

We were alike in so many ways. I couldn't imagine spending my life with anyone else.

I had no doubt that she wanted to go to Homecoming with me, however the whole wearing a dress thing really threw her for a loop. I couldn't wait to see her in a fancy dress with high heels. She had great legs and her heels would only make them look longer and sexier.

I got dressed for the dance and had my mom check my tie. She adjusted the knot and smoothed it down my chest. "You look so handsome, Chris. I wish we were going to be there to get some pictures. Can you make sure that her mom sends me the pictures she takes?"

"I will," I promised. "Do you want to follow me over and you can get your own pictures?" I felt bad that my mom was missing this.

"I don't want to seem clingy. I'm sure the pictures Tori's mom takes will be great. I can't believe my baby is so grown up." She cupped my cheek and looked at me lovingly.

My mom was so sweet. "It was bound to happen," I said. "Doesn't mean that I don't need you." I leaned down and gave her a kiss on the cheek.

Her eyes got misty. "Be good to her. I think you two are perfect. She keeps you in line... and she makes you so happy. I've never seen you smile so much."

"I love her," I admitted. It wasn't something most guys my age would tell their mom, but she already knew and there was no sense in hiding it. "How do I look?"

"Very handsome," she said. "She's a lucky girl."

"Not as lucky as me," I answered.

"Where are you taking her for dinner?" my mom asked.

"I made reservations for Andiamo's," I said.

"Very fancy." She smiled. Then she reached in her pocket and took out some money. "I love you, honey. Have fun tonight." she handed me the money and left my room.

I didn't expect her to give me money, but I would gladly take it. When football season was over, I was going to get a job.

Right now, I was dating on birthday and Christmas money, and the money I'd made cutting Mrs. Tilson's grass. I counted the bills she had handed me. There was a hundred bucks there. My mom was the best.

I raced down the stairs, grabbed my keys off the hook and then backtracked to pull her corsage from the fridge. I couldn't wait to see what Tori would look like in her dress. My dad gave me the thumbs up as I walked out toward my truck. This was it. The moment I had been waiting for since she'd told me she found a dress she loved.

I pulled up to her house and walked casually toward the door. My heart was beating erratically in my chest. I don't know what I was so nervous for. I just wanted her to be happy, and I knew the idea of going to a fancy dance was low on Tori's list of things to do.

I approached the door and knocked. Her mom answered and welcomed me into their home. Her mom had been cool with me since day one.

"Thank you," her mom whispered to me. "I don't know if anyone else would have gotten her to dress up like this."

"Am I going to be surprised?" I asked.

"I think so," her mom answered. Just then, Tori started down the stairs. She was wearing a black dress that look amazing on her. She was cautious on the stairs in her high heels, holding onto the railing as she descended.

"Wow!" It was all I could say. She looked like an angel to me! The dress hugged her curves just right and her legs looked a mile long. "I'm going to have to fight off all the guys tonight!"

Tori made it to the bottom of the steps. "You're just saying that."

"No, really! You look stunning!"

Tori blushed, and it was so damn cute. "Don't get used to it. After tonight I go back to jeans and my Converse."

"I'll take what I can get." I opened the box to her corsage and placed the tiny purple roses on her wrist. "You're a knock-out," I said. And I meant every word.

166

"Let's get some pictures," her mom said. We posed for a bunch, and I left her my mom's e-mail, asking her to forward them. Tori's mom promised she would.

After all the pictures, I took her hand and led her out to my truck. I had spent extra time washing and waxing it for tonight. Getting up into the truck was a struggle, but I helped Tori the best I could.

I slipped into the driver's seat. "You are gorgeous! I'm a lucky guy."

She shyly said, "Thank you."

I drove us to dinner and held her hand as we walked into the restaurant. She had a sexy little walk going on. Her hips swayed from side to side. I don't think she had a clue what she was doing to me. My dick was already hard. Thank goodness, my suit jacket covered that!

After dinner, we headed to the dance. "Does Kyla still have a date for tonight?" I asked.

"Yeah. She's going with Chad, but she's not super happy about it. She thinks he might be a twisted sex freak."

I was sure I didn't hear that right. "Excuse me?"

"You heard me."

"Chad Finkle?"

"Yep," she said, popping the p.

"What in the world would give her that idea?"

"Something about *Revenge of the Nerds* and worrying about the quiet ones."

I couldn't contain my laughter. "Then why did she agree to go with him?"

"She wishes she hadn't. Kyla would rather be going with Trevor. I told her to let it go and just have fun."

"That was good advice. Even though Trevor is my friend, I don't think he and Kyla would be a good match," I said.

"Why is that?" she asked.

"I don't know. Kyla is really conservative, and I don't think Trevor is. He might try to pressure her into something she isn't ready for yet."

Tori laughed. "That was my thought exactly. I just didn't have the heart to tell her."

"Let's not worry about anyone but ourselves tonight. I want to see you dance in that sexy dress. I'm not letting you out of my sight!"

"Don't worry! No one but you is interested." She blew off my compliment. I was okay with that because she really had no idea how good she looked.

We walked into the dance, and I swear heads turned. No one was used to seeing Tori so dressed up. "You're attracting attention," I said.

'No, I'm not. That's all you," she insisted. I didn't care that she didn't want to wear heels, she wore them with a flair that said *don't fuck with me*. She walked with confidence and grace. I stood by her side and with an attitude that said, *Yeah, she's mine. Fuck off!*

We danced through the night. Tori was a surprisingly good dancer. For a girl who supposedly hated all of this, she had no problem letting loose on the dance floor. I watched her sexy body move to the music and she never faltered once in her heels.

I wasn't the best dancer, but I had some moves. Most of them made her giggle. I didn't care what I looked like, as long as Tori was happy and having a good time.

We danced up a storm and decided to take a break. Tori's eyes searched the room, and I knew exactly who she was looking for. "She's over there," I pointed.

"I know I said I wasn't going to worry about her tonight, but I feel bad," she said guiltily. "I just want to check on her."

"It's fine. You're a good friend." I didn't want her to feel bad about not checking in with Kyla. I would never ever come between those two. They were more than best friends. They were like sisters.

"Thank you." She took my hand and led me through the crowd. Kyla was standing with Chad talking. She had a smile plastered on her face, but it didn't quite reach her eyes. Tori placed a hand on her shoulder. "Can I steal you away for a minute?"

Kyla looked relieved. "Sure." She turned to Chad. "We'll be right back. Don't you go dancing with someone else," she teased.

I held in my laugh, as the girls headed toward the bathroom. There was no way this guy was dancing with anyone else. He was damn lucky Kyla had agreed to be his date. I didn't really know Chad. We'd never had classes together, nor did we hang in the same social circle. He seemed nice enough, but he was a little nerdy. Chad had hit the jackpot with Kyla. "So, are you having fun?" I questioned.

"Oh yeah! Kyla's great. She's so sweet and really pretty. I hope she'll go out with me again."

Not a chance in hell! This guy really didn't have a clue. "Never hurts to ask," I encouraged. I made small talk with him and counted the minutes until the girls returned. Finally, after what seemed like forever, I saw them moving through the crowd. I let out a sigh, as I watched Tori walking in her heels. She moved gracefully, like a cat. My wild cat. I had used that name with her a few times over the past weeks. Her response was to purr. Fucking hot as hell! She had one condition for the nickname though... it stayed between us.

When they returned, the perfect song started to play. "I'm sorry, but I have to steal you back. We need to dance to this song." I laced my fingers with Tori's and led her to the dance floor. I tucked her in close and whispered, "This is how I feel about you. Listen to the words."

Tori had one arm wrapped around my neck, and her other hand held mine, tucked tight to my chest. She rested her head on my shoulder, as we swayed to Firehouse's "Love of a Lifetime". I felt like we were in our own little world, as I shut out everything else but her. She tilted her head towards my ear, "I love you, Chris."

"I love you too, Tor." My lips met hers and we kissed in the middle of the dance floor. My tongue tangled with hers in a

169

slow dance that left me breathless. When the song ended, I wanted nothing more than to be alone with my girl. "It's getting late. You wanna get out of here, so we can have some one-on-one time?"

Tori bit her lip and gave me a nod. Such a little action, but it affected me in a big way. My suit pants were fitting just a bit too snug.

I led her to the coat check, so she could get her purse. I took my jacket off and rested it on her shoulders. The night had gotten cool, and she would freeze in what she was wearing. She smiled up at me with appreciation, "Thanks."

We slipped out the side door and raced for my truck. I helped her up, then hopped in the driver's seat and started the engine. Her eyes were on me as I adjusted the situation in my pants. "I'm sorry," I said. "But I've been trying to contain this hard-on all night. I need to spend some alone time with you."

"What do you think? That I'm just going to give it up in the back of your truck?" she teased.

"Are you saying you can resist all of this?" I motioned to myself as if I were presenting a prize.

She threw her head back and laughed. "You know I can't resist you, Chris Capizzio. There's just something about you that's irresistible."

I took off toward our favorite location. I turned in, drove around the bend, and parked. "I just want to tell you that you look so sexy and beautiful tonight. I've been dying to get my hands on my wild cat."

"Kiss me," she rasped out.

We both slid toward the center, and I ran my hands up and down her arms. She was covered in little goosebumps. "You're cold. Let me kick the heat up a bit." She wasn't one to like being doted on, but I hoped it was the little things I did, that showed her how much I cared.

I reached over and flipped the switch on the heater. Warm air filled the cab of the truck. "That feels nice," she said. "Now get over here and kiss me." I wrapped her in my arms and pulled her in close. She let out a sexy little moan, as I pressed my lips to hers. I cupped the back of her head and pulled her in even closer. I nipped at her bottom lip and sucked it into my mouth. A contented sigh escaped her lips.

I kissed along the side of her face, ran my tongue along her jawline up to her ear and nibbled on her lobe. "You don't know what you do to me," I breathed in her ear. She shivered and her head dropped back, giving me access to her perfect neck. I kissed down it and glided my tongue over her collarbone and down her sternum to the valley of her breasts. I kissed each swell and ran my fingers under the edges of the material that covered her.

"What do you want, Chris?" she whispered in the dark.

"I want you. You're my wild cat. Only with me. Only for me."

"I'm all yours. Take me." She reached behind her neck and started to loosen the ties that held her dress up.

"Let me," I said, as I replaced her hands with my own. I pulled on the ends of the ties and felt them come undone. I pulled the fabric away from her tits and let it hang around her waist. "I fucking want you so bad, Tor! This dress was sexy as fuck, but you without it is even sexier."

I palmed her big tits, running my thumbs lightly over her nipples. They hardened immediately, responding to my touch. I ran my tongue over her heard peaks.

Her back arched, "Fuck, Chris!"

In the next moment, my hand was up under her dress. I pushed her underwear aside and slowly pumped into her heat. She was so fucking wet. I knew she wanted me as bad as I wanted her. I curved my fingers up inside her, and she let out a moan of pleasure. "Do you like that, baby?"

"Yessss!" Her voice was raspy and breathless. "Keep going."

I did. I rubbed over her clit with my thumb, and worked her relentlessly, until I felt her come. Her arousal covered my fingers. I slowly pulled them out of her and licked each one clean as she watched me. She grabbed my wrist and brought my fingers to her mouth, sucking each one, like she was sucking my cock. She was a dirty girl and I loved it. I watched my wild cat with an intensity that was reserved just for her. "Do you want me, Tor? Do you want me like I want you?"

"You know I do. Do you want me to blow you, Chris? I can fuck you with my mouth. Make you feel so good, baby." She ran her hand along the side of my face, down my chest and over the painful bulge in my pants. "I'll take care of you."

I cupped her face in my hands, "As much as that sounds like heaven, I want us both to get off. I'll be gentle with you. I promise it won't be like the first time in the truck. We'll do it right this time. My dick misses you."

She rubbed over the front of my pants. "I miss him too," she said giving me a little squeeze. She scooted away from me and reached her hands under her dress. "These are going to have to come off." She slid her silky boy shorts down her legs and slipped them off over her heels.

I took them from her hands and held them up to my face. I breathed in her scent, "You smell so good, baby." I stuck them in my pocket. "These are mine now."

Tori's eyes got wide, and her mouth made a little *O*. Her hands reached down to my belt and started to unbuckle it. Her fingers made quick work of the button and zipper. She reached inside my boxer briefs and started to stroke me. My head leaned against the back of the seat, a low growl erupting from my chest. She had no idea what she did to me. I didn't want to fuck her in this truck. But god, I wanted to fuck her, and this was our only option.

Still wearing her heels, she straddled my waist as I pushed my pants down my hips. "Wait up, baby." I pulled my wallet out and grabbed a condom. "We can't forget this." I ripped it open and rolled it on. With my hands under her dress, I gripped the flesh of her hips. She lined herself up and sank down on me. It was agonizingly slow. Her hands were on my shoulders, giving her the leverage she needed. Her wet pussy felt so good on my dick. It had been three weeks since our night at the hotel and my body missed her every day I wasn't inside her.

We started slow and controlled. We kissed, as she rode me up and down. I rubbed her ass cheeks and all her sexy curves. "I need more, Chris. I want to feel you deep inside me. I need it harder."

Thank fuck! I felt like I was ready to explode. I grabbed her hips harder and slammed her down onto me. All the care I had shown her earlier was gone, as we delved into animalistic territory. She was just as untamed as I was. We couldn't get enough of each other. Our sexual instincts had taken over. Her walls clenched and that was it for me. I thrust my hips up into her and unleashed everything. The orgasm ripped through my body, setting my soul on fire. I buried my head in her tits and rested there. Her hands came around the back of my head, pressing me into her.

She peppered soft kisses on the top of my head. "I love you, Chris. I love you so much."

I tilted my head up and stared into her eyes. "I love you too, Tori." Emotion tore through me. I felt like I was the luckiest guy alive, and I wished we were a few years older. "I wish we were spending the night together. I wish I could sleep with you in my arms tonight."

Her hand rubbed along the back of my head. "That sounds really nice."

I reached for the straps of her dress and tied them back around her neck, then lifted her off me. I grabbed the towel in the backseat and let her clean up, then wiped myself off. Once we were both dressed, I leaned against the passenger door. I set the alarm on my phone and brought her between my legs. She rested her head back on my shoulder as I held her tight. She closed her eyes. "Sleep, baby." I felt her body relax and snuggle back into me. And in that moment, everything was right with the world.

Chapter 24
Tori

Age 17
Senior Year of High School

"I can't believe your parents agreed to this," Chris said from the seat next to me. We were on our way up to my parents' house on Lake Michigan.

"You know my mom and Mike love you," I answered. My parents had left Monday to head up to the house. They agreed to let me stay home by myself for a few days and come up on Thursday with Chris. My mom loved Chris like a son and had practically adopted him as her own.

Chris reached over, laced his fingers with mine, and pulled my hand up to kiss it. "Yeah, I know, but still. This was perfect timing. I had to quit my internship in my dad's office anyway with football practice starting on Monday. I thought my dad was going to blow a gasket when I asked if I could leave a few days early, but he was really cool."

"Your dad loves me," I said. "He knows I'm good for you. I keep you out of trouble." I winked at him.

Chris laughed. "That's bullshit. All the trouble I get into, is with you. We just never get caught."

"Thank God we have your brother and Kyla to cover for us. If I say I'm with Kyla, my mom never questions it."

"Jim's cool. I don't think he ever thought we'd last this long."

"I don't think anyone did," I said. "Even after all this time though, Susie's still sniffing around you like a bitch in heat."

Chris rolled his eyes. "Tor, let it go!"

"I have. Doesn't mean she still doesn't piss me off." I don't know why I let that girl get to me. There was just something about her I didn't trust.

"I love you, Tori. I'm not going anywhere." Chris glanced at the GPS. "Looks like we're almost there."

"We are," I confirmed. "It's up around this bend. I can't wait for you to see the house. It's so cool. You can basically walk out the back door and you're right on the beach." I looked out the window taking in the familiar scenery. "Slow down. It's this one right here," I said, pointing to the house.

Chris pulled his truck into the drive. "Holy shit, this place is huge."

"It used to belong to Mike's parents. They rented it out during the summer. When his parents died, my mom and Mike took it over. They never wanted to deal with renters. They'll let friends use it, but not strangers."

"How big is this place?"

"Five bedrooms."

"Wow!" Chris turned the engine off. We hopped out and Chris grabbed our bags from the back of the truck.

I led him around to the back deck and through the slider. "Mom, we're here!" I shouted.

My mom came bouncing down the stairs. "You two made good time," she said as she hugged us both. "I was just getting your rooms set up for you."

"Thanks for inviting me, Mrs. Russo. This place is amazing," Chris said. "Where should I put our bags?"

"You can take them right upstairs. Tori will show you."

I led Chris up the stairs and into my room. "This is my room. Kyla and I usually stay in here together when she comes up." I took my bags from Chris and set them on the bed. Then I led him across the hall. "You'll be in this room."

Chris set his bag down on the floor. "Which room do your parents stay in?"

"Their room is downstairs on the other side of the house," I said with a mischievous smile.

"Really? They trust us up here alone?" Chris questioned.

"I guess. My mom already had the big talk with me about sleeping in our own rooms. She knows we're having sex."

"And she's all right with that?"

I shrugged my shoulders. "I guess she figures we're going to do it anyway, no matter what she says. She just wants us to be safe. She's not condoning it, but she's not naïve either."

"Now I feel a little awkward," Chris said.

"Don't." I wrapped my arms around his waist. "We'll be discreet. We've never gotten caught before. It'll be fine."

"Let's go downstairs. I don't want your mom wondering what we're doing." Chris took my hand and led me back downstairs. I had never seen him act so nervous around my parents before. We'd fooled around plenty of times at both of our houses.

We walked into the kitchen where my mom was getting stuff out to make sandwiches. "Are you two hungry? I can make you lunch."

"Thanks, Mrs. Russo. I'm actually starved."

"Chris, stop thanking me for everything. You're part of the family. I love having you here with us. Sit down and let me make you a sandwich." She started spreading the mayo on the bread and piling it high with lunch meat. "After lunch, you two should get on your swimsuits and head down to the beach."

"Sounds good."

Chris and I spent the day on the beach. It was totally private, with only the occasional walkers passing through our area. We were laying in the sun holding hands when Chris piped up. "I didn't realize how hard this weekend was going to be."

I turned my head to look at him. "What do you mean?"

"I've been looking at you all day in that bikini and it's turning me on." He flipped over on his stomach and buried his head in the towel.

I propped myself up on my arm and ran my hand down his back. "I'll take care of you later."

"I don't want to disrespect your mom and Mike," he said, his voice muffled by the towel.

"We won't. They won't ever know," I assured him.

"You're not exactly quiet, Tor."

"I can be. I promise. Let's just see how the night goes. Stop worrying."

"Easier said than done. All I can think about is fucking you," he said.

"Come on. Let's go back to the house and shower before dinner," I suggested. "Then we can watch a movie. It's supposed to storm later." I needed to get Chris out of his head. We gathered up our things and walked back to the house. I showed him where the clean towels were and promised to meet him downstairs later.

I went to my room and showered. I put on a little makeup and brushed through my hair. I threw on a pair of shorts and one of Chris's Guns N' Roses T-shirts I had stolen. I opened my door and crept across the hall to Chris's door. It was cracked open, and I could hear him talking on the phone. *Yes, mom, I'm on my best behavior.... I know.... We're going to watch a movie.... I won't.... Mom! Please!.... I know.... I love you, too. I'll talk to you tomorrow.*

I scurried away from his door and down the stairs. Plopping onto the couch, I quickly grabbed the remote and started looking for a movie for us to watch. He sounded anxious on the phone. I didn't know why. We'd dated for a year. It's not like my parents had never seen us kiss or snuggle or anything.

A few minutes later, Chris made his way down the stairs. He looked at what I was wearing. "Nice shirt." He smirked.

I tugged at the front of it. "This old thing? It's one of my favorites. So comfy and cozy."

He came over and plopped next to me. "How did you get that anyway?"

"I stole it out of the laundry basket when your mom was folding clothes," I said, giving him big doe eyes.

"Do you know I've been looking for that shirt everywhere? I thought I left it at practice or something." He seemed kind of annoyed.

I reached for the bottom hem and pretended like I was going to whip it off. I started to lift it, so my stomach showed. "You can have it back if you want it."

Chris quickly pulled the shirt back down. "Keep it. It looks better on you anyway."

"Thank you," I said, giving him a peck on the cheek. I picked the remote back up and aimed it at the TV. "What do you want to watch?"

"I don't care. You choose," he said moodily.

I scanned through the channel guide, trying to decide. "Okay, here's our choices... *Four Brothers, A Walk to Remember,* or *Varsity Blues.*" I looked over to Chris to see what he thought.

He didn't even seem to hear me. He was deep in thought about something. "Chris?"

"What?"

"I just asked you which movie? *Four Brothers, A Walk to Remember*, or *Varsity Blues*?"

"And I told you I didn't care."

I turned off the TV. "Do you even want to watch a movie? We can do something else. We could go for a walk," I suggested.

"I don't even know what there is to do around here. How would I know what I want to do?" he said sharply.

Wow! I wasn't sure what the problem was. He'd been in a funk all afternoon. I set the remote on the coffee table. "Are you regretting coming here?" I asked. "Like, do you feel trapped or something?" I moved away from him and leaned against the arm of the couch, pulling my legs up to my chest. "If you want to leave, you can. I don't want you to feel like you have to stay here for me. I thought it would be fun spending the weekend together. I thought you would like it. I guess I was wrong." I wrapped my arms around my legs and set my chin on my knees.

"Tor…" he started, with a sigh.

"I'm serious," I said. "I'm getting bad vibes here and I'm not sure why." I got up from the couch. "I'm gonna go upstairs. Think about it. If you decide you want to leave, at least wait until the morning, it's getting late in the day." I turned and started up the stairs, trying to keep the tears out of my eyes. When I got to my room, I shut the door behind me and laid on the bed.

I didn't know what the hell was going on with him. All I knew was that I had a sick feeling in my stomach. That feeling that comes right before you know something bad is going to happen. After about ten minutes, I heard Chris's door open and click closed.

I couldn't stand it anymore. I stripped off his shirt and hung it on his doorknob. I went downstairs and out to the beach, crawled up on a big rock, and stared out at the lake. What was going on? Was he ready to break up with me? Had I gotten too clingy? Had he found someone else? Maybe he met someone at his internship with his dad. I wiped away the tears that I didn't realize had been falling down my face.

I don't know how long I sat there. Everything was swirling around in my head, and I couldn't stop it. It had been the best year of my life and I felt like it was coming to an end. The end of us.

"You left your shirt on my doorknob."

I didn't turn around. "It's not mine. It's yours."

"I haven't seen it in forever, so technically, I think it's yours. Possession is nine-tenths of the law." He crawled up behind me and wrapped his arms around my waist.

"Is there someone else?" I croaked out. There was a lump in my throat that I couldn't swallow.

He rested his head on my shoulder, "No."

"Then it's just me. I'm not enough anymore."

He sighed, "You're more than enough."

"Just not enough for you," I stated.

Chris turned me in his arms and cupped my face. "Baby, I love you. You're more than enough for me. You're my best friend and my lover all in one. I don't know what I'd do without you." His thumbs rubbed along the tears that had fallen.

"Then what's going on with you? With us?"

"I'm sorry. It has nothing to do with us. It's my dad," he sighed. "He's pushing really hard right now. He wants me to get a scholarship. I can probably get one for football. But what if I can't? I don't know if I'm smart enough to get an academic scholarship. And he wants me to go into engineering. The internship was cool, but I'm not sure I want to do that forever. It doesn't seem fair that at seventeen, I'm supposed to decide what I want to do for the rest of my life." He let out a frustrated laugh. "I don't even know where I want to go to college."

I grabbed him around the shoulders and pulled him into me. "Why didn't you tell me any of this? I get it. You're stressed." I pulled back and looked in his eyes. "We'll figure it out together. Wherever you go, I go. We'll study hard. You are smart enough to get a scholarship."

"You think so?" he asked.

"I know so," I said confidently. "You can talk to me, you know? I'm not going to think less of you because you don't have it all figured out yet. Hell, I'm more in the dark than you are. I think I want to do journalism, but it isn't really practical. I mean, can I even make money doing that? And then there's photography, which I love, but again... not practical."

"You should do what you love," Chris said, while rubbing my arms up and down. "I'll take care of you. It won't matter how much money you make, as long as you're happy."

I let out a little smile, because that was one of the sweetest things he'd ever said to me. "We're going to take care of each other. We're a team."

Chris looked me in the eyes and poured his heart out. "I'm going to marry you someday. We'll have a nice house and a couple of kids. I'll hold you every night while we sleep, and I'll make love to you every morning." His lips pressed to mine, and

180

my heart nearly exploded. I opened to him, and our tongues twisted together. It was slow and passionate. A promise.

Th wind picked up and lightening flashed across the sky. "I think we should go in. There's a storm coming," I said.

"I haven't kissed you enough yet," Chris insisted. He pulled me up on his lap, so I straddled him and kissed me again. It wasn't hurried or feverish. It was gentle. It was romantic. It was perfect.

My hair whipped in the wind. Light rain began to fall. And he kept on kissing me. I felt him beneath me. His hard pushing into my soft. Suddenly the sky opened and poured down on us. "Oh, my god!" I exclaimed, lifting my face to the sky.

"Now it's time to go in." He chuckled while wrapping his arm around me, and we jogged back to the house. We were laughing hard by the time we made it to the deck. I slid open the door and we dripped all over the tile. Chris pushed my hair back out of my face. "I love you, Tori."

"I love you, Chris." I wrapped my arms around his neck, and we stood there holding each other, a pool of water collecting at our feet.

I heard a throat clear. Our heads snapped over to see my mom staring at us and smiling. "You two are soaked. Why don't you go dry off and get ready for dinner?"

"Sure thing, Mrs. Russo." Chris smiled and headed up the stairs to his room.

"Tori?"

"Yeah, Mom?"

"You two are good together. When you sneak into his room tonight, be safe, okay?" The red crept up my neck. "And try not to wake us. I like pretending to be oblivious."

"Jeez, Mom!" I squealed.

"Just keeping it real," she said. My mom was funny when she tried to be hip.

I ran over and hugged her. "Thanks, Mom." I ran up the stairs, taking them two at a time. When I got to my room, I looked in the mirror and gasped. My hair was flattened to my head and dripping. The little bit of mascara I had put on was smudged under my eyes. And the white T-shirt I had on, was totally see through, showing off my lacey bra. The best part was…Chris didn't care about any of it.

After dinner, Chris and I cuddled up on the couch together to finally watch a movie. He laid down, and I curled up in front of him. He pulled me in tight and kissed the side of my head. The storm had kicked up outside and rain pelted the windows.

I cuddled into him deeper. I felt his hard-on press into my ass. I looked up at him over my shoulder. He shrugged. "Sorry. You keep pressing back into me."

"Don't be sorry. I like it."

He kissed my forehead. "You're lucky your mom and Mike are here." He pushed his hips into me, and I giggled.

"You wanna hear something funny about that?" I asked.

"What's that?"

I whispered in his ear, "My mom kind of gave us the green light on that."

His eyes got wide, and he pulled his head back. "Are you shittin' me?" he whisper-yelled.

I put my hand over his mouth and shook my head. "She said when I sneak into to your room to be safe and not to wake them. But she's still pretending like she doesn't know."

"Oh. My. God! I'm so freaking embarrassed. How am I going to sit across from her at breakfast tomorrow?" he asked.

"Hopefully with a smile on your face." I smirked.

Lightening flashed, lighting up the room, and thunder cracked, shaking the house. It scared the crap out of me, and I jumped, grabbing ahold of Chris. He pulled me to his chest and held the back of my head. "It's just thunder, baby," he comforted me.

Chris was my safe place. In his arms, nothing could hurt me. I stayed tucked to his chest as another round of thunder boomed. I snuggled in deeper, grabbing his shirt. "This is my favorite place," I said. I breathed in his cologne and relaxed a bit.

He rubbed my back, "This is my favorite place for you to be. I'll always take care of you and protect you."

"I know."

After the movie, we went upstairs, brushed our teeth, and went to our separate rooms. I changed into my pajamas, which consisted of a pair of cotton shorts and a tank top. My mom and Mike hadn't gone to bed that long ago and I wanted to make sure they were asleep. I pulled out my tablet and started reading a smutty romance novel. It wasn't helping. All it did was make me want Chris more. After reading for about ten minutes, I gave up. *Fuck it.*

I climbed out of bed and made my way to Chris's room. I quietly opened the door and slipped inside. "Come here," he whispered, as he pulled the blankets back for me to crawl in.

I snuggled in next to him. "This feels nice. You're so warm." He wrapped his arms around me and pulled me in.

Chapter 25
Chris

I loved that we could sleep together. We'd had a few hotel nights, but this was different. I held her close and pulled her in tight, her back to my chest. She let out a contented little sigh that was sexy as fuck. I whispered to her, "Don't do that."

"Do what?"

"Make those sounds. It just makes me want you more." I started kissing the side of her head and down her neck. She started making those sounds again and I was starting to lose the control I was trying really hard to hold onto. "I want you, Tori. Do you think you can be quiet while I fuck you?"

She nodded her head and turned her face to mine so that I could kiss her. Our lips touched, and I ran my tongue along her bottom lip. She opened to me, and I pushed my tongue inside. My hands rubbed up her stomach and under her tank. I loved when she wasn't wearing a bra. I cupped her tit and ran my thumb over her nipple. It was peaked hard, and I rolled it between my fingers. She moaned into my mouth, and I swallowed the sound.

She lifted her leg and threw it over the top of mine, hooking it. I moved my hand down the front of her shorts and between her legs. She was so fucking wet. "Tor, you're soaked."

"I can't help what you do to me," she said in a raspy voice. I loved when her voice sounded like that. Like she was so turned on and all she needed was me. I couldn't imagine my life with anyone else. We were so perfect together.

I slipped my fingers into her wetness and slowly moved them in and out. She moaned, and I covered her mouth with mine. I curled them inside her and her hips began to move as she fucked my hand. I moved my thumb up to rub her clit and her walls started to clench my fingers. I kept finger fucking her and rubbing her clit. She pulled her head away from me and buried her face in the pillow as she came around my fingers, the pillow muffling the sounds she made.

Once she came down, I removed my fingers and kissed the top of her head. Even in the dark, I could see the look of contentment on her face. "Make love to me," she cooed.

I got up from the bed and went to my bag for a condom. I slipped off my shorts and slid the condom over my dick. She stripped out of her shorts and laid down on the bed. I rolled her onto her side and slid in behind her. I pulled her to my chest and wrapped my arm around her waist. Tori lifted her leg and draped it over mine. I slid into her from behind…and fuck she felt good. So tight this way. "I love your pussy," I whispered. I moved in and out of her at a leisurely pace. I wanted to feel all of her. I wanted this to last. I wanted to remember this moment with her. It was so intimate. It was so us.

All I could think about as I made love to her was that she was my forever. I couldn't imagine ever being with anyone else. She was it for me. I'd known it from that first kiss in a basement closet. I knew it from the first time her lips touched mine and fireworks exploded. I knew it the night she agreed to go on a date with me, after that asshole had pushed her to the ground. I knew it when we made out in the back of the movie theater. I knew it the first time I made her come in the treehouse. I knew it when I punched Jason in the face for talking shit about her. I knew it when she wore a fancy dress and heels for me at Homecoming. I just knew it. She was everything to me. I would never let her go.

I woke with Tori's head on my chest and my arms wrapped around her. I thought she might leave in the middle of the night, but she stayed. She wasn't worried about her mom finding us.

I felt her stretch out beside me and her honey-colored eyes met mine. She had a sexy little smile on her face. "Morning," she mumbled, her voice raspy from sleep. Her hair was a mess, but she was beautiful, and she was mine.

I kissed her forehead. "Morning. We should probably get up."

She plopped her head back down on my chest. "Why? I think we should stay right here all day."

"Because your mom is downstairs. She must be cooking breakfast. I smell bacon and I love bacon almost as much as I love you." As if on cue, my stomach rumbled.

Tori giggled. "You've earned bacon. Why don't you go check if the coast is clear for me to sneak back to my room?"

I rolled out of bed and threw a T-shirt on. I cracked open the door and checked the hallway. "Come on," I beckoned her with my head. She crept across the hall, and I made my way to the bathroom. I brushed my teeth, splashed water over my face and wet down my hair, combing it with my fingers. I looked at myself in the mirror and practiced wiping the ridiculous grin from my face. Her mom and Mike were totally going to know we slept together last night. There wasn't much I could do about it, so I sucked it up and went down to the kitchen. At least my morning wood had disappeared.

"Good morning," Mrs. Russo said, as she turned the bacon in the pan.

"Good morning. That smells awesome." I eyed the coffee pot. "Do you mind if I get a cup of coffee?"

"Chris, you don't have to ask. You're welcome to whatever we have." She reached up in the cabinet, pulled down a mug and handed it to me. "How did you sleep?"

I tried to keep my face emotionless, as I poured my coffee. "Really good. The day on the beach wiped me out."

She smirked. Yes... actually smirked at me. "Yeah, a day in the sun will do that to you." She totally knew, but she was being cool.

I couldn't take it. I started to crack. "Mrs. Russo..."

She held up her hand to stop me. "Chris don't. It's okay. Sit down." I wasn't going to argue with her. I took my coffee to the table and waited. I was nervous as fuck. This was just awkward. She sat down across from me, and I wondered where Mike was. Or Tori. Wasn't someone going to save me? "Chris, I see the way you two look at each other. You have from day one. It's been a year. I may act like I don't know what's going on, but I do. I know what love looks like." Was it hot in here or was it just me? Because honestly, I was starting to sweat. "I'm happy it's you. You two are good together. You make her a better person."

I interrupted, "She makes me a better person. I love Tori with all my heart. She means everything to me."

"I know." Mrs. Russo smiled at me. "She loves you too. I know you two are having sex." FUCK!!!! Awkward! Awkward! Awkward! I looked down at the table and wished that a trapdoor would open up and suck me into an endless vortex. She took my hand across the table. "Hey, don't be embarrassed. I was in love when I was your age and that's how Tori came to be. Please, just be safe."

I swallowed down the lump in my throat. "We are." I decided since we were having this conversation, I would ask the question that had been on my mind for a while. "Mrs. Russo? What happened to Tori's dad?" I asked hesitantly.

She sighed. "I loved him. He was everything to me. When I got pregnant, I knew he wasn't ready. He had enlisted in the Marines and was about to go off to Parris Island. I didn't tell him, and he left without knowing. I wanted to tell him, but the timing was never right. We kept in touch for a while and then he was deployed overseas. I never saw him again. It was hard raising her on my own. But now we have Mike, and he's the best thing that ever happened to us."

"I shouldn't have asked," I apologized.

"It's fine. Tori never met her dad. I don't even know where he is anymore." She had a faraway look that was a little sad.

187

"If anything ever happens… I mean, if Tori were to get pregnant," I stammered. "I wouldn't abandon her. I would be there. She's my whole world. I don't want you to worry about that."

"I appreciate that."

"I'm going to marry her someday." Talking to Tori's mom wasn't that hard. She was actually pretty cool. I felt like we were bonding, and it felt good.

She smiled. "I wouldn't be surprised." She got up and hugged me. "Thank you for loving Tori and taking care of her."

I hugged her back. "Loving her is the easiest thing I've ever done. I've loved her since seventh grade." She quirked her eyebrow up at me. "Don't tell Tori I told you. She thinks I'm nuts, but it's true."

Mrs. Russo smiled and ran her hand down the side of my face in a motherly gesture. "Let's get you some breakfast. You like bacon?"

"Yes, ma'am."

Fifteen minutes later, Tori walked into the kitchen ready for the day. I wondered what had taken her so long. "Are you two having breakfast without me?" She went to the cabinet and pulled out a mug for coffee. "Where's Mike?"

"Yes, we're having breakfast. Do you want some scrambled eggs?" Tori nodded. "Mike's out front fixing the porch. There were some rotted boards he was worried about," her mom answered.

I jumped up. "I should go help him. You know, earn my keep and all." I swiped another piece of bacon, kissed Tori, and headed to the door.

Tori ran up and grabbed my arm. "Are you alright?" She looked concerned and I had to laugh a little.

"I'm fine, baby. I had a good talk with your mom. Now I'm going to go talk to Mike about our sex life. Figure we should all be on the same page, you know?" I tapped her on the nose with my finger and kissed her cheek.

She stood there like a fish out of water. Her mouth was moving, but no words were coming out. It was rare that I could make Tori speechless, but there she stood without a thing to say. I leaned down next to her ear, "I'm fucking with you, Tor."

A look of relief crossed her face and she let out a big breath. "That wasn't nice," she scolded.

"I was only half kidding. Your mom and I did have a good talk. She's cool."

Tori looked at me suspiciously. "Yeah, she is cool. So, when you're done helping Mike, do you want to go to the sand dunes?"

"Sounds good." I motioned over my shoulder with my thumb. "I'm gonna go. Let me know when you're ready."

I headed out the back door and walked around to the front of the house. Mike was measuring a piece of wood to replace a board on the porch. "Want some help?"

Mike turned to me and smiled. "Sure, kiddo. Wanna grab those boards and bring them over here?"

I walked to his truck and started to unload the two-by-sixes. I carried them over and dropped them next to the porch. "So, how'd you sleep?" Mike asked.

I huffed out a breath. "No offense, Mr. Russo, but I just had this conversation with Tori's mom. Are guys ganging up on me?"

He threw back his head and let out a full belly laugh. "Awww shit, Chris. I'm sorry. You know we really like you, right? We just worry is all."

I dropped my head and kicked at the rocks on ground. "I get that. I would never hurt her." I went over and sat on the porch.

Mike dropped what he was doing and came over to sit next to me. "I know. I knew from the night you threw fucking rocks at my window. I knew you loved her."

I scrunched up my face. "You did?" Seemed like everybody could read me like a book when it came to Tor.

"Yep. I told Tori as much."

189

"You're right. I can't imagine my life without her. We just click. Everything is so easy with her."

Mike laughed again. "You know, you're probably the first person to ever say that about Tori. She's got a fire inside her. She can be feisty and difficult."

"It's one of the things I love best about her. She challenges me. We challenge each other. It works for us," I admitted.

"I'm not going to give you a lecture. You two are old enough to make your own decisions. We're happy to have you as part of our family." He threw his arm over my shoulder and gave me a fatherly hug. "Now, let's get this porch done. You know how to use a circular saw?"

"Sure do," I answered. The two of us got to work measuring and cutting boards. We had replaced all the rotted boards on the porch in less than an hour. Mike was a great guy. He didn't treat me like a kid. We talked the whole time, and he even told me a few dirty jokes. It was all good.

And now…everybody knew Tori and I were having sex. So much for keeping everything on the down low. The only one who might still be in the dark, was my mom. She was too sweet, and I didn't want to think about her knowing. I was happy being her baby boy, even if it wasn't the truth.

After lunch, Tori and I headed over to the Sleeping Bear Dunes. It was a quick drive, about five minutes from the house. We stood at the bottom and looked up. "That doesn't look so bad," I said.

Tori smirked. "You say that now but climbing up that sand isn't as easy as it looks. I haven't done it in a couple of years. Kyla and I used to do it every summer. Now we're more interested in getting a tan."

"Is this a shoes-on or shoes-off climb?" I asked.

190

"I think it's easier barefoot, but it's up to you," she answered.

I quickly stripped off my shoes and socks and tossed them in the back of the truck. I grabbed a couple bottles of water and handed one to her. "Let's climb this bitch." Tori tossed her sandals in the front seat with her purse. I locked the truck and held out my hand for her.

Tori laced her fingers with mine and we started the climb up the dunes. About halfway up the first hill, I was breathing hard and so was Tori. "Holy crap, this is steep," I exclaimed.

"Told ya." She took a drink of water and capped her bottle. "Let's keep going." I followed behind her, watching her ass as she climbed up the dune. God, she had a great ass. I shouldn't have been thinking about sex right now, but I couldn't help it. I was thinking about all those little sounds she made last night and how I silenced her with my mouth.

We got to the top of the first hill, and she stood with her hands on her hips. I was tired as fuck already. "We can stop here, but if we go all the way to the top, the view is amazing. I kind of want to share it with you."

If she wanted to go to the top, then that's where we were going. "Lead the way, wild cat." She smirked at me over her shoulder and then started up the next hill. After another fifteen minutes of climbing, she was standing at the top looking out over the water. Her hair was blowing in the breeze, and she had a smile that lit up her face. I wrapped my arms around her waist and nuzzled into her neck.

"Sit with me?" She sat down in the sand, and I sat behind her, placing her between my legs. We looked out over Lake Michigan. You could see for miles, and it was all water. Probably not as good as looking out at the ocean, but pretty damn close. "What did you talk to my mom about?"

"Us." I was purposely vague. I didn't want her to know all the details. I didn't know if she'd be cool with me asking about her dad. I wondered if she ever thought about him. I wondered if she looked like him or laughed like him.

Tori rolled her eyes. "I figured that much. Details. I need details," she said with exasperation.

I laughed at her. "You're kind of nosey, you know that?"

"I'm not nosey. If you were talking about us, I should know."

I kissed her neck and ran my tongue behind her ear. "I told her I love you and I'm going to marry you someday."

She tilted her head to the side, so I could kiss her more, "Oh, yeah? And what did she say?"

I continued kissing down her neck. "She said she wouldn't be surprised. Both her and Mike know we're having sex. They just want us to be careful. No babies, you know?"

"No worries. I'm not ready for that."

We had never really discussed that before. Maybe, since we were having sex, it was a discussion we needed to have. "Have you ever thought about it?" I asked.

She turned and looked me in the eye. "What? Us having babies together?" I nodded. "Someday," she said. "Not any day soon though." She dropped her head and ran her hand along my leg.

"What if it happened? What would you want to do?" I brushed her hair away from her face, so I could see her.

"I can't talk about this. Why are we talking about this?" Her eyes were getting all watery. Clearly, I'd hit a nerve with her.

I turned her face towards mine. Her glassy eyes were killing me. "Why are you getting upset? We're just talking. I think it's something we should talk about. It could happen."

"Because I'm a bad person," she choked out.

That took me by surprise. "Baby, you're not a bad person. Why are you upset?" A tear ran down the side of her face. I wiped it away with my thumb. "Don't cry. It's just a 'what if' question."

192

"Because I don't want a baby for a long time. I couldn't do it. I couldn't do what my mom did. And if she made the choice that I'd want to make...I wouldn't be here. That makes me selfish and a bad person. And the fact that I already know this without asking you what you would want, makes it even worse."

I turned her and held her to my chest. "It's okay, baby," I soothed her. "I don't want a baby either. I feel the same way."

She looked up at me with big eyes. "Really?" She wiped at her face. "You wouldn't be mad?"

I shook my head. "At this time in my life, I'm not ready. I would be there for you though. We'd get through it together. I wouldn't want you to be afraid to tell me."

"Do you think we'd regret it? Would you end up resenting me?" she asked.

I shook my head again. "No, baby. We'd need to do what's right for us. I would never resent you for a decision we made together."

She breathed out a breath of relief and laid her head against my chest. "I've thought about this for a while. Every month I hold my breath, hoping that I'm not pregnant. I know we're careful, but I still think about it."

I ran my hand through her hair and let it fall between my fingers. "I'll always be there for you, Tor. Always. We can get through anything together. You're my heart."

"I love you, Chris."

"I love you too, Tori."

Chapter 26
Tori

That night, Chris and I didn't even pretend that we were going to separate bedrooms. We crawled into bed together and talked for hours. Then he made slow, sweet love to me. I fell asleep peacefully in his arms. There was no other place, I would have rather been.

Monday, Chris started football practice. Senior year was a big deal. He wanted to get a scholarship, either athletic or academic. This would be his third year on varsity. It was his make it or break it opportunity.

I noticed him limping a little after he worked out sometimes. He never said anything about it, so neither did I. But I suspected his knee was hurting him. He knew his limits, and I trusted he wouldn't push too hard. The problem was that he really wanted to make his dad happy, and he knew that getting a football scholarship would do that. Chris was determined to be the best cornerback in the county. Determined to get a damn scholarship.

He drove right to my house after practice on Monday. We were having an early dinner and when my mom saw him, she immediately set another place at the table. Chris called his mom to tell her that he was at our house. I could tell he was busting to tell me something.

We all sat down and started filling our plates. "So, guess what happened at practice today?"

Mike bit first. "What?"

Chris's face got a big smile on it. "We got a new guy on the team. He just moved here from Bay City. He plays quarterback, so Jason's pissed because he really thought he was going to start this year. But this new guy, Tyler, he's got an arm like a cannon. Guy's good. I guess he was some kind of big deal up in Bay City."

"That's cool," I said. I was a little confused as to why Chris was so excited about this. "What does this have to do with you? I mean, you look like the cat that swallowed the canary."

"Ahhh...I haven't told you the best part." He grinned. "This Tyler kid is so good that scouts have already been checking him out. Which means...they'll be coming to our games. Coach said this is my chance."

Mike furrowed his eyebrows. "What's his last name?"

Chris thought for a minute. "Jefferson? Johnson? No, no, no... Jackson. Tyler Jackson."

"No shit," Mike said. "If it's the same kid, I've read about him in the paper. I think he's been playing varsity quarterback for Bay City High School since he was a sophomore."

"That's him," Chris said, snapping his fingers. "I don't really care who he is, but if he brings scouts to the games, that can only be good for me. It really ups my chance for getting a scholarship."

I leaned over and gave him a hug. "Have you told your dad, yet?" I asked. "This will make him really happy."

"Not yet, but you're right. He's going to be thrilled." Chris took a bite of his chicken and then pointed his fork at me. "This doesn't get you off the hook though, Tor. We're still gonna study hard and get good grades this year. And we need to start studying for the ACT."

My mom giggled. "I guess he put you in your place."

I rolled my eyes. "Yeah. He has a way of doing that."

"I'm serious," Chris said. "We need to get our shit together. If we're going to go to college together, we need to start thinking about it."

195

"I know… it's just…I don't even know what I want to do yet. You're stressing me out."

Chris grabbed my hand. "I know, but we'll figure it out. I'll help you and you'll help me. We're a team, remember?"

Mike piped up. "Chris, do you know what you want to do?"

"My dad wants me to do engineering. I like it, but I'm not totally sure. It's a big decision."

"How did your internship go this summer?" he asked.

"It was cool," Chris said. "I learned a lot about CAD, and I was good at it. It's like a big puzzle, you know? It's all space relations."

I was feeling stressed out. I knew that Kyla wanted to go to Western Michigan for their graphic design program. She and I had always planned on going to college together, but that was before Chris. I didn't want to break my promise to her. "Does Western have an engineering program?" I asked nervously.

Chris quirked his eyebrow at me. "I'm not sure. Why?"

I looked down at my plate. "Just asking." I stuffed another mouthful of chicken in so that I couldn't talk.

My mom picked up on what was going on. "Is that where Kyla is going?" she asked.

"They have a really great graphic design program. It's her first choice." I shrugged my shoulders. "We just always planned on going to college together. But things are different now."

Chris sat his fork down and gave me a hard stare. "Why didn't you say something? Kyla's like a sister to you. I don't want you to feel like you need to pick one of us over the other. I'll check out what Western offers."

"You don't have to do that," I insisted. "Kyla will understand."

"No. I should have thought about this before. I'm not going to make you choose," Chris said definitively. "It will probably be easier to get a football scholarship there, too. I mean

196

easier than Michigan State or U of M. This could actually be perfect."

I pulled up in Kyla's driveway, on the first day of school. I couldn't believe we were finally Seniors. She bounced out to the car and threw her stuff in the back. She looked really cute today, like she'd spent extra time getting ready. I was going to drive with Chris, but he was picking up the new guy, Tyler, and bringing him to school for his first day. I still hadn't met him, but Chris talked about him a lot. They seemed to have bonded.

Kyla's parents stood in the doorway waving at us. "Your parents are so damn cute," I said.

"I know it's almost sickening, isn't it? They've been together since they were seventeen. I hope I find that someday." Kyla sighed.

"Kyla, this is our year. We're fuckin' seniors, girlfriend! Time to lose that V card you hold onto so tightly."

"Seriously, Tori? Is that all you think about?" Kyla asked in exasperation.

"Not the only thing. But trust me, Kyla, you have no idea what you're missing! Since Chris and I did it, I can't get enough... of his dick that is!" I internally laughed because I knew it made her crazy when I talked like that. She got embarrassed so easily, it was almost like a game to me. I could make her blush with hardly any effort at all.

"Eww! TMI for sure!" She made a disgusted face. "I'm not going to have sex, just to do it. It's got to be right. I want it to be with someone I love. I want it all! I want the butterflies in my stomach, the stars in my eyes, the head over heels kind of love. It's out there somewhere." She sighed again.

"You're just a hopeless romantic. And I love you for it, but let's be real. The chances of you finding that here are pretty slim. There are no knights in shining armor or white horses, for that matter. Just a bunch of horny teenage boys in pickup trucks. Not that that's a bad thing." I smirked. "Pickups usually have bench seats," I waggled my eyebrows at her. I loved Chris's truck. We'd made out and fucked so many times in it, I started to get turned on just thinking about it.

Kyla turned to me. "So, what do you know about the new guy? He's playing football with Chris, right? Have you met him?"

"No, I haven't met him and yes, he's playing football. I don't really know much about him at all, except he's supposed to be some superstar quarterback." I rolled my eyes. "Chris seems to think he's cool though. I think he and Chris drove to school together today, so I guess we'll find out."

"Are you serious?" Kyla got all panicky. She pulled the visor down and unfolded the mirror. She frantically pulled her lip gloss from her purse and applied a fresh coat. She was checking her makeup as we pulled into the parking lot.

I couldn't help myself. I started laughing. "What the fuck, girl? He's a football player, not exactly your type. What's with all the primping?"

Kyla sighed, snapping the mirror back into place. "Okay. Here's the deal. I heard he's hot. Like really, really hot. And what do you mean he's not my type? Do I have a type?"

"Uhhh…yeah. You definitely have a type. All the guys you've dated have been the smart, quiet, shy type. I mean they're cute, but in a wholesome way. You know, kind of like a puppy." Kyla always played it safe. If this guy was a superstar football player, chances were, he'd been around the block a few times. I didn't want her to get her hopes up over a guy who was probably an ass. Kyla's realm of experience was minimal at best.

Kyla threw up her hands in exasperation. "What? Puppies are cute and loveable."

"Girl, you need a Rottweiler, not a Labrador Retriever." I laughed. "In all seriousness, Kyla, you need to let go a little. You spend so much time studying and trying to make your parents happy. I just want to see you have some fun. Please, just try. Be a little bad, break some rules. You're too damn nice!"

"Number one..." She held up one finger. "There's nothing wrong with nice. And number two..." She sighed, holding up another finger. "You're totally right." She slumped back against the seat. "I just don't know if I have it in me."

We pulled into our parking spot, and I killed the engine. Kyla turned to me, and I took her hands in mine. "Listen, you're beautiful, smart, and...I don't mean this in a lesbian kind of way, because I like guys way too much...you're sexy. Own it. Be open to possibilities. Expand your horizons," I pleaded with her. I loved Kyla, but she seriously needed to relax and let go.

"I'll try," she promised. "What do you think is between a Labrador and a Rottweiler, because I'm not sure if I'm ready for that?"

"I don't know. A Labraweiler?" I shrugged.

"That's not even a real thing. Is it?"

"Maybe not, but it might be just what you need."

We jumped out of the car and grabbed our stuff from the back. I saw Chris waiting for us and I just wanted to kiss the shit out of him. He was my guy. I never knew, before we started dating, that life could be this good.

"Hey, baby," I said, as I leaned in and gave Chris a quick kiss.

Chris gave me a kiss back and wrapped his arm around me. "Tori, meet Tyler. He's our new quarterback. Tyler meet my girl, Tori," Chris introduced us. "And let's not forget her bestie, Kyla."

"Hey Tori. Kyla," Tyler said. He was fucking hot! If I wasn't so in love with Chris, I'd go after him myself. The guy looked nervous a hell though, and I kind of felt bad for him.

I stopped myself from staring and finally found my words. I hoped Chris didn't notice. "Hey, Tyler. Chris says you're pretty amazing on the field. Welcome to Oak Valley," I said.

"Amazing, huh." He smiled, and hell, he had some amazing dimples. I looked over at Kyla and she was practically drooling. I bumped her with my hip and whispered in her ear, "Close your mouth." She quickly snapped it closed and blushed.

Chris wasn't even paying attention. "Yeah, 'amazing' is not what I said. Don't let it go to your head, dude. But you are pretty good. It's gonna be a great season! Hey, and Kyla is on the cheerleading team, so you two will probably see a lot of each other. Plus, these two," Chris motioned between Kyla and me, "are thick as thieves, so if you're gonna hang with me you'll be hanging with the two of them."

Kyla pulled it together and finally found her voice. "Hey, Tori could do worse for a best friend." She smiled shyly. "I try to keep her on the straight and narrow. It's a full-time job, especially since she's hooked up with you." Kyla winked and pointed her accusing finger at Chris.

"Always the party pooper, Kyla," Chris chided.

"Don't listen to him, Tyler. He knows I've saved their butts more than once. I'm their cover story for all their illicit activities," Kyla laughed.

"Well, nice to meet you, Ky. I guess we'll be hanging together, since this asshole is my only friend so far," he said as he motioned to Chris. *Ky?* Nobody called her Ky. But Kyla didn't correct him. Interesting.

"Damn right. I'm the only one who can put up with your cocky ass," Chris joked.

"Oh, you wound me." Tyler feigned hurt and clutched his chest. "Right here, man. That hurts." He pounded his fist to his chest. "Don't let this guy give you the wrong impression," Tyler said turning to Kyla. "I'm one of the good guys." He was fucking flirting with her. Again…interesting.

"We'll see," she flirted back with a coy smile. I'd never seen her flirt so shamelessly. Good for her. It was about time!

The four of us walked into the school. Kyla took off for her first class and she seemed in a hurry. Of course, she was so prepared, she didn't even need to stop at her locker. We dropped Tyler at his locker, and I noticed that it was just a few down from Kyla's. Once we got him settled, Chris and I walked toward our lockers.

"That was interesting!" I shrieked.

Chris looked at me like I had just grown horns out of my head. "What?"

"Oh, come on. You can't tell me you didn't notice." I was so happy for Kyla, that I could barely contain my excitement.

Chris looked at me with confusion. "You've lost me. What the hell are you talking about?"

I grabbed him by the shoulders and motioned in the direction we had just come from. "That! You didn't see it? Those two are totally gonna hook up."

"Who?" Chris really didn't get it. "Tyler and Kyla?" I nodded. "Are you kidding me? They're so different. He's a total jock and she's…well, she's Kyla. I think she's pretty much afraid of anything with balls."

I slapped him in the chest. "Oh, stop! She's just inexperienced. And so what if he's a jock? So are you and you're dating me."

"Well, that's different." He smirked. "You've got big tits and a great ass." He cupped my ass and gave it a squeeze. I tried to squirm away from him, but he grabbed me around the waist

201

and pulled me in closer. "Plus, you've got a wicked bad side I just can't resist." He pressed his lips to mine and pushed his tongue inside. I swear he was fucking my mouth with his tongue. "Wanna skip first hour?" he asked.

I pushed against his chest. "You're a bad influence. What happened to good grades and 'we gotta get our shit together'?" I imitated him.

Chris sighed. "You're no fun."

"Take me to your truck. I'll show you how much fun I am," I dared him.

He grabbed me by the hand, and we raced through the hall out to the parking lot.

Yeah, we missed first hour.

After school, I met up with Kyla by her locker. "Soooo?" I asked her.

She tried to hide her smile but failed miserably. "So, what?"

"Who the hell do you think you're talking to? You know what I'm asking? How did you and Tyler end up walking to lunch together?" I pressed.

"Oh, that. Funny thing," she said. "We have World Lit together." She was trying to play it so cool. I eyed her. I wasn't letting her get off that easily. Finally, she broke. She grabbed my arm and pulled me around the corner and looked around to see if anyone was listening to us. "Here's the deal," she said excitedly. "His locker is just a few down from mine and he asked me where his next class was." Her words were coming out so fast that I thought she was going to explode from her own excitement.

"Anyways, we have the same class, so I showed him. Then when we got there, I sat in the front. You know I like to be in the front. Then he sat down next to me. I swear there were like a dozen empty seats, and he sat next to me. And then he borrowed a pen from me." She jumped up and down and clapped her hands.

I started laughing. Like, full out, hysterical laughing. "You're this excited over a pen?"

She slapped me on the arm. "Shut up! He's cute, ok? No… he's not just cute," she lowered her voice, "he's fucking hot!"

"Really?" I rolled my eyes. "I hadn't noticed."

"Tori Russo! You're a liar," she accused.

I grinned. "Okay. So, I might have noticed. But I can't let Chris know I noticed. He'll go all caveman. He's kind of possessive of me." I winked at her. "That's okay though because I'm kind of possessive of him too. You didn't see that hoebag, Susie, today, did you?"

Kyla laughed. "No. Maybe she found another victim."

I grabbed my camera from my locker and walked with Kyla to cheer practice. While I was waiting for her to finish, I figured I should get some pictures for the yearbook. It would give me an excuse to hang by the guys.

I walked around the track, looking for the perfect angle. When I found Chris, I started snapping my camera. He took his helmet off and his hair was sticking up, looking just fucked.

Click!

Then he bent over to grab the ball off the ground. Nice ass shot.

Click!

He pulled his jersey up to wipe the sweat from his face, his abs on display.

Click!

Tyler walked over to talk to Chris, pulling his helmet off.

Click! That one was for Kyla.

Yeah, none of these were going in the yearbook.

Chris saw me on the sidelines and thrust his hips at me, making a lewd gesture.

Click! Click! Click!

"Get your ass over here, Capizzio!" I heard his coach yell. He blew me a kiss and then ran back to the field. I laughed. That was my man. God, I fucking loved him!

Chapter 27
Chris

Tori was so right about Tyler and Kyla. I gotta admit, I didn't see it. She was a virgin, and I didn't see her giving it up anytime soon. Ty was a jock— superstar quarterback. He'd probably had lots of pussy. The fact that he'd wait for Kyla blew my mind. Poor guy probably rubbed one out every time he got in the shower.

Tyler and Kyla were inseparable at school, and I saw the way he looked at her. Kyla had always been pretty, not my type, but definitely pretty. She didn't have the kicking curves that Tor had, but she was well proportioned. I don't even know why I was thinking about Kyla's tits, but shit…they're tits, so of course I noticed.

Ty cornered me after practice, a few weeks before Homecoming. "So…I'm thinking about asking Kyla to Homecoming. Do you think she'd go with me? She doesn't already have a date, does she?"

I narrowed my eyes at him. "I don't think she has a date. And yeah, she'd probably go with you. What's up with you and her anyway?"

Tyler pulled off his practice jersey and stuffed it in his bag. He sniffed himself and pulled out a clean shirt from his locker. Must have been one of the perks of being a quarterback. You didn't sweat as much. I, on the other hand, smelled like a rat's ass. I fucking needed a shower, and bad! I decided to wait until I got home and didn't change.

"I don't know," he admitted. "There's just something about her. She's sweet. And hot. She's got a cute little ass. There's something innocent about her that's irresistible."

I cringed. "Fuck man! I don't want to hear this shit. I've known her forever. Literally forever! And she's my girl's best friend. I can't think about her that way."

"Sorry, man! Shit! But... you think she'd go with me."

"Yeah. I shouldn't be telling you this, but she's into you. I'm gonna tell you right now though... if you're hoping to get your dick off, you're barking up the wrong tree. She's not gonna put out. And if you fuck it up...you're on your own. She's Tori's best friend. Tori's protective of her. And if I have to choose? Sorry dude, you lose!"

"I get it. I really like her though. It's not about sex. She makes me happy." Tyler rifled through his bag and acted like he was looking for something. He was fucking nervous. Mr. Football had already lost his balls to a girl he'd never even kissed. I laughed.

"I get it. Tori's had my balls since seventh grade. She made me wait forever until she'd go out with me." I shoved all my shit into my bag and grabbed my keys. "I'll tell you what though. I wouldn't trade it for anything."

Tyler straightened up to his full height with confidence. We were practically the same height at about six-two and six-three. "I'm gonna ask her."

I fist bumped him. "Good luck, man!"

Tori and Kyla were getting ready for the dance at Kyla's house. Tyler and I were meeting them there. That meant that Tori and I would have to go to her parents' and my parents' houses for pictures. I could have given a fuck less because Tor and I had a hotel room waiting for us at the end of the night. Thank you, Jim! In a few months, we'd both be eighteen and could get our own room. Tori's parents were cool about us having sex and so were mine, but we tried to be respectful. Fuck… it's not like we could really let loose under their roofs. I wanted my girl screaming my name. God, I fucking wanted her, and the night had barely started.

Tyler and I pulled up at the same time. We walked to the door and rang the bell. "Don't fuck this up tonight," I told Tyler.

"Fuck you, asshole," he said. I kind of loved this guy.

Kyla's mom answered the door, and I turned on the charm. "Hi, Mrs. O'Malley." I gave her my panty dropping smile.

"Hi, Chris." She smiled back. I had a way with moms. She invited us in, and I introduced Tyler to her. I'm not too much of a man to admit that he had the looks. He was built and his panty dropping smile rivaled mine. I was used to being top dog around here and this guy was giving me a run for my money. He charmed Kyla's mom in about ten seconds.

The girls came down the steps and they were gorgeous. That black, strapless dress Tori had on, made me want to peel it off her. I knew what was hiding underneath and my dick got hard just thinking about it. She had on fuck-me heels that made her legs look miles long. I bit my lip and tried to suppress the growl rising from my chest.

After the requisite photos, I pulled Tori out to my truck. "I don't think we're going to make it to the dance," I told her. "You look way too hot tonight."

"Let's make the rounds and then I'll give you a blow job on the way to the dance," she chided. We stopped at her house for pictures and then went to mine for pictures. It seemed to take forever but making the moms happy made our lives that much easier.

On the way to the dance, I had to pull onto the side of the road. Tori had my dick out and was fucking me with her mouth. My girl knew how to please me, that was for sure. It didn't take long for her to get me off. I came hard and relaxed my head back against the seat. She was every wet dream I'd ever had, come to life.

"I love you, Tor," I whispered, as I came back to reality.

She wiped her mouth on the back of her hand. "I know, baby."

We headed into the dance ten minutes later. Kyla and Tyler were on the dance floor, and I swear people were looking at them. What the hell? So what if he was the quarterback and she was the captain of the cheerleading squad? New guy had game. I couldn't believe they had been crowned Homecoming King and Queen.

Fuck them! Tori and I would attract our own attention. They may have been the new power couple, but we weren't chopped liver. My girl was hot, and I wasn't so bad myself. Together we made one hell of a good-looking couple. They had the all-American good looks, but we had that exotic Italian thing going. Way hotter!

Tori and I moved to the dance floor and it was a sex show. I danced with my legs between hers, inviting her in. She rode my leg, rubbing up and down. We ground up against each other in a shameless display of want and need. I grabbed her hand and twirled her around. She giggled like crazy while spinning. Then I dipped her down low and kissed her neck. All of this was foreplay. Only one thought crossed my mind... hotel room tonight!

I needed to piss bad, so I left Tor with Tyler and Kyla. I walked around the corner to the bathroom, trying to calm my hard-on so I could pee. Out of nowhere, I felt a hand wrap around my arm. My head snapped to the side. Fuckin' Susie. "Hey, Chris. You look hot tonight," she flirted.

My hands got clammy, and my hard-on disappeared. I didn't like the situation she was putting me in. "Hey, Susie. Umm, thanks?" It came out more as a question. I tried to pull away, but I felt her hands tighten around my arm.

"You know what I was thinking about the other day?" I shook my head. "Remember that time when we were at Trevor's party and you fucked me in the bathroom?" she continued, with lust-filled eyes. "Remember how you made me come while I was sitting on the bathroom counter? You really knew how to work my body."

My eyes widened in shock. I did remember. She's thrown herself at me that night. I was horny and drunk. I had fooled myself into thinking it meant something. I pried Susie's hand off my arm. "What the hell? You know I'm with Tori. Why are you bringing this shit up?"

She ran her hand along the side of my face. "Because we were good together. The sex was amazing," she cooed.

"Yeah. So good you let someone else stick their dick in you less than three weeks later." My words came out harsher than I intended. I didn't know why what she had done still bothered me. It was a long time ago.

Susie pouted at me, "I made a mistake, Chris. One I've always regretted. We can get it back. You just have to give us a chance."

I took two steps back. "Not gonna happen. I love Tori."

Susie crossed her arms, pushing her small tits up. "For now. I'm not giving up." She winked at me and turned on her heel to leave. I watched her walk away as Tyler came around the corner. Susie "accidently" bumped into him. Tyler reached out and grabbed her waist to steady her. "I'm so clumsy," Susie said sweetly. "Thank you." Then she rubbed her boob on Tyler's arm and disappeared.

Tyler's eyes went wide as he looked from Susie to me. "Who was that?"

"Trouble. And my past. She wants back in my pants."

"Oh...and?" Tyler questioned.

I shook my head. "Not happening. Can you do me a favor and not mention this to Tori? She'll fucking blow a gasket."

"Sure, man. It stays between us."

I fist bumped him. "Thanks."

I finally made it to the bathroom and back to Tori. "What took so long?" she questioned.

"There was a line," I answered nonchalantly.

"Hmm. I thought only girls had to wait in line for the bathroom," she said.

I shrugged my shoulders and grabbed her hand. "Come on. I want to dance with you." I leaned down next to her ear. "Did I tell you how fucking sexy you look? Tonight, I want you in those heels and that pearl necklace. Nothing else. I'm gonna make you come so hard you're going to forget everything but my name."

Her eyes hooded and filled with lust. "How much longer are we staying?"

"A while. The anticipation will only make it better." I led her to the dance floor and pulled her against my chest. I held her close as Boys II Men's "I'll Make Love to You" started and it couldn't have been more perfect. I wanted to make love to her tonight. And to fuck her. I had every intention of doing both. I would never stop doing everything in my power to make her happy.

She let out a little gasp as I pushed my hard-on into her softness. Her lips met mine in a gentle kiss and then Tori snuggled into my chest. I loved her there. Right where she belonged. All I could think about was the life I wanted to have with her.

Tori tapped me on the shoulder, breaking me out of my trance. I looked down at her and she pointed over my shoulder. Tyler was leading Kyla out of the dance. Tori pulled me in their direction. "Whoa! Where do you two think you're going? Cutting out early on us, is not cool," Tori teased.

Kyla looked at Tyler and then at the two of us. "Tyler and I are just... well the dance is almost over anyway. Talk to you in the morning?" Kyla said over her shoulder.

"Definitely. And I'll want details girl!" Tori yelled. And then they left.

I leaned down to Tori's ear. "Let's get out of here."

She nodded her head, and we practically ran out to my truck.

By the time we got to the hotel, my dick was so hard it actually hurt. "You're mine tonight," I told Tori.

She backed up toward the bed, pulling me by my tie. "I'm always yours."

I stepped toward her, shrugging out of my jacket, as she started to sit on the bed. I grabbed her hands and pulled her back up. "Not yet." I loosened my tie and slipped it off.

I slipped it down over her head and her eyes got wide. "What are you doing?"

"You'll see." I smirked. "Well, no. Actually, you won't." I put it around her head, so it covered her eyes, and tied it. "Can you see?"

She felt the front of her face with her hands. "No," she breathed out. "What are you going to do to me?"

"Do you trust me?"

"Always. Be gentle with me, okay?"

"I would never hurt you, baby." I led her over towards the opening that served as a closet and backed her in. I took her hands and lifted them above her head. I wrapped her fingers on the overhead bar. "Whatever happens, don't let go," I whispered in her ear.

"I won't." She completely trusted me.

211

Chapter 28
Tori

I completely trusted Chris, but not being able to see made me apprehensive. We had talked about doing some kinky shit, but nothing compared to this. "What are you going to do to me?" I gasped out.

"Wouldn't you like to know. Just hold on, baby, and let me take you for a ride." I felt Chris's hands at the back of my dress. He slowly slid the zipper down and the material fell to my feet. I stood there in my black strapless bra, silky black boy shorts, high heels, and that damn pearl necklace. "Lift your feet," he instructed. I did, and I felt my dress brush my ankles. "You look sexy as fuck, like this."

Chris kissed the space between my neck and shoulder. I tilted my head and moaned. "If you keep making those sounds, I won't be held responsible for what I do to you," he growled. I moaned again. "Fuck me," he growled again.

I felt a soft tickle down the side of my face. I didn't know what it was, but I liked it. It traveled down my neck, across my collarbone, and down between my breasts. I bit my lip and sighed.

Gentle kisses covered my neck, while Chris's hands quickly undid the clasp on my bra. It fell away and I felt extremely exposed. "You're perfect," he moaned.

The soft tickle found my breasts and circled my nipples. "Chris," I gasped. Then his tongue was on me, tracing circles around my nipples and flicking my taut peaks. He palmed one tit and sucked my nipple into his mouth. My hand went to the back of his head and pressed him to my chest.

"Nuh uh. Hand on the bar." He grabbed my wrist and wrapped my fingers back around the smooth metal. "Don't let go."

He continued his assault of my breasts and I whimpered. I was so turned on and soaking wet. I couldn't see him, but I was tuned into the sound of his breathing. I felt a soft tickle run down my stomach and then more gentle kisses followed. I threw my head back in anticipation of him moving lower. His hands ran down my back as he kissed my stomach. They dipped into the back of my panties and gripped my ass. "Fuck me, Chris," I gasped.

"Not yet, baby." I felt my panties move down my hips and over my thighs to my ankles. He wrapped his hand around my ankle "Lift." I lifted one foot, then the other as Chris removed my panties. I was standing there naked. In my black heels and pearl necklace. Just like he had promised. I felt the cool air move over my body and a shiver ran through me. "Spread your legs," he demanded, while holding my ankles. I was more than happy to accommodate him.

I stepped my feet to the sides. "Wider," he growled. I opened my legs wider for him. "You look so fucking perfect right now." His breath was warm on my ear. His hand slid down my stomach and down through my folds and then lower to the space between my legs. He slid his fingers in. I'm not sure how many, but it was more than two. He stretched me wide, as he finger fucked me slowly.

"Please, Chris. I need more," I begged. I felt like I was about to combust. "I need to come," I gasped.

"Oh, you will," he promised. I pushed my hips forward, trying to ride his hand. I needed to increase the pressure.

"Need it so bad." I felt like he was teasing me.

"Stay still," he ordered.

He curled his fingers inside me, hitting that spot that always made me whimper. While his fingers worked me from

213

the inside, I felt his tongue lash out and lick my clit. I whimpered again. "Please...please...make me come!" I was so needy and horny. "Don't stop!"

He removed his fingers and pushed my legs further apart. Next thing I knew his tongue was in my pussy, licking me up. He fucked me with his tongue and rubbed my clit with his thumb. The pressure was building. It was a slow burn. I felt my walls starting to clench. I was almost there. And then... nothing. He stopped. "What the fuck!" I gasped out.

Chris laughed. Fucking laughed at me. "Honest to God, Chris, if you don't make me come, I'm not gonna suck your dick for a month!"

He laughed again and then pounded his fingers into me. I sagged back, clutching the bar above my head. "So damn greedy. Always wanting more. And me, I always want to give you what you want. Don't ever doubt that." Then his tongue was back on my clit. Relentless. I felt the pressure building again. More intense this time. I didn't know how much more I could take. The sensation of his fingers filling me and his tongue on my clit were too much. And then he went in for the kill. He sucked my clit into his mouth. He sucked and sucked. The pressure reached its peak, and I knew I couldn't hold on any longer. "I'm gonna come!" I gasped. One final, long, hard suck and I fell over the edge. He kept sucking and pumping me. My body convulsed, and waves of pleasure took over. They kept coming and coming. I felt my fingers slipping and then Chris's arm was around my waist holding me up. I wrapped my arms around his neck. I was spent. My head fell to his shoulder.

"That was the most beautiful thing I've ever seen," he whispered in my ear. He lifted me, scooping one arm under my knees and the other supporting my back. He set me on the edge of the bed and removed the tie from my eyes. His shirt was off, but his pants were still on. He made quick work of the button and zipper and stripped everything off in one fluid motion. His dick was long and hard against his stomach. His hand wrapped around his cock and stroked it up and down. I watched him intently, as he stroked himself. "What do you want, wild cat?"

"I want your big, hard dick in my pussy," I said as I kept my eyes on him. He loved when I talked that way. It made him crazy. Chris growled, and I pushed myself back on the bed. He grabbed my legs and pulled me back to the edge, as I let out a giggle. He grabbed a condom off the nightstand and ripped it open with his teeth. Rolling it on, he stepped between my legs and rubbed his hands down my thighs. I pulled my legs up and set my heels on the edge of the bed.

His fingers ran over the straps of my shoes. "Don't take these off." I wrapped one leg around his hips and pushed the heel into his ass, bringing him closer to me. "I'm gonna fuck you now. I need to be inside you." And then he was. He reached his hands under my ass and lifted me to him as he thrust into me. I was so sensitive from my orgasm, and it felt so amazing. It was animalistic and untamed. No thinking. Just feeling.

He pulled out and flipped me on my stomach, so I was leaned over the bed. He continued to pound me from behind. He reached his arm around my stomach and his fingers went to my clit. He rubbed my clit quickly as he fucked me. I felt the build up again, taking me higher and higher as another orgasm peaked. And then I shattered. Wave after wave consumed me and my eyes rolled back, as a blinding light obscured my vision. I felt myself squeezing him with each wave of ecstasy. "Fuck, Tor! I'm gonna come so hard!" And then he slammed into me harder, holding my hips with both hands, pushing me into the mattress. His body stilled and then collapsed over the top of me. "Fuck, baby!" His breath was warm on my neck. I was exhausted. I was physically spent from the pleasure he had brought me. "That was intense. I never get tired of being inside you."

Chris pulled out of me, and I just laid there, barely able to move. "Get up, baby!" his voice was urgent. I cracked one eye

215

open, my face pushed to the bed. "I'm serious, baby. Get up!" His voice was frantic now. I pushed up on my hands. He quickly pulled me up off the bed and against his chest. He grabbed the comforter and shoved it down off the bed and onto the floor. "I can't believe we just fucked on that thing!" He cringed, and his body shook in disgust. "Shower! Now!" he insisted.

"But I'm so tired," I complained.

"I don't care. You could have someone else's cum on your face. I'm not kissing that!" I rubbed my hand down my face and he quick pulled it away. "Don't touch it!" He moved us to the bathroom and started the shower. I sat on the toilet seat and carefully removed my shoes.

We stepped into the shower. He used the hotel shampoo and conditioner to wash my hair. The way he massaged my head felt incredible. I moved under the spray to rinse. "Tor?" I looked over at Chris. My eyes scanned his gorgeous body. His muscles were defined. He'd gotten hotter over the last year. I watched the water roll down his broad chest and over the ridges of his abs, down to that perfect V at his hips. My eyes moved lower to his hard dick. He was stroking it again, staring at me. "I wanna fuck you in the shower."

I'd always wanted to have shower sex with Chris. I bit my lip. "So do it."

"Spread your legs and put your hands on the wall." I did. I pushed my hips back and up, offering myself to him. He ran his hand down my back, over the arch and down my ass. "I gotta get a condom."

"Just pull out," I said over my shoulder. "I wanna feel you. All of you." Screw the condom.

Chris blew out a breath. "You sure?"

I nodded, then changed my mind. "Don't pull out. We'll stop at the drug store in the morning and get the morning after pill. I want to feel you deep inside me." It was reckless and impulsive, but we would still be protected, right?

"Shit! I wish I knew that fifteen minutes ago." We'd never had sex without a condom. I wanted... no needed to feel him, and only him, in me. "I don't know, Tor. This seems risky."

I couldn't believe he was telling me no. I thought he would jump at the chance. "Fine! Go get a condom. But I'm going on the pill." I was frustrated, and I couldn't hide it. I don't know why I was getting pissed. Using a condom never bothered me before.

Chris stepped up behind me. "Hey," he whispered in my ear.

"I'm sorry," I huffed out. "I don't know what's wrong with me." I dropped my head against the shower wall. So much for shower sex. I'd just ruined it for no reason at all.

He turned me in his arms and lifted my chin. "It's okay. I wanna go bare with you. We just can't risk it. I'm not gonna put you in that position. Put us in that position."

"I know. You're just looking out for us. Being the smart one," I admitted.

Chris pulled me into his arms. "Let's get out of the shower and get in bed."

I nodded. He turned off the water and handed me a towel. I patted my hair dry and then wrapped the towel around my body. We laid in bed, and I rested my head on his chest. "I'm sorry. I didn't mean to get shitty with you."

Chris ran his hand through my hair. "I know. Do you want to talk about it?"

"No. I think I already talked enough." What would I even say? I couldn't explain why I had reacted the way I did.

"Do you wanna smoke. I've got some weed in the truck," he suggested.

"Yeah." Getting high was the perfect solution to get me out of my head.

He popped up and threw on a pair of shorts. "I'll be right back."

After he left, I went through his bag and found one of his long-sleeved tees. I pulled on a pair of underwear and threw his shirt over my head. I opened the slider and walked out onto the balcony. I held onto the railing and looked out over the parking lot. It was late, and no one was around. It was quiet. Really quiet. The air was cool, and it felt good on my bare legs.

What was wrong with me? I'd seen that slut, Susie, at the dance tonight. It made me physically ill to think of her and Chris together. Maybe that was why I didn't want to use a condom tonight. I wanted to have something she never had. I wanted all of Chris. I wanted to be marked by him. I shook my head. It was a stupid thought. I knew he was mine.

The door behind me opened and Chris came out. He sat in one of the chairs and I sat on his lap. "Are you okay? You know I love you, right?"

I nodded. "I love you too," I said.

We sat on the balcony and smoked the whole joint. I was stoned, and I was horny. "Make love to me." Chris picked me up and carried me to the bed. He pushed into me slowly. Gently. The urgency from earlier was gone. This was all about us connecting. Sharing something intimate and personal. Having Chris make love to me felt so amazing. Not just physically, but emotionally. Then, I realized he had already marked me a long time ago. He had marked my heart. It belonged to him.

"Do you want me to come over after practice, so we can study for our physics test?" I asked. I was leaning against the locker next to his.

He spun the combination on his locker and pulled it open. "That's cool. We can study in my room." He waggled his eyebrows at me.

A folded-up piece of notebook paper fell out of his locker and landed on the floor. I leaned down to pick it up and went to hand it to him. That's when I noticed his name written on the front in fancy handwriting. Definitely a girl's handwriting. I pursed my lips and took a deep breath, trying to control the heaviness in my chest. I handed it to him. "I'm gonna go. I'll see you at lunch."

I turned and walked away without even giving him a kiss. I needed to get out of there. I didn't give him a chance to answer before I was gone. I headed right for the girl's bathroom, went into the last stall, and shut the door. That was when I started hyperventilating. My chest hurt, as if someone had punched me. I tried to remember what I had read about panic attacks.

In the through the nose.
Out through the mouth.
In the through the nose.
Out through the mouth.

Finally, the pain in my chest started to subside. *It was just a note,* I told myself. *It doesn't mean anything. It doesn't mean he's cheating on me.*

I pulled out my phone.

Tori: I think Chris is cheating on me.
Kyla: He isn't.
Tori: Some girl left a note in his locker.
Kyla: What did it say?
Tori: I don't know. I ran away.
Kyla: He loves you! Talk to him!
Tori: I can't!

After my English Comp class, I didn't feel any better. *Who would be leaving notes in Chris's locker?* I could only think of one person. And that thought made me even crazier. She was never going to give up until she won.

I decided to skip lunch. I couldn't stomach eating or seeing the guilty look I was sure would be on Chris's face. Instead, I went to the yearbook room and started going through some of the pictures I had taken. There were a lot of Chris. I pulled a flash drive out of my backpack and saved them all. They were only for me in the first place.

My phone buzzed.

Chris: Where are you?

Tori: Sorry. Got stuck doing yearbook stuff.

Chris: I'm on my way.

Tori: No…I'm really busy.

Chris: No, you're not.

Shit! Now I needed to look busy. I pulled up the page I had done for Homecoming. It was already finished, so I sat and stared at it. I was nervous. Why was I nervous? My leg was shaking, and my heart was thumping.

It didn't take long for Chris to show up. He peeked his head in. "Hey."

I didn't look up from the screen I'd been looking at for the past five minutes. "Hey."

"Are you avoiding me?"

I still didn't look up. I couldn't look at him. I was afraid he'd be able to see the hurt on my face. "No. I'm just finishing up this page from Homecoming."

"You finished that two days ago." He walked toward me and looked at the screen.

"Revisions," I answered lamely. Lie.

"It looks exactly the same, Tor." He lifted my chin, so I had to look at him. "Is this about the note?"

"God, no! I just needed to do this is all." Lie. I couldn't let him know how much that note affected me.

"I thought we agreed not to lie to each other." He stared at me, calling my bluff.

"I'm not lying." Lie.

Chris pulled me up out of my chair. "Come here, baby."

I felt the sob well up in my chest. I wouldn't let it out. I let him snuggle me into his warmth. I tried to keep my voice level. Tried not to show emotion. "Was it from her?"

"Yes," he answered honestly.

"She wants you back, doesn't she?"

"Yes." He never lied to me. Sometimes I wished he would. I didn't want to know this shit.

"I hate her!" Truth.

"I know." He pulled me in tighter. "I'm not going anywhere, Tor."

Chapter 29
Chris

Susie wasn't kidding when she said she wouldn't give up. The notes kept on coming. I always showed them to Tori. I let her read them, even though I knew it pissed her off. I wouldn't hide this from her. Better to have her pissed from reading the notes, than pissed about me keeping them from her.

It was hard to believe that after all this time, she was still insecure about us. I knew Tori hated Susie. Tori didn't want me to have a past. I couldn't change what had happened. Honestly, Susie was nothing but a small blip of my past. I had so many more memories of Tori. Tori was my past, my present... my future.

We were sitting in my room doing "homework". We had finished our actual homework twenty minutes ago. Now we were laying on my bed. My hand was up under Tori's shirt rubbing her tits, while she laid next to me looking at the ceiling. "Did you finish your application for Western yet?" she asked.

"Yep. Put it in the mail yesterday." What I didn't tell her was that I also sent an application to Michigan State. With all the scouts showing up at the games and the grades I was getting this year, I couldn't help myself. Part of me hoped I wouldn't get accepted. It would make life easier. Make my decision easier. But I had to know. I needed to know if I was good enough. I was pretty sure Tyler was going to State. It would be cool for us to play football together there.

It would break Tori's heart if she knew I was keeping this from her. There was no sense in telling her until I knew what was going to happen.

"I hope we get to be in the same dorm next year. Even if we don't, we'll get to sleep together every night, if we want. Kyla won't care if you crash in our room."

I silenced her with a kiss. I didn't want to hear about the plans she was making. Plans that wouldn't happen if I got a scholarship to State. No one, but my dad, knew about my application to State.

What I did next, I did out of guilt. I didn't keep secrets from her. Just this one. And it was killing me. I unbuttoned her jeans and moved my hand down the front of her pants. She bent her knees and moved her legs apart. My hand slid lower until I felt her wetness on my fingers. I slid them inside of her and she moaned. My mouth covered hers, as I finger fucked her hard and rubbed her clit with my thumb. I worked her relentlessly, taking her higher. She arched her back and grabbed my shoulders. She was almost there. "Stay quiet, baby," I whispered. When we started dating, she had been so worried that I wouldn't be able to make her orgasm, but now, I barely had to touch her, and she fell apart. I knew what she liked. What made her squirm and what made her scream.

With my other hand, I pushed up her shirt and pulled down the cup of her bra. I took her nipple in my mouth and sucked it. Hard. She loved when I sucked her tits. She bit her lip and her hips bucked off the bed into my hand. I felt her pussy clamp tight around my fingers as she came. Tori threw her arm across her mouth to silence herself. Her hips eased back to the bed, and she let out a contented sigh.

"What was that for?" she asked, trying to catch her breath.

"Because I love you." It was the truth.

We'd made it to the State Championship. That son of a bitch, Tyler, promised us we would. And we did. I loved that asshole. He'd become like a brother to me. The best friend I ever had. It didn't hurt that Tori and Kyla were best friends and we all spent a lot of time together. But it wasn't just the girls that connected us. There was something more. We were alike in a lot of ways. Our girls having our balls, being one of them.

It was at these away games that I really missed my girl. Especially when I saw Tyler and Kyla sitting together on the bus. Tori had to drive downtown to Ford Field with some of our friends. I didn't like her driving in Detroit. The downtown area was all right, but there were a lot of seedy areas along the way, and I worried about her car breaking down. She'd be ripe for the picking for the drug dealers and gang bangers. She was tough, but not that tough.

I made her text me when she was inside the stadium, otherwise I'd be a damn wreck for the whole game, which was about to start. We were playing against Cass Tech, and they were intimidating. They'd been here before, we hadn't.

We ran onto the field and the pain I'd felt for the last few months in my knee was a dull ache. I ignored it like always. I could ice it after the game. I wasn't going to let a little pain get in the way of getting a scholarship and playing college ball.

During the first half of the game, we easily outscored Cass Tech. They tried to play catch up, but by half time we were in the lead. My knee was throbbing, but I needed to push on. Mind over matter, right?

Coach pulled me aside. "Capizzio, you've been with me for three years. It's hard to believe this is our last game together."

"It's been a good ride. I'm hoping to play next year."

Coach patted me on the back. "You will kid. You've come a long way since you were a sophomore. With Jackson being here, you've gotten the exposure you deserved. Where do you want to go?"

"I applied to Western." I contemplated telling him the next part, then thought *What the hell? Why not?* I took a deep breath and continued. "I haven't told anyone, but I also applied to Michigan State."

Coach's eyes went wide. "No shit! You know, that's probably where Jackson is going? It would be great to have two of my boys playing together there. I can't really take any credit for Jackson, but you, Capizzio, I've watched you grow. I watched you train hard. I'd like to think I've had a hand in your success."

"You have, Coach. Thanks for putting up with all my bullshit over the years."

"You're a good kid. You've got passion. Sometimes it just gets the best of you." He pulled me away from everyone. "Honestly, Chris, how's your knee?"

I pulled back in shock, "What do you mean?" I thought I had hidden it well.

"You think I don't notice, when one of my best players is favoring his other leg. Or the subtle grimaces during practice. I know you, Chris. And I know you'll push through the pain, even if you shouldn't. So, I'll ask you again… how's your knee?"

I let out a deep breath. "It hurts like a bitch. No one can know. The scouts are out there watching."

He motioned to the bench, "Have a seat and let me look at it." I sat down and pulled up the leg of my pants. He ran his hands over the joint and pushed on it. I clenched my jaw and ground my teeth. "It's swollen. Let me wrap it to get you through the game, but you need to see a doctor. If you let this go, you're going to mess it up to the point that you won't be playing college ball. Trust me, you need to get this checked out."

I nodded my head. "I will. Just get me through this last game."

225

"We will," he assured me. Then he went to work on my knee taping and wrapping it to give it extra support. It felt good. I only had to get through the second half of the game. I could do that.

Cass tech came out strong in the second half. They quickly tied up the score. I kept tackling their receiver to prevent them from getting running yards, but it wasn't enough. This game was going into overtime. I was sure of it. There were only a few minutes left in the game and Cass Tech took possession. My job was to keep them from scoring. Their quarterback threw a perfect pass, and the receiver caught it. I hit him hard and then he fumbled the ball!

I caught the ball as it flew from his hands and started to run. The adrenaline kicked in and I felt no pain. I was fucking fast, and my team was clearing me a path to the end zone. They tackled players right and left. I hardly noticed as I focused on the goal line. I zigged and zagged around Cass Tech and kept running. I was down to thirty yards, twenty yards, ten yards…the clock ticked down… touchdown! I threw the ball to the ground and started my happy dance!

I did the cabbage patch round and around in a circle. It was a ridiculous choice of dance, but being the cornerback, it wasn't like I ever actually got to be in the end zone. Seconds later my teammates were jumping on me, patting me on the back, and high fiving. This was my moment. My fifteen minutes of fame.

Back on the bus, I sat down behind Kyla and Tyler. I could hear them talking about the game. I popped up over the seat. "I heard the word *amazing*. You must be talking about me!" I said with a shit-eating grin.

"I was," Kyla said. "That was really great! I'm so happy for you." She turned and gave me a quick peck on the cheek.

"You guys are coming out to celebrate with us, right? We're all going to IHOP. Tori's going to meet us there."

Kyla didn't hesitate. "Of course, we're coming! We wouldn't miss it!"

"Cool! I'll let Tori know you'll be there." I sank back into my seat and began texting.

Chris: We're going to IHOP to celebrate. You're coming, right?

Tori: Of course. Are Ty and Kyla coming?

Chris: They'll be there.

Tori: We can't stay too long. I need to congratulate my man. He's a big deal, you know?

Chris: Your man? Do I know this guy?

Tori: He's tall, dark, Italian. Kind of cute. Big muscles. Even bigger dick.

Chris: Sounds like a catch. I'm jealous!

Tori: You should be...I'm going to fuck his brains out!

Chris: I love you!

Tori: Love you too!

I was laughing to myself as I put my phone into my bag. Then I felt the seat next to me dip. I didn't have to look to know who it was. Before I could stop her, Susie's arms were around my neck, and she kissed me on the cheek. Her voice came out shrill and loud. "I'm so proud of you, Chris. You totally saved that game. You're a hero."

I looked to the seat in front of me and Tyler was staring at me, shaking his head. He kissed Kyla on the head and turned back around. I was a shit for letting this happen. If some guy was hanging on Tori, I'd fucking knock him out. I don't know why I found it so hard to be mean to Susie. But it was obvious she wasn't going to stop if I didn't make things clear.

I unwrapped her arms from around my neck. "Susie, you gotta stop this shit. I know you think you can change my mind about Tori, but you can't. She and I are solid. I'm not breaking up with her."

"What does she have that I don't? Why can't you give me a chance?" Susie pouted.

I stared at her incredulously. She couldn't possibly be that thick. "Give you a chance? Are you fucking kidding me? I gave you my virginity. You're the one that walked away. Wanted to be with someone else. I was crushed at the time, but you know what? I moved on."

"Things can be different this time," she insisted.

"You would have never had all of me anyway. You know why? Tori was my first love. And now, she's my only love. And you know what she has that you don't? My heart."

Susie pouted again. "You'll change your mind. She's going to hurt you. She's a born bitch. It's inevitable. And when she does, come find me. I'll make it all better." Susie scooted out of my seat and across the aisle.

I shook my head. How did it even get this far? Better question...How did I *let* it get this far? I should have shut her down months ago. No... a year ago.

Tori met the bus back at school and jumped out of her car when I hopped off the bus. She ran at me and leaped into my arms. I picked her up and swung her around. "I'm so proud of you, baby!" she exclaimed.

I kissed her hard, setting her back on her feet. She loosened my tie and undid the top few buttons of my shirt. "God, I missed you," I told her. Susie was wrong, Tori would never hurt me.

We went and dropped her car off at home, so we could go to IHOP in my truck. It would be practically impossible to mess around in her beetle. And I was thinking about her text, and messing around, and being between her legs.

228

We got to IHOP, and everyone showed up, Coach included. I was the center of attention for the night. Trevor pulled his phone out and shoved it in my face. "You're on YouTube, dude."

He pressed play and I watched myself running down the field. It was cool watching myself. But it was even cooler living it. I'd made a seventy-yard run, scoring the final touchdown in the State Championship game. I guess I was a big deal.

Tori sat next to me with her head on my shoulder, watching the video. I wrapped my arm around her and kissed the top of her head. "Ready to get out of here."

"I'm ready when you are. It's your night. We can do anything you want."

"Anything?" I asked.

"Anything," she whispered.

That was all I needed to hear. We rushed out to my truck and hopped in. I drove to our secret spot where she did anything and everything I wanted.

December was our month. My birthday was on the fifteenth, hers was on the twentieth.

I'd bought her a necklace with a heart-shaped pendant. You know…because she had my heart. Her birthday was almost a week away, but I'd already made us reservations at a fancy restaurant, scheduled a night at the hotel and wrapped her gift. I couldn't wait to give it to her.

I picked Tori up for school on Monday. She opened the door and hopped in. "Happy Birthday, baby!" She leaned across the seat and gave me a kiss. "Do you want your gift now or later?" she asked.

"Depends. Is there sex involved?"

229

She rolled her eyes. "There can be, but that's not your gift."

I pulled her over to me and kissed her harder. "That's all the gift I need."

She reached into her backpack and pulled out a large, flat box wrapped in black and gold paper. "I guess I can get rid of this then." She rolled down the window and lifted the gift toward the opening.

I reached over and snatched it out of her hands. "I want it!" I was like a little kid turning eight, instead of eighteen.

She laughed and leaned against the window. "I didn't know what to get you. I hope you don't think this is lame, but it's the thought that counts, right?"

Holding the box in my hands, I squinted at her. "Nothing you could give me would be lame." Now, I was even more curious about what she had gotten me. "Can I open it now?"

Tori bit her lip and nodded. She was kind of nervous and it was cute. I ripped the paper off and pulled the top off the box. In the box sat a black leather photo album with our names embossed on the front in gold script. I opened the book. The first page didn't have any pictures, but a letter.

Chris~

Happy eighteenth birthday, baby! We've been together almost a year and a half now, but my heart has belonged to you since that first kiss in the closet back in seventh grade. I knew when I kissed you that night, and fireworks exploded, that if we ever got together, it would be something great. I didn't know you that well back then. We were just two kids that had been in the same class forever. That night changed everything for me. Even though it was many years until we became official, every kiss I had from that point on, was compared to you.

When we decided to try this, you know I was skeptical. I didn't want to ruin the friendship we had built. You assured me it

230

wouldn't, and so I agreed. I just want you to know, that giving us a chance was the best decision I've ever made.

You've been my rock, my anchor, and my best friend for the last year and a half. I honestly don't know how I survived before you. You get me. You complete me. You are my heart.

Putting together this book for you was a walk down memory lane. I tried to capture all the great times we have had together, although the best memories live in my mind. They are only for us. There are several blank pages in the back because I know we have so many more memories to make, and I want to capture all of them.

I love you, Chris! Forever and Always~ Tori

I felt a lump in my throat, as I read the words she wrote. I leaned over and kissed her. "Thank you."

"You haven't even opened it yet," she said.

"If this is all there was, I'd still love it."

She smiled at me. "Turn the page."

I did, and I was blown away. There was page after page of pictures of us. Not just pictures, but ticket stubs from concerts, movies, and dances, and even a couple of mementos from hotels we'd stayed at. Next to every picture, she'd written dates, places, and captions. Each page was decorated and scrapbooked to perfection. I didn't even know what to say. This must have taken forever for her to create. "How long have you been working on this?"

"Since the summer. Do you like it? It's not too lame?" She bit her lip.

"Baby, I love it. It's perfect." I didn't want to go to school right now, so I took her back to my house.

"What are you doing?" Tori asked when she realized we weren't headed in the right direction.

"Getting the second part of my gift." I pulled into the driveway and dragged her out my side of the truck. We raced up to the house and straight to my bedroom. Everyone was at work, and we had the house to ourselves.

We didn't make it to school until third hour. It was the best birthday ever!

We finally got to school and went our separate ways. I could have spent the whole day in bed with Tori.

I was at my locker after fourth hour, when two hands covered my eyes. I smiled, because my girl, she always made me smile. She flipped me around and kept my eyes covered with one hand. I snaked my arms around her waist and lowered my head towards hers. Our lips touched and started to move, but something was wrong. Something was very wrong. I could taste cherry. Tori never tasted like cherry.

I pulled back, but it was too late. "Happy birthday, Chris!" Susie was standing in front of me, smiling from ear to ear.

"What the hell, Susie!"

Chapter 30
Tori

I came around the corner and froze. I couldn't believe what I was seeing. Chris had his arms around her waist, and he was kissing her. Not a little peck, but full out kissing.

I quickly stepped back around the corner and held my books to my chest. He wouldn't! He fucking wouldn't! I slid down the wall until I was sitting on the floor.

This couldn't be happening. Not after the morning we had together. He wouldn't! There had to be an explanation. None of it made sense!

All the little notes she'd been sending him flashed through my mind. The way she shamelessly flirted with him boiled my blood. Maybe she'd finally worn him down. I was going to find out what the fuck was going on. One way or another this had to end.

I finally pulled my shit together and stood back up. I straightened my shoulders and pretended that nothing was wrong. Sucking it up, I turned the corner to head to my locker. I scanned the hallway, but he was gone. And so was Susie.

After school, Chris took me home. I looked out the window, staring at the trees that flew by. "Are you okay?" Chris asked.

I kept looking out the window. "I'm fine." I wasn't fine. I was far from fine.

"Are you feeling okay? You haven't said much since we left school."

I gave him a weak smile. "I'm fine. Just tired, I guess."

Chris got a cocky grin. "I wore you out this morning, didn't I?"

I gave him another weak smile. "Something like that." *Nothing even close. You fucking broke my heart today.*

He pulled up in my driveway and I reached down to grab my backpack. "You should try to take a nap. I'll pick you up at five. My mom's making her famous lasagna for my birthday."

"I'll try." I leaned over the seat and gave him a quick peck on the cheek. I didn't want to put my lips where hers had been.

I jumped out of his truck and headed into the house. I was halfway up the stairs when my mom stopped me. "Hey, sweetie. How did Chris like his present?"

I internally groaned and then turned to face her. I plastered on a fake smile. "He liked it. I'm kind of tired and I have a headache, so I'm going to try to take a nap before I go to Chris's for dinner."

"I'm sorry," she said. "I know how hard this time of the month hits you. I was the same way when I was your age."

I shook my head. "It's not...." *Fuck!* I stopped and started mentally counting the days. *Shit...this can't be happening!*

I ran down the stairs and into the kitchen. My mom yelled after me, "Tori?!"

I pulled the calendar off the wall and flipped back to November. I counted the weeks. And then I recounted the days. I fell to the floor, holding my head in my hands and started crying. My mom's arms went around me, holding me close. "How late are you?"

"Ten days." I couldn't look my mom in the eye right now. I already knew what I had to do.

234

My mom let out a breath. "It'll be okay, Tori. We can handle this. But we need to know for sure."

I nodded and dropped my head back to my knees. My mom stood and went to her room as I sat there in shock. She came back with a pregnancy test in her hand. She reached out her hand to me and I took it. She pulled me to my feet. I buried my head in her shoulder and sobbed. "I'm scared," I admitted. "I don't want a baby."

Mom smoothed back my hair. "You have choices, sweetheart."

I cried harder, "But you..."

"Tori, I made the choice that was right for me. That doesn't mean it's the right choice for you. We'll figure this out, okay?"

I sniffed hard and wiped at my eyes. The garage door opened, and Mike walked in. "How are my girls?" He set his keys on the table and then realized what he'd walked in on. I was in tears and mom had a pregnancy test in her hand. "Aww, shit!"

"We're not sure, yet. We were just going to do the test," my mom answered his unasked question.

Mike came up behind me and rubbed my shoulders. "Does Chris know?"

I shook my head. "I just realized I was late." Then I started crying again.

Mike pulled me into his arms. "It's going be okay. Do you want me to call Chris? Do you want him here?"

"No!" My response came out harsher than I intended. I swallowed down the lump in my throat. "It's his birthday. I don't want to ruin his birthday," I insisted.

"Yeah, okay," Mike begrudgingly agreed.

My mom led me to the bathroom and handed me the test. I didn't want to take it. If I just ignored it, it would go away, right? My mom took my hand and put the test in it. "You know what to do?"

"Just pee on it," I answered.

"Pretty much. Put the cap on and set it on the counter when you're finished."

I nodded, walked into the bathroom, and shut the door. This could change everything. I was scared shitless. I wished Chris was here holding my hand, but then again, I didn't. If he was into Susie, I didn't want to tie him down. I wouldn't tie him down. We had discussed what we would do if this ever happened, but the reality was so much scarier than the hypothetical. I wanted him here. I wanted him to hold me tight and tell me it would be okay. I wanted to smell his cologne and let it relax me. He was my safe place... and right now I was freaking out.

My mom knocked, and I startled out of my thoughts. "Tor?"

"I didn't do it yet," I said through the door.

"Just get it over with, sweetie."

I took a deep breath and undid my pants. I sat and held the test between my legs. My hand was shaking, and I almost dropped the damn thing into the toilet. Finally, I relaxed and peed on the stick that was going to determine my fate. I capped it and set it on the counter.

I opened the door and sat down on the floor outside the bathroom. "How long? How long until we know?"

Mom sat down next to me and put her hand on my knee. "Three minutes."

I tilted my head and rested it on her shoulder. "I'm sorry. I swear we've been careful. We always use protection. I'm sorry I'm putting you through this."

My mom rubbed my head. "This is what moms are for. We help our kids, especially through the rough times." We sat like that for what seemed like forever.

Mike cleared his throat, and we looked up at him. "It's time."

236

"Do you want to do it, or do you want me to do it?" my mom asked.

I pushed myself to my feet. "I'll do it." I felt like I was walking towards my death. Whatever this test said, could change my life. I knew what Chris and I had decided, but the fallout could destroy us…if we weren't already destroyed.

I lifted the test off the counter and looked at the results. Tears started to run down my cheeks. I held the test to my chest and slid down the wall, crying silent tears.

Mom came in and took the test from my hand. "It's negative."

I nodded. "I know."

Mike let out a relieved, "Thank God!"

Mom kneeled in front of me and pushed my hair back over my shoulder. "I'm going to call and make you an appointment. We're going to find out what's going on and get you on birth control."

"Thanks, Mom… for being you. I love you."

"You don't have to thank me." She ran her hand along the side of my face. "You're my baby." She hesitated and then continued. "Are you going to tell Chris about this?"

I looked up at her. "Probably, but not today." I stood and left the test on the counter. "I'm going to go lay down for an hour."

I slowly walked up the stairs to my room and crawled under the covers. The tears wouldn't stop coming. I closed my eyes, but all I could see was Chris kissing Susie. It made me physically ill. I rushed to the bathroom and emptied my stomach. I brushed my teeth and laid back down, but the tears never stopped.

After an hour, I decided I should get ready for dinner. Looking in the mirror, I gasped. I looked like shit! My eyes were puffy and red. I pulled out all my makeup and beauty products, most of which I barely used, and set them on the counter. I filled

237

the sink with cold water and stuck my face in it. I counted to ten, pulled back, took a breath, and then did it again. By the time I had done it a couple of times, some of the puffiness had disappeared. I patted my face dry and started applying concealer. If there was one thing I was good at, it was hair and makeup. Ironic, because I didn't wear that much makeup. I'd use the excuse of Chris's birthday dinner, for going beyond my usual mascara.

Thirty minutes later, I was finished. I looked in the mirror. Not half bad. There was still a little puffiness around my eyes, but it was barely noticeable. I went downstairs to wait for Chris.

"You all right, sweetie?" Mike asked. I nodded. "You look nice."

I walked over to Mike and wrapped my arms around his waist. "I'm sorry about earlier. I'm sorry I made you worry and I'm sorry that you walked in on that."

Mike hugged me tight, holding me to his chest. "Don't be sorry, Tor. You're my daughter. I'll always be there for you."

I wiped at my eyes and let out a little laugh. "Don't make me cry. It took a long time for me to pull this together." Mike had always been there for me. He'd bandaged my scraped knees when I was a little girl, held me tight when I had nightmares, and gave me advice when I needed it. He taught me how to ride a bike and how to fish. He was my dad. The only dad I ever knew. I pulled back and said something I don't think I'd ever said before. "I love you, Mike."

Mike wiped at his own eyes. "I love you too, sweetie."

We were in Chris's truck on the way to his parents' house. I was looking out the window again. The words were stuck in my throat. They wouldn't come out. I was waiting for him to say something about it, but then I realized, *Why would he?*

Chris reached over and grabbed my hand. I let him lace his fingers with mine because that's where they should be. We were supposed to be together. "You look pretty tonight."

I gave him a small smile. "I wanted to look nice for your birthday."

He picked up my hand and kissed the back of it. "You always look nice, but tonight you look extra pretty." A light snow started to fall and covered the windshield. He turned on the wipers. "We're supposed to get like ten inches of snow tonight. Could be a snow day tomorrow. What would you want to do?"

I sighed, "Lay in bed with you all day. Snuggle under the covers and watch movies. What would *you* want to do?" *Snuggle with Susie?* I couldn't help it. I hated her before, but now I loathed her. I was afraid that if I saw her, I would probably lose it.

"Lying in bed, snuggling sounds nice. I don't know about watching movies though," he said with a wolfish grin.

We pulled up in his driveway. I lifted the hood of my coat over my head, so that my hair wouldn't get soaked. Chris and I walked to the door hand in hand. He opened it for me, and the smell of lasagna filled my senses.

I walked in, took off my coat, hung it on the hook, and headed towards the kitchen. Chris's mom wrapped me in a warm hug. "Hi, sweetheart."

"Hi, Mrs. Capizzio," I hugged her back. "Everything smells great." I pulled the apron from behind the pantry door, which had become my norm since Chris's mom had started teaching me how to cook. "What can I do to help?"

"Why don't you make the salad?" She pulled all the things from the fridge that I needed. I started chopping and slicing. Imagining that the cucumber was Susie, I sliced furiously. "Are you all right, dear?"

239

I kept slicing and looked up at her. "I'm fine." The pain ripped through my finger, and I sucked it into my mouth. "Damn it!" I pulled it out and inspected the cut. It wasn't that deep, but it hurt like hell.

Chris's mom put a hand on my shoulder. "I'll finish this up. There are band-aids in the bathroom, under the counter."

I nodded and headed towards the bathroom, searching for a band-aid. I pulled out the box and started cleaning my finger under the faucet. The blood ran down the drain, but all I saw was my bleeding heart. I watched the blood drip from my finger. It was almost therapeutic.

Chris broke my trance when he popped his head in. "Do you need stitches?"

"No, it's fine."

Chris took my finger and dried it with a towel. He carefully wrapped the band-aid around my finger and kissed it. "All better," he said. If only it were that easy to mend my broken heart. But the longer we played this game... him pretending like nothing happened... me pretending not to know what happened... the more my heart broke.

During dinner, I put on my happy face. I smiled when I was supposed to. Laughed when I was supposed to. Participated in conversation when I was supposed to. How could I look at the people sitting at the table and tell them what their son and brother had done? And so, I continued to play the game.

"I was looking through the book you gave me," Chris said, while driving home. The snow was falling hard and there were a few inches covering the road. The plows hadn't come through yet, and it was slick.

His eyes were focused on the road, trying to maneuver through the falling snow. Mine were focused on him. "You don't have to keep it. I can take it back if you don't like it."

He scrunched up his eyebrows and looked over at me. "Of course, I like it. I love it. Why wouldn't I want to keep it?"

I tried to keep the bite out of my tone. "I just think it means more to me, than to you. That's all." I crossed my arms over my chest and stared out the window.

"What the fuck is that supposed to mean?" I could hear the irritation in his voice.

I turned and gave him my best bitch look. "It means I saw you today."

Now he was pissed. "Saw what?" he spit out.

"Are we really going to play this game?" I asked him.

His jaw clenched, and he focused back on the road. "What game?"

I threw my arms up in the air. "The one where I pretend I didn't see you kissing Susie and you pretend like you have no idea what I'm talking about!"

He glared at me. "I didn't fucking kiss her!"

"I saw you!" I yelled. I tried to fight the tears that were coming. "I saw you," I said softer this time.

"I didn't fucking kiss her! She kissed me!"

"I saw your arms around her waist. Your lips on hers. I saw everything!" I was staring out the front window, watching the snow fall around us. The tears crept down my cheeks.

His voice was loud in the small cab of the truck. He was mad, as if he had any right to be. "Obviously, you didn't see..."

"Chris! Deer!" I screamed.

His head snapped back to the road. He locked up the brakes. The truck started skidding across the ice. Chris's hands worked furiously to get the truck back under control. It was fishtailing all over the road.

I held onto the door handle and pushed myself back against the seat, waiting for the impact. My eyes were wide, hoping the huge deer would move. But he just stood there, mesmerized by the headlights, as the truck got closer and closer. Finally, the deer started to leap out of the way, but it was too late.

The truck clipped its hindquarters and began to spin. There was no controlling it. The truck spun around twice and came to a stop sideways in the middle of the road.

"Son of a bitch!" Chris yelled, pounding on the steering wheel. He finally looked over at me. "Are you all right?"

I released my grip from the door handle and breathed what felt like the first breath since I'd seen the deer. I nodded my head.

Chris opened the door and got out to inspect the damage to his truck. After a few minutes, he got back in and brushed the snow out of his hair. "It's not that bad. Mostly the headlight and the casing."

"I'm sorry," I spit out. "This is all my fault!"

"Come here," he said.

I unbuckled my seatbelt and scooted towards him as he scooted towards me. He wrapped his arms around me and hugged me tight. "I didn't kiss her. She kissed me, and I pushed her off me, but I'm guessing you didn't hang around to see that part."

I shook my head. "All I saw was her lips on yours and it fucking broke my heart." The tears flowed freely now down my cheeks.

He pulled back and grabbed my face in his hands. "I would never, and I mean never, cheat on you, Tori. Do you understand me? Never!"

"I love you, Chris. It broke my heart to think that you wanted her instead of me."

"You're all I want, baby. All I'll ever want."

Chapter 31
Chris

With the deer and the sliding and the spinning and the truck hitting the deer, I forgot that my truck was sitting sideways in the middle of the road. I was holding Tori in the front seat, when I saw the headlights over her shoulder, coming straight at us. With the snow falling and the truck turned sideways, there was no way they would see us. There was no time. All I could do was hold onto her.

I squeezed her tight. "Hold on, baby!" The car hit the side of the truck. I covered our heads and pulled her down into me. Glass sprayed across the inside of my truck. It rocked up on two wheels and Tori fell into me and screamed, as I fell into the driver's side door. My head hit the window and my left knee twisted and smashed into the dashboard. I felt it pop and the pain was excruciating. I knew it was bad. Then, the truck fell back to the ground with a jolt.

I still had Tori in my arms, her breath coming in rapid spurts. I pulled her away from me, so I could inspect her for injuries and pull the pieces of glass from her hair. "Are you okay, Tori?"

She looked at me with tears in her eyes. "My back hurts. It really hurts, Chris."

I turned her to look at her back. There was a six-inch piece of glass stuck in her back and her white coat was turning red. "You're going to be okay, baby." She was looking at me with fear in her eyes. She wanted me to help her. To do anything to ease the pain. I knew I couldn't pull the glass out, or she was going to bleed more. "Don't move and don't lean back, okay?" She nodded her head as tears poured down her cheeks.

I ignored the pain in my knee and searched for the phone in my coat pocket. My first call was to 911. My second to my dad. And my third to Mike. Help would be here soon. She just had to hold on a little longer.

"Tor, hold on, baby. I've got to check the other driver. Make sure he's okay." I pulled her off me and tried to open the door.

"Chris, don't leave me! I need you!" She was breaking my heart, but I had to know what happened to the person who hit us.

"I'm not leaving you, baby. I'll be right back." I opened the door as she reached for me. "I'll be right back. I promise." I hobbled around the front of my truck to the passenger side. The front end of the other car was smashed up, smoke pouring out the hood. The snow was coming down harder, covering me. I went around to the driver's side door and pulled on it. It wouldn't open. I brushed the snow off the window and knocked on it. I saw the man inside lift his head off the airbag that had gone off. Thank God he wasn't dead!

The door opened, and the man cautiously stepped out of the car. "I tried to stop. But it was too late. The car just kept sliding." I could hear sirens approaching. Help was almost here.

"Are you okay?" I asked him. "We hit a deer and the car spun around," I explained.

The man patted down his body, "I seem to be okay. Thank you, airbags! How about you?"

"I'm fine. I've got to get back to my girl. She's bleeding pretty bad." I limped back to the truck, which was destroyed on the passenger side. I reached through the door and held Tori's hands. "Help's almost here, baby."

"Chris, it hurts so bad." I turned her, so I could see her back. The entire back of her coat was covered in blood. She was still bleeding. "And I'm so cold." I rubbed her hands between mine and blew on them, trying to warm her up.

Two sets of headlights pulled up simultaneously from opposite directions. My dad and Mike. They rushed out of their cars and towards us. "Help is here, Tor. You're going to be okay." I met them around the front of my truck.

My dad grabbed my shoulders, checking me out. "The back of your head is bleeding, and your hands are all cut up." I reached back and touched my head. I stared at my hand. It was covered in blood.

"I'm not worried about me. It's Tor. She's got a piece of glass sticking out of her back. She's losing a lot of blood and I think she's going into shock."

Mike raced to my open door and leaned inside.

"What the fuck happened?" my dad asked.

I swallowed down the lump in my throat. "We were fighting. And then there was a deer in the middle of the road. Tori screamed. I slammed on my brakes." I shook my head trying to remember everything. "And the truck was sliding. We clipped the deer and the truck started spinning. It stopped in the middle of the road and then the other car. It didn't see us. And it smashed into the side of the truck." I don't even know if any of what I said made sense to him.

He grabbed my face. "It's going to be all right. Calm down."

I pulled his hands off my face. "Tori's hurt. I have to help her."

"Mike's got her." The ambulance, fire truck, and police cars started pulling up to the scene.

"I have to help her. She needs me." I hobbled back to the truck and squeezed in next to Mike. "Help's here, baby. You're going to be okay," I assured her.

She reached for my hand. "Don't leave me."

I held onto her tight. "I'm not going anywhere." Mike looked at me with worry and fear in his eyes.

The paramedics had Tori out of the car in a matter of minutes. They placed her on her stomach on a gurney and rushed her to the ambulance. I climbed in after her and grabbed her hand. Mike and my dad followed behind the ambulance.

I never let go of her hand the whole time.

We were both in the ER. Tori was whisked away so they could deal with the glass in her back. They shaved the back of my head and put in a couple of stitches, then sent me for an MRI. My knee was fucked. The cartilage and ligaments were torn, and the kneecap was chipped. I was going to need surgery to correct the damage. Not today, but eventually. Today they fit me with a brace for extra support as a temporary fix.

I knew I would care about it later, but right now I didn't give a fuck about my knee. I begged to see Tori, and they wheeled me over to where she was. My mom, dad, and I moved into the small space where Tori was recovering. Mike and Mrs. Russo were sitting with her. She had an IV hooked to her arm and her eyes were closed. "How is she?" I whispered.

"She's going to be fine," Mrs. Russo smiled weakly at me. "They had to knock her out, to get the glass out of her back."

Tori's eyes fluttered and when she saw me, she reached out her hand. I carefully stood and limped over to her bed. I picked up her hand and kissed it.

The doctor came in next. "You're a very lucky girl, Ms. Russo. One more inch to the left and the glass would have gone through your spinal cord. We removed the glass, but you have stitches on the inside and the outside. You'll be fine. We'll make sure you get some pain killers before you leave." The doc was very matter of fact, and then he was gone.

I leaned down and kissed her head, then sat in the chair Mike offered. "How's your knee?" he asked.

"It's fucked."

My mom slapped me on the shoulder. "Language, Christopher Michael!"

Tori giggled. "You got full name on that one." It was the first real smile I had seen from her since this morning when we'd been in my bed. That seemed so long ago. It was hard to believe that a little over twelve hours ago, she was screaming my name and now we were both in the hospital.

I held Tori's hand, as the adults around us talked. The curtain pulled back and two uniformed police officers stood there. My dad was the first to react. He was a big guy, six-three and wide. He folded his arms across his chest and took a step forward. The officers took a step back. "What is it that you need?" my dad asked.

The smaller of the two spoke first. "We need to get a statement for our report."

"Now?" my dad bellowed. "Don't you think these kids have been through enough tonight?"

"Yes, sir. We need to get it now."

My dad, reluctantly, stepped aside and eyed me. I knew what he was telling me. *Don't mention the fight.* I went to open my mouth, but Tori spoke before I had a chance. "It was snowing, and the roads were slick. A deer jumped out in front of the truck. Chris did everything he could to stop, but we kept sliding." She took a deep breath. "We clipped the deer and the truck started spinning. That's how we ended up in the middle of the road. Before we knew it, the other car slammed into the side of us. I'm sure he didn't see us with how hard the snow was coming down. It was all an accident. One horrible, awful accident."

I knew Tori felt guilty because we were fighting. She felt responsible. She wasn't. I was. This shit with Susie was out

247

of control. I wasn't sure how I was going to handle the Susie situation, but I needed to do it fast.

Tori didn't mention the fight and said the deer had *jumped* in front of the truck. It wasn't exactly true, but it sounded better. More out of our control.

The taller officer asked, "Who was driving?"

I raised my hand. "I was."

"Were you drinking?"

"No, sir. I was driving Tori home from a family dinner at my house. There was no alcohol involved."

The officer pulled out a breathalyzer machine. "Could you blow into this? We need to make sure."

"Seriously?" my dad said incredulously. "You think I'd supply minors with alcohol?"

"Just doing our job, sir," the officer responded.

"It's fine, dad," I assured him. I took the machine and blew into the tube. The machine made some beeping noises, and I handed it back to the officer.

"Zero point zero," he read. "I think we have everything we need. Looks like this was just an unfortunate accident. Good luck with your recovery." They turned and left us alone with our families.

Next came the nurses. They gave both of us paperwork on follow-up care and prescriptions for painkillers. They handed my mom a list of doctors who specialized in knee injuries.

After the nurse left, Tori spoke up. She looked at all the adults. "Can Chris stay with me tonight? I need him with me. We won't have school tomorrow, not like either of us would be going anyway."

My mom spoke first. "Does this make us bad parents if we say yes?"

Mrs. Russo laughed. "Hell, if I know. What I do know, is that keeping these two apart is next to impossible."

My mom nodded her agreement. "They are adults now and they've been together a year and a half."

"These *are* special circumstances," Tori's mom said.

"But we're not making this a habit," my mom added.

In the end, they let us have our way, even if it was against their better judgment.

That night Tori and I laid in her bed, staring up at the ceiling. My knee was propped up on a pillow and Tori was lying on my outstretched arm, her head nestled into the space between my arm and my shoulder. My arm wrapped around her, my hand resting on her stomach.

"How's your back?" I asked.

"It's fine, as long as I don't twist too much." Then nothing. The silence between us was deafening. "How's your knee?"

"Like I said, it's fucked. I need to see a specialist. Probably need surgery."

"I'm sorry about tonight," she whispered.

I kissed the top of her head. "It wasn't your fault." Then the silence again. It stretched between us, as the minutes ticked by.

"When I saw you kissing her, it felt like I was being stabbed in the heart. Like I was losing you."

She was so fucking frustrating. "Number one, I didn't kiss her. She kissed me. She came up behind me and covered my eyes. I thought it was you. When I realized it wasn't, I pushed her off me. Number two, I'm a little disappointed that you don't know me better than that. I thought we were solid. Did you really think I'd make love to you all morning and then kiss her when your back was turned?"

"I'm sorry," she said again. "But she won't let it go. She's wanted you forever."

"It's not about what she fucking wants, Tor. It's about what I want. And I've wanted *you* forever."

Tori turned in my arms, and I heard her let out a hiss from the pain. Then, her soft lips touched mine. Our lips and tongues moved together in a slow, seductive kiss. She pulled back and rested her head on my chest. My fingers ran through her hair as she laid there.

"How bad is your truck?"

"Pretty sure it's fucking totaled," I sighed. "But that's what insurance is for, right?"

"This was a sucky birthday, wasn't it?" I could hear the guilt in her voice.

"Actually, the first part was amazing. Just so you know, I love my gift. I know it must have taken a lot of time to make it. It means everything to me. I love you, Tori."

"I love you too, Chris."

Two days later, I was fucking wasted. I'd grabbed a bottle of Jack and headed to my room after my doctor's appointment.

There was old scar tissue in my knee, indicating that the damage had already been done. I should have never let it go as long as I did without seeing a doctor. But the accident… that was the nail in the coffin, so to speak. The way my knee had twisted and popped…I was done.

All I could hear were the doctor's words, *college ball is out of the question.* Sure, after my ACL surgery I'd be able to run again. Play sports for recreation. But the intensity and demands of a college practice schedule, would be too much. If I tried, I'd probably end up blowing my knee out for good, doing permanent damage.

And just like that, my dreams of playing college ball were shattered. What made it worse, were the two envelopes

250

waiting for me when I got home. Michigan State and Western both were offering me scholarships to play football for them. Now those letters were worth nothing more than the paper they were written on.

I picked up the letter from State again. The words blurred before my eyes as I read:

Mr. Christopher Capizzio,

We are pleased to offer you a full athletic scholarship to play football for the Spartans.

Yada, yada, yada. Fucking ironic. I'd kept it a secret thinking I wouldn't get it. Then when I did get it and should have been happier than a pig in shit, I still wouldn't tell anyone, because I couldn't play anyway.

I raised the bottle up in the air, *Here's to you, you fucking loser.* I moved the bottle to my lips and took another swig. I rested back against the headboard and closed my eyes. *How did I get here?* Tori and her fucking jealousy. This was all her fault. If we hadn't been fighting, maybe I would have seen the deer. Maybe I would have been able to stop the truck. Maybe my dreams wouldn't be falling apart. Coulda, woulda, shoulda. None of it mattered now.

I heard a soft knock on my door and then Tori stuck her head in. "I came to check on you. How did your doctor appointment go?"

I raised my bottle in salute. "Just fucking peachy!"

"You're not supposed to drink while you're taking pain meds," she scolded.

I narrowed my eyes at her. "I'm not supposed to bring you here during the day to fuck you either, but you don't seem to have a problem with that."

Tori looked shocked by my words. "Are you drunk?" she questioned.

"Not drunk enough to deal with this," I snapped at her and took another sip. I could barely look at her right now.

251

She couldn't take a hint, instead she came over and sat on my bed. She picked up the letter I had just been reading. "You got a football scholarship? To State?"

"Don't look so fucking surprised. Ty's not the only one who can play football you know."

She pulled back, her eyes wide. "I didn't say he was. I just didn't know you applied. You never said anything."

"Why the fuck would I? You were so intent on going to Western, so you could be with your best friend. Never once did you ask me what I wanted. Where I wanted to go. And me?" I let out a self-deprecating laugh. "I just followed you around like a goddamn puppy. It's pathetic really."

"So, go to State. Play football. Do what you want to do." It was too late for that.

I lifted the bottle again and took a drink, then pointed it at her. "Aaaah. This is where it gets good. That little accident we had. You know, the one that happened because you were accusing me of cheating on you." Her face dropped. "Yeah, you know exactly what I'm talking about. Well, that little accident fucked up my knee for good. There'll be no college sports for this guy. So, I fucking hope it was worth it!" I yelled. "Cuz right now, I'm not sure you're fucking worth it!"

"You don't know what you're saying. You're drunk," she croaked out. "I don't deserve this."

"Well, you know what they say. Alcohol is like truth serum." I glared at her. "*I* don't deserve this!"

Tori started to back away off the bed and headed towards the door. "I'm gonna go. I'll talk to you when you're not drunk." She wiped the tears from her eyes. "I'm sorry you think I ruined your life."

"Run away, Tori. Isn't that what you always do? Things get tough and you run away. And I always chase you. Not this time, baby!" I yelled after her.

I hobbled off the bed and into the hallway. I passed my mom and dad and stood at the top of the stairs. I saw Tori by the front door and yelled down to her, "Tori?" Her head snapped up to me and our eyes met. "If you leave, don't bother coming back! And don't let the door hit you in your fat ass!" And that was my kill.

Tears streamed down Tori's face as she opened the door and Susie stood on the doorstep. "I just wanted to check on Chris," she said in her sickeningly sweet voice.

"Come on up, Susie!" I yelled down the stairs. "Tori was just leaving."

Tori looked up at me one final time, the hurt marring her beautiful face. She shook her head and turned to Susie. "You win. He's all yours." Then she pushed past a stunned Susie and left.

My mom flew down the stairs and after Tori. The door slammed shut, closing out all of it. Susie included.

My dad slammed me against the wall, pinning me with his forearm against my throat. "What the fuck is wrong with you?"

I laughed in his face. "What the fuck is wrong with me? My truck is fucked. My knee is fucked. And my scholarship is fucked. And you want to know what the fuck is wrong with me? Everything!"

His arm pushed deeper into my throat. "You're pissed off? I get that. But you don't treat her like that! That girl would do anything for you, and you just treated her like shit! You're her whole world."

"Yeah, well, maybe I shouldn't be," I spat out.

"You better think long and hard about that, son. Because she's the best thing that ever happened to you. And you probably just blew it! Quit feeling sorry for yourself and look at what's right in front of you! 'Cuz you know what? Your truck. Football. Your goddamn scholarship. They aren't going to mean a damn thing, when you're sitting alone, trying to figure out where it all went wrong. Why you let the best thing in your life walk out that door."

My dad released me and grabbed the bottle out of my hand. "And by the way," he said, "this is mine." He lifted the bottle to his lips and walked away, leaving me in the hallway with my regret.

Chapter 32
Tori

I left Susie standing on the front porch and ran to my car. I opened the car but stopped when I heard the front door slam. I looked up to see Mrs. Capizzio with her arms crossed, staring at Susie. "What do you want, Susie?"

She put on her best fake smile. "I came to see Chris. I wanted to check in on him."

Mrs. Capizzio didn't mince any words. "My son has a girlfriend. You're not wanted here. Go home, whore!" I covered my mouth to hide my surprise.

Susie just stood there, a look of shock on her face.

Chris's mom stood her ground. "You heard me. Go home and don't come back to this house." Susie backed away like a scared dog with her tail between her legs. It must have been a change to have something besides a dick there. Even though the tears were still streaming down my face, I released a giggle into my hand.

We watched Susie drive away, and then Chris's mom walked towards me. I sniffed back my tears. "That was…great. Thank you."

She wrapped her arms around me, and I hugged her back. "I don't know what's gotten into him, but you can bet, I'm sure as hell going to find out. You didn't deserve any of that."

I blew out a breath. "I guess he's been holding some stuff in. Please tell Chris's dad I'm sorry about what happened here today. I don't think I'll be seeing you for a while, but I wanted to thank you for accepting me as part of your family. I'm going to miss you."

She pushed my hair over my shoulder and grabbed my chin, lifting my face to hers. "Don't you dare apologize. And you're still part of my family. Right now, I'd trade you for him in a heartbeat." Then she kissed me on the forehead.

I gave her one last hug and then, headed home.

I sat in my car, in the driveway, for a long time. I didn't want to face my mom. I didn't want to face my life.

I tried to figure out what I had done so wrong. I should have believed him about Susie. I should have known. But I kept pressing. Kept pushing. But it was hard to ignore what I'd seen with my own eyes.

I didn't know he wanted to go to Michigan State. He'd never said a word about it. I guess I should have figured that out too. Of course, he'd want to go wherever Ty went. They were best friends.

He'd been so mean. So nasty. I didn't even know who that boy was today. He wasn't *my* Chris. My Chris would never, ever talk to me that way.

A fresh set of tears rolled down my face. I needed to accept that it was over.

A knock on my window, pulled me from my thoughts. My mom was standing there with her arms wrapped around herself, trying to stay warm. I rolled down my window.

"Trina called," she said. "She told me what happened. She wanted to make sure you got home safe." More tears. "Why don't you come inside?"

I rolled up the window and opened the car door. My mom wrapped her arm around me as we walked up to the house. I shrugged out of my jacket and hung it on the hook.

"Do you want me to make you some soup?" my mom asked.

I shook my head. "I'm not really hungry." I plopped down in the kitchen chair. "I don't want to go to school tomorrow. I know I had today off for my appointment, but I don't think I can see him. It's too soon."

My mom nodded. "It's been a stressful week. I think you've earned it. Take tomorrow and Friday off. Monday starts winter break. You can start fresh after that. Maybe you'll be feeling better by Saturday. It'll be your birthday, after all." She was trying to cheer me up.

"I don't think it's going to be that great of a birthday," I huffed out. "I'm going to go upstairs and sleep for like…I don't know…forever."

"Do you want me to wake you if Chris calls?" she asked.

"He won't be calling," I assured her.

I trudged up the stairs, changed my clothes, and crawled between the sheets. This whole week had fucking sucked. Chris's words echoed through my head.

Never once did you ask me what I wanted.

I just followed you around like a goddamn puppy.

Run away, Tori. I always chase you. Not this time, baby!

Don't bother coming back!

Don't let the door hit you in your fat ass! That one really hurt.

Come on up, Susie!

What hurt the most was that I never saw it coming. I thought we had cleared things up after the accident.

I wished Chris and I had never dated in the first place. Then, I wouldn't be lying here with a broken heart. I gave him so much of myself, that I didn't even know who I was without him anymore. In the span of a few minutes, he took everything I gave him, shred it, and threw it back at my feet. I hated him, and I loved him all at the same time. Over time, I was sure the love would fade, but I doubted it would ever completely disappear. I thought we were soulmates. That he was my mirror. My other half.

257

How could he have done this to me? How could he have been so careless with my heart? I could feel the gaping hole in my chest where he had reached in and pulled it out. It throbbed. The pain was like nothing I had ever felt before.

Thankfully, the doctor confirmed today that I wasn't pregnant. It turned out I had cysts on my ovaries that needed to be surgically removed. In ten days, they would be cutting me open and hoping that the cysts were benign. It could be more, but they wouldn't know until the doctor biopsied them.

I hadn't gotten to tell Chris any of this. Now, I was glad. I didn't need his pity. Although, I'd be lying if I said I didn't want him to hold me and tell me everything would be okay. But that wasn't going to happen.

I was in love with a boy who didn't love me the way I loved him. I wondered if this was how my mom felt when my dad left her. When she realized she wasn't enough to keep him. When he walked away without a second glance. God, *I was just like my mother.*

The thing was... I knew better. I knew from the beginning he was going to destroy me. And I let it happen anyway. I was a fool.

I wrapped my arms around myself and let the tears fall. Just for tonight, I would let myself wallow in my own misery. Then I would begin to rebuild that wall around my heart. I wouldn't let this happen again.

I stared at the ceiling, replaying the scene over and over again in my head. My phone buzzed on the nightstand. Without bothering to look at the screen, I reached over and turned it off. My tears hadn't stopped. And when I was all out of tears, exhaustion finally took over.

Chapter 33
Chris

I sank down against the wall in the hallway, with my head in my hands.

I hurt her.

Bad.

I was a total fucking asshole to her.

Hurt wasn't nearly a strong enough word. More like I had annihilated her.

I don't know why I said she had a fat ass. I loved her ass. It fit in my hands perfectly. I took a hit at her biggest insecurity.

And then inviting Susie up? Man, if that bitch didn't have perfect timing. Bam! I slammed Tori again. Rubbed Susie right in her face.

I destroyed the only girl I had ever loved, and I didn't even know why.

Pushing off the wall, I dragged my sorry ass to the bathroom and stared in the mirror. I rammed my fist into it and the glass shattered. I didn't even recognize the guy looking back at me. I only had one question for him.

Who the hell are you?

Chris and Tori's story continues in
Secrets of the Heart.

Song List on Spotify

Magic Man~ Heart
Sorry~ Buckcherry
Can't Fight This Feeling~ REO Speedwagon
Slow Ride~ Foghat
Stranglehold~ Ted Nugent
All Along the Watchtower~ Jimi Hendrix
Bitch~ Meredith Brooks
Love of a Lifetime~ Firehouse
I'll Make Love to You~ Boys II Men

Listen and Enjoy!

Acknowledgments

Being a full-time educator, leaves me little time to write during the school year. However, I look forward to coming home each day and writing about true love. My husband and I joke that right now, I'm making less than ten cents an hour writing. The funny thing is, I couldn't be happier. I enjoy what I'm doing and the creative outlet it provides me. Writing romance novels has been one of the most fulfilling experiences of my life. My dream is to walk into a book store and actually see one of my novels on the shelf. One day…

To my husband~ I could have never done this without your love and support. Thank you for putting up with my endless hours of writing, all the take-out dinners, and my hounding of you to read and offer input. I knew I had done something right when we were sitting on an airplane and you were reading *Wild Hearts* for the first time. Every once and a while I would hear you laugh out loud or a "Holy Shit" would escape from your lips. I know I've made you crazy, but you were a trooper through it all! Thank you for believing in me!

To Ari, Denise, Kristy, and Amy~ You girls are the best beta readers anyone could ask for! You supported my journey and spent endless hours reading and rereading. Your suggestions, critiques, and encouragement helped me in ways you'll never understand. Thank you for listening to my obsession day after day!

To Jill~ You've been a great friend! I was wishy-washy about what I wanted for this cover, yet you came up with something amazing. Thank you for the beautiful cover of *Wild Hearts*… I absolutely love it!

To my readers~ Thank you for supporting me in this journey. Please spread the word and leave a quick review on Amazon, if you have enjoyed this book. Without you, writing would still be a dream.

About the Author

Sabrina Wagner lives in Sterling Heights, Michigan. She writes sweet, sassy, sexy romance novels featuring alpha males and the strong women who challenge them.

Sabrina believes that true friends should be treasured, a woman's strength is forged by the fire of affliction, and everyone deserves a happy ending. She enjoys spending time with her family, walking on the beach, cuddling her kittens, and great books. Sabrina is a hopeless romantic and knows all too well that life is full of twists and turns, but the bumpy road is what leads to our true destination.

Want to be the first to learn book news, updates and more? Sign up for my Newsletter.

https://www.subscribepage.com/sabrinawagnernewsletter

Want to know about my new releases and upcoming sales? Stay connected on:

Facebook~Instagram~Twitter~TikTok
Goodreads~BookBub~Amazon

I'd love to hear from you. Visit my website to connect with me.

www.sabrinawagnerauthor.com

www.ingramcontent.com/pod-product-compliance
Lightning Source LLC
Chambersburg PA
CBHW070903180626
46817CB00003B/892